ROB WILLIAMS

Rest in Brandon Springs

Rob Williams
Second Edition 2023

In dedication to ministers who have dedicated
their lives in service to God and others:
In particular, in memory of

Walter Swetnam

and

Jim Summers

Chapter 1

LARRY CHATTERSON SAT at his desk staring at his hands, hands which had brutally taken the life of another individual. The blood spatter across his shirt that night was still clear in his mind. The sickening rattled sound of a man struggling to breathe through a crushed face played as vividly in his memory as when it was heard that evening. More than feelings of guilt, he was haunted by concerns that he might still be capable of losing control if threatened. Those thoughts triggered others; back to his childhood, and of an abusive father violently beating him in a drunken rage. All his life, Larry feared he and his father shared the same demon. His nervous fingers straightened the nameplate on the desk, which read,

"Larry Chatterson
Associate Pastor - Director of Missions."

Those hands had now found a more constructive use. Still, he found it difficult to forget such a violent experience. Now safely seated at his desk during what should have been a peaceful morning, visions of washing his hands until they became raw that evening were replaying in his mind. Though the bloody shirt had long been discarded, it was more difficult to remove the stain he sensed tainting his soul.

Like a shadow, it seemed to stubbornly cling to him. Glancing at his watch for the ninth time in twenty minutes, he breathed out a heavy sigh and rose from his chair. Larry closed his eyes and attempted to mentally prepare himself for the duties of the day. He checked his coat pocket for prepared notes, and then exited his office.

Evelyn Reynolds sat at her desk in the mission reception area just outside Larry's office. She paid particular attention as Larry moved past her post.

"You've been the director of this mission for two years, and I have never seen you leave the office without speaking," she admonished. "Are you on your way? It's an hour earlier than when you said you would leave."

A widowed wife of a minister, Evelyn had taken the job as administrative assistant for the center. During the many years of her husband's ministry, she sat in on his sessions while he counseled women. The purpose of her presence was to ensure no woman accused her husband of engaging in inappropriate conversation or behavior. Being privy to years of advice given by her husband, Larry found her to be rich in wisdom and sound judgment. She became a valuable asset to Larry's work at the mission for the homeless. He often consulted her in matters of counseling.

"I'm sorry," Larry replied, as he halted and turned his attention to the aging woman. "I have a lot on my mind, and I'm nervous about today. I can't sit around here any longer. I need to do something – I need to get on the road."

"You've been an ordained minister for three years. There's no reason for you to be nervous."

"I just can't seem to concentrate today," he answered. "I'll be speaking to an unfamiliar crowd."

"You're an exceptionally intelligent and gifted man. This mission was adopted by a very wealthy church because the leadership wanted your success to be theirs. They have complete confidence in you, and so do I. You'll do fine."

As Evelyn gave his large frame a quick hug, she felt

tension in the muscles spanning his lean, broad back. She wished him well, but her encouraging smile hid her growing concern.

Once Larry was on the road, he placed a call on his cell phone to his best friend, Ryan Walker. The two men were very different in background, but complemented one another like two connecting pieces of a puzzle.

"It's way too early, man," Ryan answered.

"What? No cheerful greeting?" Larry questioned. "I expected a pleasant greeting offered to me, possibly in song. A tune along the line of Snow White's *Whistle While You Work* would be appropriate."

"You're ridiculous," Ryan responded. "Okay, what's up?"

Larry's voice took on a more serious tone.

"I have an interesting day ahead of me. Remember my telling you of that prestigious treatment center in the mountains? Remember how Dr. Stevens asked me to accept an invitation to speak to the patients there?"

"Yeah, I remember," Ryan replied.

"Well, today's the day."

"You speak to people all the time. You sound a little nervous. So, what's the big deal? Is everything okay? Is it Patsy? Is she all right? Has she had any complications with the pregnancy?"

"She's fine; it's me. The guys at this exclusive center are different. This isn't like talking to the homeless; these are accomplished people in need of treatment. I'm not really sure what to say to them. I mean, I have a message laid out; but I just feel a little edgy."

"For such a tall athletic guy, you can be an absolute wimp," Ryan replied. "If I had half your intelligence, I would be running for President of the United States."

"Okay – cut the crap!" Larry exclaimed.

"Cut the crap? – is that a phrase they taught you in seminary?" Ryan poked.

"I'm not your pastor," Larry replied. "You're my best friend, and it is perfectly acceptable to tell my best friend to cut the crap."

"You caught me just before leaving for work," Ryan answered. "I'll pray for you today; and I'm sure Patsy will be in prayer for you. When I get to work, I'll call Layla and ask her to pray. You'll be fine. God's got to do the communicating, and you just need to be the mouth piece. Remember, He's a lot bigger than those guys. To tell you the truth – they aren't so big. You told me that all of them are trying to break some form of addiction. I'm sure they've been humbled a bit by all that. Besides, if they give you a hard time, just tell them to cut the crap."

Larry chuckled at the thought of telling his audience to "cut the crap."

"You're right. Maybe I just needed to hear that…I really appreciate the prayers today…But there's something else."

Larry was silent for several seconds. The sound of tires against the highway seemed almost deafening.

"Isn't it ironic that it was five years ago, today… that I killed Keith Turner?"

"I didn't remember, but I guess something like that sort of sticks with you," Ryan replied.

"Well, yeah. It's not like I make a habit of beating a man to death with a brick. That was no small thing. Maybe one day I won't even remember the date when it rolls around, but I guess I'm not there yet."

"You can't let that get to you," Ryan replied. "You saved your brother's life. That guy had a knife, and he intended to use it. He would have killed Ronnie, for sure. You're fortunate that he didn't kill both of you."

"I know. But I can't explain what that did to me. I second-guess myself. I question what would have happened if I had just beaten him really bad, instead of ... Maybe, I could have been more threatening …"

"Keith Turner would have found Ronnie later, and he

would have killed him. The guy was a vicious animal, and he wanted Ronnie dead. Let it rest. I'll be praying for you, and so will everyone else."

"Thanks," Larry said. "I'll let you know how things go."

MOST CONVERSATIONS WITH his best friend caused Larry to relax and be himself. Today, he longed for a life less complicated. As he traveled the curves and slopes of mountainous roads, the countryside reminded him of a cherished secluded place in the Appalachians. Ryan had inherited a farmhouse and hundreds of acres near a little village called Brandon Springs. The house was just outside town and had been the home of Ryan's Uncle Andrew. Each visit with his friend to this remote place had brought a type of inner healing to Larry. There was something real about this plain dwelling. Pristine woods behind the house rekindled enjoyable childhood memories of playing in the forests of south Alabama. Beneath the protection of giant oaks, he had always found relief from the continual belittling and physical abuse of his father. To Larry, spending time in this place was always like visiting a dear friend. His soul ached for the peace he felt there.

As he drove, Larry's thoughts carried him to his favorite place in all the world. His mind wandered to a path through Appalachian woodlands that led up the side of the mountain that overlooked the farmhouse in Brandon Springs. In his imagination, he took in the view from the top. He breathed in fresh summer air, and he listened to leaves of ancient trees rustled by the wind. In his mind, Larry smelled the subtle bittersweet fragrance of hardwoods and the musty smell of disturbed earth beneath his feet.

The ringing of his cell phone interrupted this fantasy trip to the mountain. It was his pastor, wishing him well in his upcoming talk. He was not in Brandon Springs; he was on his way to speak to the type of men who had once looked down on him. Raised relatively poor, his hope as a young adult was to make a better living working on the docks. Failure at that forced him to wash dishes in an inner-city Boston café. He was to be the speaker today, but he dreaded seeing arrogant glances from powerful and successful men. He tried reminding himself that he had been blessed with his own form of success, but for the next several miles Larry longed for the company of his wife. She made him feel like a giant. With Patsy on his arm, he knew he could enter the room with a swagger that spoke volumes.

Larry thought about the nights that he, Patsy, Ryan, and Layla played cards and board games at the old Brandon Springs house. He remembered sharing meals and listening to the pounding of rain on the tin roof during storms. The old home and woods were a harbor of peace and relaxation, surrounded by a world filled with strife and ugliness.

"I want to spend time in Brandon Springs, so badly that I can almost taste it," thought Larry. *"It's more than a farmhouse, surrounded by acres of woods. There seems to be something spiritual about entering a place where departed souls once lived. It's as though I can almost sense a type of residue left by former residents of the home. A mystical presence seems to permeate the wooden walls; almost like the way burned incense leaves a physical trace in the fabric of curtains and bedspreads. Some might think of it as the presence of ghosts. I don't believe in ghosts, but there's something special about that place. The only real peace I found as a child was while walking alone in the forest. I felt an overshadowing protection from those large and ancient trees. They had outlived so many people. As a child, they seemed to be eternal. There was a calming presence about them. I was safe under their care. There is also something very similar about a home that has been in one's family. It's common for the sights and smells to trigger memories of past experiences. Laughter and voices from the*

past echo through time in the minds of those remembering and are heard again. There's a link to one's roots. Although the place has no connection to my family, I feel more at home there than anywhere on earth."

"I would love to raise my child in a place like that!" Larry shouted out loud. "Did you hear me, God? I said, 'I would love to raise my child in a place like that!'"

As he made his way, he became reconciled to the fact that his children would be spending a good bit of time around the indigent souls in his care at the mission. Larry compared the surroundings of his soon-to-be-born child with those of Ryan's adopted daughter. Kaylee, was the only child from Layla's first marriage. He thought back to Kaylee's early childhood. He remembered her heartache and the poor treatment by her natural father. From a young age, she had managed to deal with her own private hell.

"Okay, God," he prayed. *"You made your point. She deserves the peace Brandon Springs affords. She deserves the love she now has from Ryan, but his love may never make up for her birth father. My child will have it good. From birth, my daughter will know love from both natural parents. No matter where we live, she will never have to suffer like Kaylee. You're right. Kaylee deserves Brandon Springs."*

Larry had plenty of time for thought during the five-hour drive from Charlotte to the plush center in the Appalachians. The center had once been an exclusive camp for boys during the 1930's. When very few had money in the United States, aristocratic "old money" families pooled contributions to build this camp for their children. They viewed it as a place where their offspring could take in fresh air and escape the daily worries of the Great Depression. The problem with freely roaming daydreams is that they continually evolve and mutate into newly imagined creations. Without conscious discipline of the mind, they are left to wander. Throughout Larry's drive, peaceful thoughts of ancient trees and an old house in a rural setting were periodically interrupted by mental images of Keith Turner's crushed face. Without warning these thoughts rudely interrupted and invaded his tranquil mind. Pleasant daydreams were suddenly seized and brutally beaten into submission by flashes of horror and rivers of remorse. The blood of another man once coated his hands. They had long been scrubbed clean, but Larry still carried a stain within. He remembered seeing a bubble of blood grow beneath a nostril as the dying man struggled to exhale. Worst of all was the raspy rattle the air made as it exited the broken body with each breath. That sound seemed to be etched in his mind and soul with intensely clear fidelity. Larry spotted the sign indicating the approach to the rehabilitation center and purposefully cleared his mind of incriminating thoughts. He focused on his present surroundings.

As he entered the long private drive, he admired the large open expanse of grass that had once been a polo field. After parking in the circular drive, he sat for a moment examining the large oak front door. The finely built door sported a cheaply made sign marked "Entrance," which appeared somewhat out of character with the original solid brass latch and hinges. Stepping out of the car, he was impressed with the view leading to a distant wooded area that hid the complex from the road. The regally designed main lodge was constructed of stone, and a matching stone chimney rose elegantly through the steep pitched roof. From the outside, the building looked to be the residence of a wealthy aristocratic family. Now, this well-respected facility provided services to professionals suffering from various forms of addiction.

Larry felt he was out of his comfort zone. It wasn't that he had little understanding of highly motivated and successful professionals; he once had a successful career in finance before entering the ministry. He understood them all too well.

I know what they are thinking. Why would a wizard in

finance waste his time dealing with the homeless on a daily basis? He must have screwed up royally to leave that career for this.

Although Larry and this audience shared an understanding of the business world, he felt that his speaking to this success-oriented group would most likely be a real waste of time.

It may be obvious to most of the homeless that I might be someone with a few answers. Most are in need of sound work ethics and self-discipline. What could I tell a group of well-educated, career-minded men that they don't already know?

He took in a deep breath, and the pleasant familiar smell of hardwoods temporarily calmed his spirit. He opened the front door to a reception area, where a round faced, middle-aged woman sat at a desk. Her warm, soothing voice welcomed him.

"You must be Reverend Chatterson."

"Yes, I'm Larry Chatterson. I'm here to see Dr. Whitfield."

She promptly picked up a phone and dialed three numbers. "Reverend Chatterson is here," she softly spoke. "All right, I'll tell him."

She slowly returned the phone to its place. "Please take a seat; it will be about five more minutes," she said, while pointing to a couch against the wall.

While enroute to the couch Larry noticed emergency evacuation floor plans posted on a wall. The building housed a central dining area and a fully equipped kitchen. The left side of the building provided offices, and the right end housed living quarters for staff. The second floor contained the primary living quarters for those receiving services and secondary quarters for other staff members.

Larry took a seat on the couch. After a moment, he took the notes for his prepared message out of his coat pocket and began to review them. Although the words were well-written, he found it difficult to concentrate. He seemed captured by the elegance of the building's architecture.

The door directly behind the receptionist opened, and a stocky man with broad shoulders stepped into the reception area. "You must be Larry Chatterson," he said with a deep-throated voice. "I'm Howard Whitfield."

"Yes sir," Larry answered, as he held out his hand.

"Well, it's a pleasure to have you," Dr. Whitfield announced, while grinning from ear to ear. His teeth were particularly large, and he reminded Larry of Teddy Roosevelt. He didn't at all appear to be the type of person one would expect as director of an exclusive rehabilitation center. The man's shirtsleeves were rolled to just below his elbows, and he wore no tie. As Whitfield took the younger man's hand, Larry sensed a subtle power in the handshake. This was not the forced grip of a man attempting to prove his manliness to another male but rather a firmness indicating unspoken confidence and inner strength. Although Larry's athletic hands were larger, Dr. Whitfield's clasp implied a man of natural and well-established leadership.

"I appreciate your invitation," Larry responded.

"Come on in," Dr. Whitfield invited, as he opened the door leading to the commons area of the facility.

They entered a large room to find his audience seated in wooden folding chairs arranged in a semi-circle, facing a plain wooden lectern. The commons area sported a massive stone fireplace, and the lectern stood directly in front of it. Dr. Whitfield placed a hand on Larry's shoulder and escorted him to the lectern. The faces of the seated men showed little response to his presence. He could not tell whether he was truly a welcomed visitor or whether he was just someone to fill another hour in the day of each man's life.

"Men, this is Reverend Larry Chatterson from Charlotte, North Carolina," Whitfield began. "He comes to us by recommendation from an old friend of mine."

With the short introduction, Dr. Whitfield took a seat in

a plush chair just to the right of the lectern. Larry almost cringed each time he was addressed by the term "Reverend". Though he was an ordained minister, he never thought of himself as being a person whom people should revere. *"Recommendation?"* Larry thought. *"I thought I was invited; I can't believe I was set up to speak here by my senior pastor, Dr. Stevens!"* It was at that moment that he realized that he had "been "volunteered" to come to the rehabilitation center.

Taking the prepared written message from his coat pocket, he unfolded it and laid it on the lectern. "My name is Larry Chatterson, and I am the Minister of Missions to the Community at a church in Charlotte," he began. "I would like to..."

Larry stopped in mid-sentence and glanced down at the paper before him. His eyes rose from the text to the men who had been placed in front of him. Scanning the faces of those seated on the wooden chairs, he recognized something familiar in the eyes of most of them. Though these were not persons of the streets, these were successful men whose addiction had become public. They had become humbled before people whom they had once commanded respect. Personal weaknesses had been laid open to those who had once looked to them for guidance and strength. Whether they were CEOs of corporations, doctors of those in need of healing, or pastors of those needing spiritual guidance, they were all fallen men. Their sin had become public, and their shame widespread. Their gifted abilities of leadership had given way to heavy loss of personal self-worth. Each dreaded going back to the people whom they had failed. These were not men accustomed to following others, and each felt like his gift to the world had been crushed by poor judgment and personal weakness. Each pair of eyes ached for hope. Each pair of eyes seemed to be asking *"Will I hear something that will help me continue to live? Are you going to show me something worthwhile about my life?"*

Larry quietly folded the paper and placed it back in his coat pocket. The eyes of those men were now fixed on the man before them.

"I had prepared something to say to you, but I've changed my mind," he said.

Larry was silent for a moment. Soon the initial questioning eyes of the men began to harden. He had their full attention. For a moment, he stood in silence.

"Instead, I want to share something very personal with you," he said. A few stares softened somewhat, but all eyes continued to be locked on him.

"I have not always been the Minister of Missions to the Community; or even a minister to anyone," he began. "I have a personal history of great change. Before I was a minister and the director of a shelter for the homeless, I had a career in finance."

Larry glanced over in the direction of Dr. Whitfield, hoping to obtain assurance that he was on the right track with his message. No indication was given. Silence filled the room, and inwardly he questioned whether it would have been better to stick with the prepared script. Facing the men before him, he quickly received his answer. Every eye was still locked on him.

"Even the career in finance was a huge change from my earlier life," he continued. "As you can probably guess from my speech, I am originally from the Deep South. I grew up relatively poor. I was raised by a real mix of parents. I had a saint for a mother, and my father abused alcohol. He didn't just abuse the bottle; he eventually abused everyone in the family. The man wasn't all bad, but he never really got past the drinking. That's just about all I plan to say about him, except for the fact that he died of cirrhosis of the liver a while back. My mother and my baby sister still live in the old house. I left home at an early age, and soon afterwards married. At first, it seemed like I was living in a heaven on earth. I was earning honest wages as a dock worker in

Mobile, Alabama, and my new wife and I were having great weekends. That all ended when I walked in on her with another man."

Larry was completely honest in sharing his personal life experiences. He was silent for a moment, as he maintained eye contact with most of the men in the room.

"That's when things seemed to dive into a fast tailspin," Larry softly spoke. "I ran. I lived in my car on the beach for a while, and then moved in with a fellow dock worker. I thought I was adjusting fairly well until I ran into my ex-wife at a grocery store. I couldn't handle it. The next day I pulled every dollar out of my bank account and drove to Boston. I ran like I had never run before."

At that point, Larry stepped from behind the lectern. Spotting a folded metal chair leaning against a wall, he picked it up. He silently headed in the direction of the other men. Unfolding the chair, he placed it directly in front of one of the men and motioned for them all to pull their chairs in close. Once the men moved closer, he took his seat in the midst of them.

"I left my mother, sister, and little brother to suffer the abuses of my father," he continued. "All I could think about was getting away. No one else mattered, and once I was gone, those family members were pretty much gone from my mind. I was unable to get on with crews working the docks in Boston, so I took a job washing dishes at a café. To make a long story short, I became friends with someone who convinced me to go to school at night. It was after I finished school and had a promising job in finance that I felt I could return home with my head held a little higher. I had been away for years. In my vanity, I thought people would be impressed by my newly achieved success. Focused on the change in me, I gave little thought to the change in others. I was not prepared for the carnage that had become of my family. My old man was dying from cirrhosis of the liver, my unwed sister had given birth to a son, and my little brother had become a drug dealer. My mother was still a saint, but a difficult life had aged her significantly. She was the only family member who seemed happy to see me. I don't blame them. I had abandoned them; I left them defenseless under the brutality of my drunken father. It was like a cancer had taken hold of my family, and I had left them to die."

He was unlike any preacher those men had previously heard. He had no pretense of being pious or spiritually superior to them. They held on to every word as he openly spilled personal pain and faults before them. One of the men seated in the group was David Clarkston, a pastor who had fallen under the power of alcohol abuse. Larry's experience of having an unfaithful wife had intimately captured him; and the statements about an abusive alcoholic father exposed his heart as though he were under the scalpel of a surgeon.

"My younger brother had felt betrayed during my absence, but over time our relationship began to heal," Larry continued. "He got away from drugs and began a new life in Charlotte. His new profession showed promise, and personal situations in his life caused him to consider matters of the soul. One of the happiest days of my life was when he became a Christian. Afterwards, we drew closer than ever. Not long after his commitment to Christ, I found him with his throat slashed. In a pool of blood, he lay dead in front of his apartment. I can't tell you how I felt as I looked into his lifeless eyes, and I can't really explain what that experience did to me.

Months before, I had gone to extraordinary lengths to protect him. I would rather not discuss what I did, but I thought he was safe. In the long run, it turned out that my efforts offered little protection. At first, I was extremely angry with God for allowing drug dealers from Ronnie's past to find him and brutally take his life in such a senseless and horrible way. Within a short time, it was sort of like I died with him. All the hope I had for my little brother was gone;

our newfound rich relationship was gone. My vision for my own future died with him, and all my expectations of God went with his death. I was numb. For months I was empty. I performed well enough at my job, and I seemed to be a success to those who didn't really know me. However, nothing really mattered anymore. People who loved me didn't matter, and a Savior who gave His life for me no longer mattered. I focused on my work in finance. I had no intentions of losing my career as well.

I turned inward, and eventually I cut myself off from all personal relationships. I was slowly building a wall around my soul. Just as I was about to mortar in the last brick, someone walked in with a sledgehammer and began to beat that wall. Patsy, the woman who is now my wife, would not let me go. She violently beat that wall with a vicious hammer of love, and the bricks began to crumble. I allowed her to enter that breach in the wall, but I still kept God at bay. It wasn't that I no longer believed--I just wanted nothing to do with Him. I felt I could no longer trust Him. I tried to shove God aside, but it didn't mean that He abandoned me. He didn't go away. Everywhere I went, He was there. I saw Him in people, I saw Him in situations, and I saw Him even when I closed my eyes at night. He would not leave. I can't explain it to anyone else; it was a personal thing. I knew He was there, and I know that He is here now. His presence penetrates any building, and He can enter through any breach to our soul that we allow to exist.

Some of you may have successfully built that wall; some of you may have sealed the world off from the innermost part of your being. I also believe there may be some in this room who have not yet placed the last brick in your wall. I would ask you to stop your work. Drop the brick from your hand and abandon your mortar-filled trowel. Let it go. Leave the opening and allow your fortress to be unprotected. Allow your Creator and your Savior to have access to that opening. Even if you find it painful, allow God's hand to reach in and begin to pull the wall down. Let it go, and live. You haven't died; it isn't over yet. He has plans for you. He still has a life for you, and He is bigger than anything that has beaten you in the past. Contrary to how you may feel, your real enemy is not a situation or any person. You may not be able to fend off your true adversary, but God can handle anything."

Larry opened his Bible and began to read from Ephesians Chapter 6, "Above all, taking the shield of faith, wherewith ye shall be able to quench all the fiery darts of the wicked. And take the helmet of salvation, and the sword of the Spirit, which is the word of God:"

"Open up your faith in God, and let it shield your soul," he continued. "It is a living, breathing shield that allows the Spirit of God to flow through it to give life to the innermost part of you. Still, it offers protection. Once the proper protection is held for defense, then saturate your soul with words from the Bible. God's words are like a sword to use in fighting off any spiritual enemy who intends to take you down. More is going on than you may realize. An unseen spiritual war goes on around and within each of us, and we should never lose sight of that."

Looking down at the Bible, Larry began to read again. "For our struggle is not against human opponents, but against rulers, authorities, cosmic powers in the darkness around us, and evil spiritual forces in the heavenly realm."

"Look beyond the situations, circumstances, and people who seem to mean you harm," Larry said. "There is a power behind much of what you see, and this power means you real harm. Without that shield of faith, faith in God's personal work in your life, you will have little real defense. There is more to it, than what we see with our eyes and touch with our hands. Trust that your Creator can help you become the man He intends you to be."

Larry closed his Bible and placed it on his left knee. "Guys, this is all I wanted to share with you," he said. "I'm going to end with a quick prayer; and I will be around for about a half hour, in case anyone wants to talk a little more."

Closing his eyes and dropping his head, he began "God, we ask you to help each one of us sitting in this room. You knew us before we began a physical life in our mother's wombs. Help us to be the men You intend each of us to be. We ask for direction in our lives, for strength to help us do what we should do, and for the wisdom needed to trust You. Open the right doors before us and close all the wrong doors. Each day, from this day forward, we commit ourselves to humbly walk with You. Amen."

With his Bible in his left hand, he stood and folded the metal chair using his right hand. Larry carried the chair back to its original location against the wall. Turning back, his eyes met those of David Clarkston. The man had moved several paces toward Larry, separating himself from the rest of the other men. Several of those behind Clarkston were quietly talking among themselves, and some were exiting the large room to make their way back to their quarters. Larry slowly walked over to David. Reaching out his right hand, he said, "In case you don't remember my introduction, my name is Larry Chatterson."

David took the extended hand in a firm handshake and said, "I remember your name. Over the years I developed the skill of quickly picking up on the names of individuals I meet. I've been a minister for several years, but I'm a pastor who has picked up a few bad habits."

"I would guess most of us have a few poor habits," Larry continued.

"I'm an alcoholic," David plainly stated.

"So, where do you plan to be a year from now?" Larry asked.

"We sort of take one day at a time," David explained. "We begin each day making the decision to remain sober for the remainder of the day."

"That's good," Larry replied. "That's a good short-term

plan, but what about long term plans? Where do you see that daily short-term plan leading you?"

"The leadership in my congregation said that they are open to retaining me as their pastor, but I don't know how well that will work out."

"Great! Take them at their word. Humbly accept the gracious hand they are extending to you, and humbly accept the grace God is extending to you through them. You're very fortunate, and it is obvious that you mean a great deal to your congregation."

"I don't know why, but I sense you are a man who can be trusted," Dr. Clarkston sincerely said. "I have never told anyone what I am about to say to you."

Larry quietly swore an oath to the man standing before him. "I promise that your words will not leave the two of us."

Because of the issues within his own home and because of the public revealing of his own personal problems, David's arrogance and pride had become broken. Everything was on the line, and he saw no reason to retain secrets with Larry.

"I'm having marital problems, as well. My wife still attends our church regularly, and I don't believe anyone in the church knows about this particular personal problem".

"You don't think she will stay with you? I guess you think she will leave you, and that will be the beginning of the end of your career in the ministry. Do you think the church is hanging on to you for her sake?"

"Possibly. I don't know. I don't seem to have much insight into much of anything, now. There was a time when my confidence was high, and I was brimming over with answers to just about everything; but not now. I've failed the church, failed God, and I've failed myself. I have no idea as to how the future will turn out."

"Well, to be honest, did you ever really know what the future would hold? Did you really know, or did you just think you knew? Did you really have all the answers, or did you convince yourself by your intelligence and your studies that you had the answers?"

"Maybe I really never knew answers to anything," David responded in a tone of deep grief and desperation.

"You have the unique opportunity to lead an honest life now," Larry firmly stated.

David's downtrodden countenance now began to take on a scowl. His eyes narrowed.

"I might have had a drinking problem, but I wasn't a liar," David retorted. "I wasn't the strongest person in the world, but I did have a few redeeming qualities."

"I would guess that you probably weren't honest with the church about your drinking problem, until you had no choice. I doubt very seriously that you were honest with yourself about your problem with alcohol, until confronted. I lived with an alcoholic father, and I'm well acquainted with cover-ups and lies associated with the condition. Alcoholics lie, first to themselves and then to others. I'm not really sure how open and honest you have been with your wife. That is something only you know. What about it? Do you plan to live an honest life now, or are you going to try to play a game of arrogance and lies again?"

Now the conversation had turned very personal, and somewhat confrontational. Larry was a bit surprised at the words he heard coming from his own mouth. Becoming keenly aware of the tension between them, he nervously shifted his Bible from his left hand to his right. He considered whether he had overstepped his position with a man he met only moments before. Quietly, he searched within himself as to whether he should apologize for his accusations. The two men stood staring silently into one another's eyes.

At last, David broke the silence. "You're right. I haven't told blatant lies; but I haven't been entirely honest, even with myself. I'm anything but perfect. Maybe I am not really cut out to be a minister."

"Why do you say that?" Larry asked. "The respect and loyalty shown by members of your church indicate that you are loved and well respected. It's obvious that you must have been doing something right."

"People are looking for someone perfect to trust with their confessions and personal problems. Now that the church has come to know how screwed up I have been, I will need to go back and really prove to them that they haven't made a mistake by giving me a second chance. The problem is that I know I'm going to blow it. Before, they would have given me the benefit of the doubt for goofing something up. Now, any mistake will only confirm to them that I am unfit to be their pastor. I really don't know what to do. I don't think I stand a chance."

"Don't sell yourself short. You studied hard and long to obtain knowledge to equip you in helping people with their situations. You don't have all the answers, so, don't pretend. Be yourself, and just be honest with people. Just cut the crap with the pious arrogance and highbrow 'holier than thou' stuff."

"I've congregation is well aware that I'm not perfect."

"Remember who you are. You are a remarkable mix of greatness and the lowest thing on this planet. The Bible states that God made Adam out of dirt, but it also says that God Himself breathed life into man. You're basically warmed-over dirt, but you have also been graced by an intimate touch from God. Don't think too highly of yourself, but don't underestimate the power of the Creator of the universe. Never underestimate the Spirit of God in your life, and the fact that He is bigger than anything that may come your way."

"I've let God down. I'm not so sure that He's still interested in using me in ministry. I'm pretty much a soiled item."

"God is never surprised at anything. His vision is not

limited by time, like ours. God saw your entire life at the time He called you into His service. He foresaw the things that you would do in life, and He still called you to do His work. He sees a much larger picture. I truly believe God's hand is on your life, and I know He hasn't left you. He said that He will never leave or forsake us, and God is not a liar."

In almost a whisper, David asked "Will you pray for me?"

Swapping his Bible from his right hand into his left, Larry placed his large right hand on the back of David's neck and drew him close. He prayed for God's strength and anointing to be on the life of this struggling pastor. Before parting, the two men exchanged business cards, and Larry wrote his personal cell phone number on the back of his.

"Anytime, day or night, you can call," Larry promised. "You, know, if you just want somebody to talk to – call me. I mean it. I'm no better or worse than you. Each morning, I have to fall into God's grace."

There was honesty in what Larry said, and David saw it.

THE NEXT MORNING, David Clarkston arose at the same appointed time and ate his breakfast at the same table as he had each day while at the center. This morning, it was as if a weight had lifted from his soul. The personal demons of despair and intense sorrow were no longer pulling at his heart and mind. He walked with purpose, and with hope.

ROB WILLIAMS

Chapter 2

IT WAS ALMOST 11:00 PM when Larry wearily stepped from the doorway of the center in Charlotte. It was "lights out" time for those living at the mission, and he was relieved to find that nothing had gone badly while he was away for the day. An overwhelming sense of responsibility caused him to stop there on his way back from speaking at the exclusive rehab in the mountains. He had to make sure everything was alright before going home. Outside the center the night was still. Thoughts of the day flashed through his mind as he walked down the broken sidewalk to his car. Larry considered whether his talk with the men at Whitfield's center had made any lasting difference for anyone. His reflection of the day's activity was broken by the sound of his cell phone.

"Well, how did it go?" questioned the caller, without any sort of introduction. No introduction was really needed, for Larry could never mistake the voice of Ryan.

"I hope it went all right, but I guess you never really know," answered Larry.

"I sort of expected a call from you this evening," Ryan replied. "It's not like you. Are you sure that everything is okay?"

"Yeah, I'm fine, just a little tired" Larry said.

"Thinking about Ronnie?" his best friend questioned. "You have that same tone of voice when he's been on your mind."

"I told the guys at the place about my brother, so I would have to say that I've thought about him," answered Larry. "To tell you the truth, I put away the prepared message. I sort of just sat down with them and talked. It probably wasn't very professional of me, and it probably wasn't what Dr. Whitfield wanted. Honestly, I don't care."

"Man, you really sound down," Ryan said. "Did someone say something to you about it? You said that you weren't given a topic or a format before going there. No one should hold you to a specific manner of speaking. But I don't think that's really it. What's going on?"

"I told them about a lot of things," whispered Larry, as he opened the door of his car and slowly sat in the driver's seat. "I told them about my first wife. I never think about it, and the talk just stirred up memories of painful stuff. Patsy is the most wonderful woman in the world. I should never even bring up my previous marriage. That is all in the past. I was really messed up back then. I talked to them about Ronnie and the rest of my family. What a depressing and screwed up bunch! I don't know if my sister will ever get her life together. My poor mother is getting old. Since Ronnie and Dad died, she only has my dumb sister and my sister's little boy. Poor kid will probably end up as messed up as his mom. She leaves him with my mother, and she spends nights with a collection of different men. Can you imagine having a slut for a mother? Sometimes it gets to me."

"Hey, why don't you and your family spend weekend after next with us in Brandon Springs?" Ryan offered.

"I'm just tired," Larry replied with a chuckle. "When I'm tired, I have a tendency to concentrate on crap rather than what is good. I really sound pretty bad, don't I? I'll be fine after a good night's sleep."

"One of the reasons I called was to invite you and Patsy," Ryan explained. "Layla and I are planning to leave out around noon that Friday and return home Sunday night. I want to cook on the grill and see if the old house needs repairs. We promised Kaylee that we would go, and Joey is now old enough to enjoy the place. Kaylee is excited."

"I don't know," Larry replied.

"The other reason that I called was to tell you that I plan to accept a job offer in Knoxville, TN. Besides the pay increase, it will be closer to Brandon Springs and closer to Layla's relatives."

"I should congratulate you on the job, but I hate the thoughts of you moving away."

"I almost turned the job down, but it was pretty much settled after talking with Layla. She wants her mother to be able to see Kaylee and Joey more often. The move makes sense for a number of reasons."

"I was away from the mission all day. I'm not sure the church would want me to leave again so soon. You're planning to take your boy Joey out there? He just turned three years old a couple of months ago. Since marrying Layla, you've become a real family man. Kaylee even calls you Daddy. "

"We take little Joey almost everywhere we go," stated Ryan. "I really have to watch the little guy, as he can get into things pretty fast. It's all good. You had better get used to the idea. You're going to be a Daddy in just a few months."

"That's another thing; Patsy doesn't have morning sickness anymore, but I'm concerned that there isn't a hospital in Brandon Springs," Larry explained. "If something happened with her pregnancy, it might be bad. I'm not sure she would want to go."

"I doubt Patsy is as nervous about it as you are," accused Ryan. "She's a nurse. She would know for sure if she should go. Like I said earlier today - for such a big guy, you can really be a wimp."

"I just want to be careful," Larry explained. "I guess I do worry more about the pregnancy than she does."

"Well, ask her; and ask the church. I bet she will want to go, and I'm pretty sure the Senior Pastor won't slap you around for asking. He doesn't appear to be the violent type."

"I don't want to put too much on Evelyn," Larry replied. "She runs a tight ship when I am away. However, she is getting pretty old for an administrative assistant at a mission for the homeless. Situations are unpredictable with the people there. They can sometimes be volatile. I have this guy, George, who lives at the mission. I made him supervisor of the work crews, and he's dependable. He usually handles things that come up at night, without calling me in. If a situation isn't serious, George just lets me know about it after I arrive in the morning. This guy has really taken a load off me, and I usually get a good night's sleep. I have to be careful, because it has only been a little over a year since he was a drunk. He has natural leadership abilities, but I don't want to put him in a difficult position or push him to the edges of what he can handle."

"You are not pushing him, and you know it," Ryan retorted. "You've given George a second try at life. He takes it very seriously when you trust him with things, and he is as loyal a man as I have ever seen. I believe that it means a lot to him that you trust him with responsibility. Without that mission, and you, he would probably be on the streets again."

"If I take another weekend off, I should really use the opportunity to visit my mother," Larry said. I haven't seen my mother since we told her that Patsy was pregnant.

"I want to buy her airfare to come up," Ryan said. "I know you don't have the money right now, and you really should save it for the baby. In fact, tell her to bring your sister's son. Let me bring them up to Charlotte, and they can ride over with you. It would give them an opportunity to visit with you and Patsy. Your mother probably could use the break from your sister. The last time we brought her to the place, your mother loved it. Are you still planning on bringing her to Charlotte when the baby is born?"

"That's the plan. Patsy wants to take off work at the hospital during the ninth month, and she should have time off until the baby is two months old. Honestly, I'm not sure if my sister's son would be a good influence on Joey. He might learn a few words that you would want left out of his vocabulary."

"Kaylee will take care of that," Ryan replied. "She's a lot tougher than you think. She will look out for Joey, and she won't put up with bad behavior from your nephew. You need to remember her situation before I married her mother. Her dad was a real jerk. The guy never played a serious role in his daughter's life. She protects Joey like a mama bear. She will play mama to both boys. It'll be fun."

"Okay, I'll ask Patsy first and then I'll approach the Senior Pastor. I won't call my mother unless everything is settled. Are you sure you can afford the flights for both of them?"

"I got a raise a couple of months ago; we're good," Ryan explained. "I'll expect a call tomorrow night. The sooner I buy the tickets the cheaper they will be, so don't mess around with this. It's going to be fun."

As soon as the call ended, Larry placed the key in the ignition. Before he started the car, he felt the vehicle shake, and then heard a pop at the rear of the car. Looking in the rear-view mirror, he saw nothing out of the ordinary on the poorly lighted street. This was not the type of neighborhood where it would be safe to experience car trouble in the middle of the night. Turning his head to the left, he was somewhat startled by the grin of a disgusting face just outside of the driver's side window.

"Why don't you go home, preacher?" the toothless man shouted through the glass.

Rolling down the car window, Larry replied "Don, I was thinking about doing just that until you beat the trunk of my car. Why don't you come inside the mission for the night? We have a spare bunk, and I can get George to fix you a plate of food. We always have a few leftovers."

"I don't want no leftovers," the man replied. "I have everything I need in this brown bag, right here."

The smell of alcohol was extremely strong on the man's breath, and the fellow was close enough for Larry to discern that it had been some time since the man had shared a relationship with a shower.

"Good grief, Don!" Larry exclaimed. "Why don't you just leave the bottle behind the shrub over there, come inside, take a nice hot shower, and bed down for the evening. I won't throw the bottle away; just put it behind the shrub."

"You know, preacher, you're a good man," Don stammered. "I trust you not to take my bottle, but everyone knows you have people put their bottles behind that old shrub. I don't trust the people outside the mission. Heck! I've even looked behind that shrub when I have been hard up for something to drink. Didn't find none though. Can't blame a guy when he's hard up, can you? If you got to have it, you just got to have it. Naw, I just wanted to say 'Hi'. Did I scare you a little bit?"

"When I heard you pound the back of the car, I thought it might be you," Larry replied. "Are you sure you won't stay the night?"

"No, go on home, preacher," Don replied. "If I had a wife of my own, that's what I'd be doing. She hadn't had that baby yet, has she?"

"No, the baby is still in the oven," Larry replied.

Don took a sip from the contents of the brown bag and stammered, "You're gonna be a good Daddy to that child; I know you will. You got a kind heart, you been around a little, so I know you will keep a good eye on him. Is it gonna be a boy or a girl? Do you know yet?"

"Don, we just decided to let be a surprise," Larry answered.

"Well, that's the way it should be," Don stated. "Doctors and people shouldn't be a poking around too much before a baby's born. That might be what's wrong with some of the young people now. Folks may have been prodding around way too much and messed some of them up. You never know. I think the good Lord intended some things to be a surprise. I think you done the right thing. Well, I'm not gonna keep you. I will probably be taking you up on that hot shower and bed when the weather turns cold. You know what I mean? Yeah, you know what I mean... you know all about it. And on a real hot day, I might take you up on that shower. On a hot day, it can make you be sorta smucky in betwixt."

"Sort of what?" questioned Larry.

"Smucky in betwixt. You know, smucky in betwixt your arms, betwixt your legs...it gets so hot that it makes you miserable. You go on home to that wife now."

With that, the indigent man continued on his way down the street. Larry had talked with Don on several occasions, but he had been successful in convincing him to stay at the mission on only four nights. Larry wondered if the man would last until the weather turned cold. It was spring, and colder weather was months away. Since working at the mission, he had seen a number of indigent people pass on. He once found a dead man behind the same shrub he often suggested as a place to stash liquor. The man was found early in the morning, and it was obvious that this soul had passed on during the night. He thought about what it must be like to die alone behind a bush, having no one to know or even care.

He started the car. The traffic was very light during that time of night, and within twenty minutes he was home. Before leaving his car, he rolled the driver side window down and took in the cool spring air. He noticed that a light had been left on in the living room, but there was no movement from inside the house. The night was quiet, all but the muffled sounds of traffic in the distance. Larry thought about Ryan's inherited property just outside Brandon Springs. That small Appalachian town had caused a great change in his friend, and the change was certainly for the better. Without the impact of the people in that place on Ryan, Larry was certain that things would not have gone so well for himself. It was Ryan's friendship and influence that gave him the courage to go to school at night. It was through his best friend that Larry had found his wife Patsy. That farmhouse and pristine property in that calming rural setting had been the source of so much good in so many lives. Just the thought of going there brought a sense of peace to his tired mind.

A slight breeze drifting through the window reminded him that morning would come soon and that he needed sleep badly. His body expressed weariness as he slowly stepped from the car. All he wanted to do was to slip into bed beside Patsy.

He found her asleep on the couch. He knelt beside the couch and kissed her on the forehead. Patsy took a deep breath and sleepily stared at him through squinted eyes.

"What time is it," she whispered.

"It's time to come to bed," Larry replied. "It's late, come on."

She placed a hand over her swollen belly and pushed herself into a sitting position with the other. Still half asleep, she slowly obeyed. After a few seconds of sitting with her eyes closed, she opened them again and lifted herself to a standing position.

"Here, take my arm," he coaxed.

Slowly they walked to the bedroom, where Larry pulled back the covers and helped her into bed. Placing them over his wife, he gave her a second kiss on her head. With the lights still off in the bedroom, he returned to the living room to turn the lights off there. Carefully he made his way back to the bedroom. After undressing, he snuggled up behind Patsy.

"What a day," he thought as he closed his eyes. *"I was probably a disappointment at the rehab center, but it's just as well. I really don't have the time for remote speaking engagements. I have my hands full at my own mission. I should make sure my traveling is reserved for needed down time with my family, like to Brandon Springs."*

Thoughts of a trip to Ryan's place in the country calmed his racing mind. Placing his face near his wife, he breathed in her familiar smell. This was all he needed, Patsy, his child on the way, and his ministry at the mission. Drifting off to sleep, one thought pressed.

"Hopefully, tomorrow will be uneventful."

ROB WILLIAMS

Chapter 3

STILL EXHAUSTED, Larry entered the mission the next morning. Without saying a word, he gave Evelyn a dutiful wave as he passed by her desk in the reception area.

"You can't get away with that," Evelyn warned. "How did it go yesterday? You could have called. For all I knew you ran off the road and hit a tree. Don't you do me that way anymore, you hear?"

Larry silently nodded his head in agreement and motioned for her to follow him back to the office.

"I really don't know," he began. "I can't even put into words how tired I am. I dropped by the mission before going home last night and had a conversation with Don Rivers. I hadn't seen him in some time. I couldn't convince him to come in for the night. Evelyn, I'm afraid I'll probably find him dead one cold night."

The phone rang. Larry answered it and Evelyn returned to her desk.

"Well, you certainly made an impression yesterday," the voice on the phone exclaimed.

"Is that a good thing, or a bad thing?" Larry questioned.

"You have to be joking," Dr. Stevens replied. "Dr. Whitfield said you made a huge impact on one man, and he has called several of his friends to tell them about you."

"Tell them about me?" Larry questioned. "What is he telling them? What are you suggesting?"

"I'm not suggesting anything at this time," Dr. Stevens replied. "I am just letting you know how well you were received. He said that he had a long talk with one man yesterday afternoon, a pastor. A half hour later others began coming to his office to talk. Each one referred to you, and each of them said they would like a return visit by you at some point."

"I'm glad things went well, but I'm not sure what else I would share with those men."

"If you ever decided to return, you would have my full support."

"Dr. Stevens, I have an unrelated request," Larry began. "I know that I've been away from the mission all day yesterday, but I would like to take weekend after next off. A friend has invited Patsy and me to visit during that weekend. I think Evelyn and George could take care of things for a couple of days, if it's all right with you."

"Sure, I trust your judgment regarding the capable hands of Evelyn and George," Dr. Stevens answered. "With the birth of your first child, you and Patsy are about to have your lives changed forever. It's perfectly fine for you to spend some time in a relaxing environment."

As Larry hung up the phone, he remembered that he had not discussed with Evelyn or George his leaving for the weekend. In fact, he had not even had a conversation with Patsy on the matter.

"*First things first,*" he thought.

Larry called Patsy, and she was excited over the idea of spending a weekend in Brandon Springs. She was almost giddy over it. He then discussed it with Evelyn and George.

"I know that you aren't stupid, but you are running out of time in a big way," Evelyn chided.

"What?" Larry replied, almost shocked by the statement.

"The window is closing on you and Patsy," she scolded.

"If you intend on having a free weekend with your wife, you had better jump on it. Once that baby is born, the care of that child will determine much of what you do. This may be your last opportunity to travel for a while. Do you understand me?"

"Yes, I guess so," Larry replied.

He could tell that George felt respected by the confidence Larry showed by leaving the mission in his hands. The man's eyes almost sparkled.

The phone rang, and Evelyn and George excused themselves from Larry's office. On the line was a probation officer.

"I believe I have someone who could use your assistance," the caller began. "My name is Tom McKinley. I'm a probation officer, and I think you're a man who could be counted on to help."

"What's up?" asked Larry. *"What I need is a ten-minute power nap,"* he thought. *"Just ten minutes. I'm dying here, this morning."*

"Before you say anything, I need to explain," continued McKinley. "This is not a simple matter. I have a young woman who is about to be released from prison. She served time on a drug charge. Her name is Tiffany Jennings. I know the truth of the matter, but it may not make a difference to you. I know that it was really her boyfriend who possessed and sold heroin. The police have been trying to bust him for some time, and there was a large amount of heroin in the apartment. Russ Boyd has a long criminal record, and another arrest would put him away for a long time. I believe she took the rap for him, and she did the prison time. She knew she would receive a shorter sentence than Boyd. She didn't want to be separated from that jerk Boyd for a lengthy time. At the time Tiffany didn't know that she was pregnant. Her daughter Brandy was born in prison and was immediately given to a family member until Tiffany's release. I'm asking you to take this woman and her twenty-one-month-old daughter into your center."

As Larry realized what was being asked of him, it was though a shot of adrenaline exploded throughout his body and mind. He immediately became fully alert.

"Wow!" Larry exclaimed. "I don't know. I've never housed children before."

"Well, actually she would only have the girl every other weekend for the first six weeks," McKinley explained. "After that point, she would be evaluated as to whether she is a fit mother to have full custody of her daughter. Tiffany needs a place to live, and she must stay out of trouble. Right now, the little girl lives with Tiffany's sister and has only visited her mother every other weekend at the prison. The daughter has to be made available to her father on the alternate weekends. He only takes her about half the time, but the little girl must be made available."

"When would this begin?" asked Larry.

"Tiffany would begin this weekend, as she is to be released at 8:00 AM Friday," Tom answered. "The daughter is to be with her father this weekend, but I have arranged to have Brandy accompany her mother to meet you Friday morning. After you meet them both, I will take the girl to spend the weekend with her father. She is to be returned to her mother at your mission at 6:00 PM Sunday."

"How long would she need to stay with us?" Larry asked.

"In my opinion, she needs to get a job and show that she is capable of taking care of herself and her daughter," Tom answered. "I would ask that she stay in your program at least six months, but would prefer she stays a year. This is why I am asking you to take her. She needs to be reintroduced back into society slowly, and she needs a stable environment. Tiffany certainly doesn't need to be placed in a position where she might live with her old boyfriend anytime soon. Things could go very badly for her and her daughter, should that occur. Russ Boyd is bad news. Think about it. What kind of man would allow his girlfriend to go to prison for him? What kind of man would leave her there after finding out she was carrying his child? The guy is cold, and he is dangerous. I hate the fact that Tiffany decided to allow him visitation rights. In my opinion, this child has no business spending that kind of time with her biological father."

"We have an empty room next door to Evelyn's bedroom," Larry explained. "I could probably move a couple of twin beds in that room for her and the little girl. Let me call my Senior Pastor and first discuss the matter with him. Since becoming a part of that church, I don't call all of the shots anymore. I'll get back with you soon."

"Oh, one more thing," McKinley said. "The woman is a knock-out. She's really easy on the eyes. Those looks may help her find a job, but they will probably cause trouble for you. She'll probably be a distraction for the men you currently serve at the mission."

Before consulting with the church leadership, Larry first asked the advice of his wife. Patsy believed it to be a good idea.

"Besides helping Tiffany, this could be a life changer for that little girl," Patsy said.

Within fifteen minutes of calling the Senior Pastor, Larry gained the approval. Larry placed a call to Tom McKinley and made plans to take the woman and child into the program. Evelyn was particularly excited about having the mother and daughter stay in the room next to hers. It was when he discussed it with George that he began to realize the complications of this commitment. While he and Patsy visited Brandon Springs, George would have the new situation entirely in this lap. The sparkle in George's eyes gave way to apprehension.

"George, I don't have to go to Brandon Springs that weekend," Larry suggested.

"I can handle it," George cautiously responded with a nervous smile.

He was now in a tight situation. Ryan and Layla were

thrilled that Larry and Patsy had decided to come to Brandon Springs. Evelyn had scolded him for not already taking his wife on a weekend prior to the birth of the baby. Patsy was on cloud nine at the thought of going. Now he had placed a struggling individual in charge of handling the mission on a weekend that included a mother and child for the first time ever. Larry called Patsy.

"Patsy, I don't know what I was thinking!" Larry blurted. "Under normal circumstances, I would be laying a lot on George in handling the mission. Maybe I should just tell Ryan that we can't go. I'm not sure what to do. I really don't feel good about leaving all of this on George. Then, if I don't go, he will think I don't trust him."

"So, let's take the woman and little girl with us to Brandon Springs," Patsy replied. "The mission would be left with George, and he wouldn't be in such an abnormal situation. It would present you with an opportunity to size up the mother and daughter before they are firmly entrenched in the mission. You and I could still go. The little girl might have a great time with Kaylee and Joseph. The woman would be away from her crappy boyfriend, and I am sure she would see a trip to the country as a nice change from prison."

"You really think this would be a good idea?" Larry asked.

"Sure," Patsy replied.

"You are an absolute genius," Larry answered.

Larry called Ryan to make sure the extra visitors would be welcome. He thought it to be a great idea. Immediately after the conversation with his best friend, he called Tom McKinley.

"Tom, I have a question for you," he began. "What are the rules regarding taking Tiffany and her daughter out of town? I have a friend who has property in a rural area and has invited my family to join his for a weekend visit and cookout. He is agreeable to my bringing Tiffany and her daughter along."

"Whoa! Slow down a little," Tom pleaded. "You haven't even met this woman and her little girl."

"I know it may sound rushed," Larry replied. "The people making the invitation are good people. They have an eight-year-old daughter and a three-year-old son. I think it would be good for Tiffany to see a stable family in a relaxed environment, and I think the kids will have a great time."

"There is nothing in her release that prevents her from going out of town; she just has to clear it with me," Tom explained in a more relaxed tone.

"That's what I am doing," Larry replied. "Does she have your permission to do this?"

"Okay, it's your call," Tom stated. "I'm not sure what she will think about it, but I would guess that she might enjoy a weekend with her daughter in the country. I'll talk with her about it. I'm still not sure that you know what you're doing."

"You must have had a degree of confidence in me," Larry said. "Remember, you called me. You asked me to take them in under my care."

"I can't argue with that" McKinley admitted. "You just don't know Tiffany. She will be on her best behavior since she will have been so recently released. She will not have been able to size things up yet, and she certainly doesn't want to do anything to lose her daughter. She will understand your plans for the weekend before she arrives. I'll call you tomorrow to confirm things."

"Good," replied Larry.

As the call ended, he realized that he had not considered the fact that Tiffany would be sizing him up, as he was doing the same with her.

Maybe McKinley is letting me know that she is more intelligent than her choice to spend time in prison for a boyfriend would indicate.

TIFFANY PEERED THROUGH the bars of her cell in silence. Deals she made with inmates had kept her alive and free from permanent injury. A significant loss of self-respect was the price paid to make sure she obtained what she wanted. There were two sets of rules; rules made by those in charge of the facility, and those established by the inmates. She gracefully traversed them both like a tight rope walker schooled by a long line of circus family artists.

A lifetime of practice prepared her for an almost flawless performance. From a very young age she had found that her unusual physical attractiveness could be used to subtly work her will on others. Tiffany masterfully honed these skills to passively manipulate even the most vicious of convicts. A similar approach was taken with the prison staff, but tailored to satisfy those rules. Her keen mind was cloaked beneath an appearance of submissive sensuality. Invisible to everyone, deep within this seductive and manipulative exterior, resided her most powerful desire. A life with her daughter meant everything, and now her release was in sight.

EARLY FRIDAY MORNING, Larry sleepily arose from his desk and made his way to Evelyn's administrative area. She smiled as he approached.

"Evelyn, would you please put on some coffee?" Larry requested.

"Preacher, you look a little slow this morning," she replied. "Sure, it will be ready in just a few minutes."

Hearing the ringing of the phone on his desk, Larry turned and retreated back into the office. It was his Senior Pastor letting him know that Dr. Whitfield had contacted other centers around the country and Larry was now in demand.

"Well, I don't know what Dr. Whitfield thinks I can do about it," Larry said. "I have a job here. I can't just go bopping around the country."

"I've given this some thought, and I have also talked with the Committee on Missions," Dr. Stevens continued. "I bear some responsibility for this. The Committee has agreed to allow you to have six out of town speaking engagements per year if you are inclined to do so. What do you think?"

"What about the center?' Larry asked.

"You said yourself, that Evelyn and George were capable of handling the mission during your short absences. I want you to think about it."

"All right, I'll give it some consideration and prayer," Larry said.

After the call, Larry poured himself a cup of coffee and thanked Evelyn. He took the cup with him as he made his rounds at the mission. Some of the men were cleaning up after breakfast, and a few second phase people were just leaving for jobs outside the mission. Larry had placed one man at a local grocery store, stocking shelves. He found a job for another as a janitor at a private Christian school. The third phase involved people working and living in a low rent apartment. Not many entered the third phase, and few found success while living apart from the mission.

Larry had gotten little sleep the night before. He had lain awake for hours thinking about the fact that he would now be responsible for a mother and child at the mission. There had been a couple of occasions when a child had stayed overnight in Evelyn's room, but both situations involved a child waiting to be picked up by representatives from Child Welfare. One child was a runaway, and the other had been left by a parent who was running from legal problems.

Tom McKinley had promised to bring Tiffany and the little girl to the mission at 10:00 AM, and he was on time. In fact, Larry found the three of them waiting for him in his office when he returned from his morning rounds at the mission.

"You have visitors," Evelyn advised as he neared her desk.

"Thanks, Evelyn," he replied.

"Mr. McKinley, I am sorry to have kept you waiting," Larry said, as he extended his hand.

"You said 10:00 AM, right?" questioned Tom.

"You're right on time," answered Larry. "And this must be Tiffany Jennings."

She rose from a chair, holding her little daughter on her left hip. At once he understood that the probation officer had not exaggerated. Larry found her strikingly beautiful. Her bright blue eyes seemed to be flawlessly framed by her unblemished skin and black hair. She seemed to have just recently stepped from the pages of a magazine, rather than a prison. She gingerly slipped her delicate right hand into his.

"Mr. Chatterson," she whispered.

He felt a distinct sensual surge flow from Tiffany's stimulating touch, and he could not help but look deeply into her eyes. She was captivating. There was a mix of invitation and aloofness in her manner, such as could cause a man genuine confusion. Most men would immediately be drawn to desire her, yet thinking men would be slightly uneasy in her presence. Like most men, Larry initially sensed his ego stir with the sensation of her touch, but being a man of God, he quickly became uncomfortable.

"This is my daughter, Brandy," she continued.

Catching the smile of innocence from the child, the tension brought about by the mother subsided. He felt relief and was refreshed by the welcomed purity of the daughter. Though the little girl was a smaller and younger version of her mother in physical traits, she was still an innocent child. Brandy had the same blue eyes and black hair, but she had not yet learned how to use her looks to obtain what she wanted from men. This was an honest and sweet child contained within a shell which held promise to grow into the beauty owned by the mother. With the little girl's smile,

Larry completely forgot the physical power of the mother. Instead, his instinct of a soon to be father was drawn to the innocent little person being held on her mother's hip. He could not help but return Brandy's smile. Realizing the goodness of the man before her, the little girl instantly held out her arms to be taken into his. As he took her, her little head seemed to melt into his chest.

"Well, she seems to like you, Mr. Chatterson," Tiffany said softly.

"Please take a seat," Larry offered as he made his way to the chair behind his desk. "You do understand the provisions of your stay here, don't you?"

"She was told that she and Brandy would have a room together, and she understands that the little girl's father still has visitation rights every other weekend," Tom explained.

Larry placed the little girl on one knee as he took his seat. Bending down close to her ear he said, "I want to show you something."

She nodded her head and smiled. Larry opened a desk drawer and retrieved a small snowflake filled globe, containing a mother polar bear and cub within. He gently put it in her small, cupped hands. Placing his large hands on each side of hers, he guided her in giving it a slight shake. Brandy stared in amazement as the artificial snowflakes swirled around the two bears. He then turned his attention back to the little girl's mother.

"The policy here is that I will attempt to find you employment during the first four weeks of your joining the mission," Larry began. "You must understand that your independence will be limited, due to your history of serving time in prison?"

"I understand," Tiffany replied.

This time there was no aloofness in her manner. Her demeanor had suddenly changed. For the first time Larry caught a glimpse of the personal brokenness within the woman. Now, she seemed to be more like a thankful servant seated before a gracious king, rather than someone in control. He found her even more attractive than before. Larry immediately began to doubt the wisdom of taking this woman to Brandon Springs. He began to question his ability to maintain absolute control of the situation. Larry sensed she had a natural ability to control the emotions of men, and he found himself uneasy. Yet he had already set the plans in motion to take her and the child to the country for the visit.

"I understand that Brandy is to be with her father this coming weekend?" Larry asked.

"Yes," Tiffany answered.

"I talked with Mr. McKinley about taking you and your daughter with me and my wife to visit friends in the country over the following weekend," Larry said. "This is a good family, with two children of their own.   They said they would love to have you and Brandy along.   It's probably been a while since you've been to a place like that. What do you think?"

"It sounds really nice, but I really don't want to be any trouble for you," she replied.

"It won't be any trouble," Larry said. "I'll bring my wife by this afternoon to meet you. We are expecting our first child."

"Okay, I look forward to meeting her," she responded.

"Any poor judgment, in word or action, on your part will cause real problems for your probation," Tom sternly said to her. "If you were to cause Larry Chatterson and his wife problems on this trip, or if you cause problems at this center, you could go back to jail. Then again, good behavior on your part might go a long way in the court acknowledging you as a good mother for your child.   Reverend Chatterson is stepping out on a limb for you."

"I understand, and I appreciate the help," she replied.

Larry escorted the three from the office and into the reception area.   Evelyn chuckled when she saw Larry carrying the little girl past her desk.

"You look like a natural Daddy," she teased.

"Soon enough," he said, as he returned the child to her mother. "Please show Tiffany the room and help her get settled in. Brandy will be leaving with Mr. McKinley."

As she followed Evelyn from the reception area, Tiffany glanced back at Larry and silently mouthed, *Thank you.*

WITHIN A FULL day Tiffany easily adjusted to the routine at the mission. However, she was somewhat apprehensive about traveling to a rural setting with people she hardly knew, to visit people she had never met. Tiffany hoped that she was doing the right thing. Her time in prison had reinforced a distrust of fellow human beings.

At noon on the next Friday Tiffany and Brandy accompanied Larry and Patsy to Brandon Springs. The conversation among the three adults was so natural and enjoyable that the trip seemed to take little time. Patsy and Tiffany hit it off, and Larry thought he was beginning to see the real person who lived inside that gorgeous exterior. Brandy remained quiet during the majority of the drive, as she sat in her car seat and watched the changing landscape along the route. As they drove up to the house in Brandon Springs, they found Kaylee and Joey playing in the front yard.

"They're here!" Kaylee shouted, as the car came to a stop.

The screen door of the home opened, just as the visitors exited Larry's car. Kaylee and Joey began running toward the car. Within minutes of introductions, Ryan's two children were walking on each side of Brandy – each holding a hand. They were careful to steady her steps, as she had just begun to walk a few months earlier.

Patsy, Layla and Tiffany kept watchful eyes on the kids, as Larry and Ryan began to start the grill.

"All three children seem as though they have always

been the best of friends," Layla commented. "This isn't always the case when three kids play. Often two will team up and leave the third as an outsider."

Layla understood that the lack of conflict was because of her daughter Kaylee. She was the oldest, and her leadership established the environment of play. Kaylee played, but she also took on the role of mini mommy.

It had been years since Tiffany enjoyed a burger cooked on an outdoor grill, and she enjoyed every bite. Tiffany closed her eyes and imagined that it had been cooked and served to her by a handsome husband of her own. She envisioned that this country home was theirs, and that her life was much different than it was. Opening her eyes to reality, she felt satisfied for the time being just to reflect on how her daughter enjoyed laughing and playing with the other kids. Night settled, and soon the three children showed signs of fatigue from the hours of play, Layla and Tiffany gave baths to the youngest two. Kaylee readied herself for bed. An inflatable mattress was placed on the floor of the living area between the fireplace and a couch, and the three children talked and giggled before drifting off to the world of dreams. Brandy was soon fast asleep, lying between her two newly found friends.

Tiffany looked in on the kids. Comforted that the children slept peacefully, she rejoined the other four adults to play board games on the kitchen table. Just after 1:00 AM, the five exhausted adults left the kitchen for their assigned sleeping arrangements.

Tiffany's place was the fold-out couch near the children. Earlier in the night, this piece of furniture had been opened to reveal its alternative use as a double bed. Sheets, a couple of pillows, and a quilt had transformed it into a welcoming place for sleeping. Seated on the bedding she watched the slow shallow breathing of each child sleeping on the inflated mattress. She scanned elements of this plain and rustic room. Everything was clean, but imperfections could easily be observed in the worn wood planking that made up the flooring. There was a faint musty smell emitted from the fireplace. The evening was slightly cool, but the atmosphere of the house was filled with warmth. The still night was lightly touched by the faint murmurings of conversation drifting down the hall from one of the bedrooms.

A calm peace filled her mind and heart. She closed her eyes, allowing herself to be more fully immersed in the sensation. As Tiffany slipped between the sheets, she felt a security that she had not known since sleeping with her mother as a child.

"This is how it should be," she thought.

Tiffany slowly ran her hands across the texture of the quilt, sensing each stitch and each patch. Looking up at the high ceiling, she listened to the sound of her own relaxed breathing. Pulling the old quilt up around her shoulders, she turned on her side and snuggled up with a spare pillow.

"The only thing that would have made this day more perfect would have been if this pillow was a man," she thought.

She closed her eyes and tried to imagine the perfect man. The father of her daughter didn't fit the mold. Since spending time in prison, and since giving birth to her daughter, she viewed her former lover differently. An irresponsible and reckless man may appeal to some single women, but those are rarely the men trusted to care for a child. She pulled the pillow tight against her breasts and imagined a strong kind-hearted man with the physique of an athlete. In her imagination, the two of them lay nude, and she imagined touching his firm and powerful body. In her mind, she kissed and caressed this imaginary figure.

She imagined lying with Larry.

ROB WILLIAMS

REST IN BRANDON SPRINGS

Chapter 4

DAVID CLARKSTON THOUGHT back
to the first time his wife told him that she was going out and
that he should not wait up for her return.

"Rebecca, where are you going?"

"Just out to see a friend," she replied.

The lack of eye contact, along with her distant manner,
caused him to doubt she was being truthful. Still, he
attempted to convince himself that he should give his wife
the benefit of the doubt. By eleven that evening he began
to suspect that his trust was in vain. He attempted to contact
her on her cell, but the mechanism had been turned off.
Nervously he paced around the den of the parsonage.
Attempting to calm himself, he dropped into his favorite
chair and turned on the TV. However, a different set of
visual images played within his mind. Scenes flashed by
as if someone within his head was operating a slide show.
First were mental pictures of her suffering or dying from an
auto accident, then came the scenes of his wife enjoying the
company of another man. In vain desperation, he attempted
to concentrate on the broadcasted programs. It was no use,
for his emotions gravitated toward the mental pictures. Soon
he lost consciousness of anything emanating from the screen
before him. Moving to the kitchen, he busied himself with

items in the house that could be better cleaned or arranged. By 1:00 AM he had managed to fall asleep in a chair facing the TV. He awoke just after 2:00 AM. David nervously went to the bedroom hoping to find Rebecca sleeping there. The undisturbed bedding caused heavy emptiness to gnaw at his gut, and panic gripped his heart and mind. Attempts to reach his wife by cell phone continued to fail. Again, he busied himself; he brushed his teeth and set his alarm clock. A horde of feelings stampeded through his soul. Moments of terror were replaced by worry, which were replaced by anger, and then terror.

At last, he heard the unlocking of the front door. Hope and gratefulness replaced negative emotions, and he hurried to find Rebecca entering the home.

"Where in the world have you been?" he asked.

"I told you I was going out to see an old friend," she coldly replied. "Why aren't you asleep?"

"I couldn't sleep while you were still out!" he exclaimed.

Almost angrily she said, "Don't be ridiculous. You have to get up early, and you will have had almost no sleep. I'm not a little girl."

Astonished, he just stared blankly at his wife. She turned from him and proceeded to prepare for bed. After they both were in bed, David attempted to continue the conversation.

"Why were you out so late?"

"We just had things to talk about."

"Who is this friend?"

"It's late and I'm really tired" she abruptly answered. "I need some sleep, and so do you. Please just let me sleep."

She was fast asleep within a couple of minutes, but David finally drifted off about an hour before the alarm rang.

From that point on, her evenings out became more frequent, and her explanations were given less frequently. His last inquiry into her outings was answered by a cold statement from his wife.

"You have your life, and I have mine. Just live yours

and let me live mine. We have nothing in common; we just happen to live in the same house – that's all. That is all we have, nothing else. I don't care what you do, and I owe you no explanation regarding what I do."

David suffered from depression and exhaustion. He began to drink a glass of wine at night to help him sleep. Without it he would lay awake for hours listening for her return. Each noise in the night caused him to anticipate the unlocking of the front door. When David closed his eyes, he was often haunted with imaginary mental pictures of his wife making love to another man. He would lay awake, filled with emotion. His momentary feelings of anger towards her betrayal would shift into that of fear. Dr. Clarkston's once stable life was completely slipping away from him.

At the end of each day both husband and wife returned home from work. He returned for the evening, but she returned only to shower and change clothes. As he watched her leave for the evening, stress caused his hands and body to tremble. David's nerves were constantly on edge. Her absence at night consumed his thoughts, and he began to question his calling from God.

Still, members of his congregation came to him for counseling and comfort. They spilled their grief, horrors, and sins upon his aching soul attempting to rid themselves of personal troubles - never knowing of the deep despair that bore down on the man to whom they spoke. He felt trapped in a no-win situation. David would never think about spilling out his heart to a member of the congregation. He was supposed to be the spiritual and emotional rock, the man with all the answers. Dr. Clarkston had just begun to climb in his profession. A year prior he accepted the job as head pastor of a large and wealthy suburban church. If he confessed his situation to those in the administrative higher realms of his denomination, they would begin to view him as a liability. In time he believed they would make arrangements to place him in a less visible and less damaging position. In his eyes, this would be a setback for his career. Being in the area only a year, he knew of no other pastor locally that he could trust with the matter. It had been years since he allowed himself to make close friends within his church because he knew that he could not afford to show favoritism among members of a congregation.

He also felt he could not confide with members of his family. His father resented his going into the ministry, for he had hoped his son would attend law school and become a partner in his firm. He recalled his father's reaction to the decision to serve God.

"You're intelligent and gifted. I have the means to help you become great in a variety of fields. With these benefits going for you, why would you waste your life as a preacher?"

David knew what his father's advice would be, and he did not want to leave the church. He loved Rebecca and at the same time he hated her. He wished for a miracle; he wished for her to suddenly wake up from her world of lies and destruction and to appreciate his love for her. His mother would have never kept the matter to herself; she would have immediately confronted Rebecca. If she did, there would be no hope of working things out. The marriage would be over. He believed he was very much alone in dealing with the situation, and the massive internal struggle continued to consume his mind and emotions.

Over time, a glass of wine before bedtime became a bottle. Eventually, the drinking moved into his daytime hours. His habits became noticeable to others on staff at the church. Eventually, he was confronted by members of the pastoral committee at a special meeting. The Chair of the committee gave him a clear choice.

"The committee has notified the denominational administrative leaders of this situation, but we made it very clear of our wish to retain you as our pastor. However, if you wish to remain as the pastor of our congregation, you must enter a rehabilitation program. We have selected one for you, and arrangements have been made."

David never told them about the behavior of his wife, but agreed to go into the program for alcoholism. It would mean that he had to leave the church in the hands of the associate pastors for the six weeks needed to complete the first phase of the program. The second phase required him to attend counseling twice each week for six months; and the counseling sessions would be reduced to once a week for the third phase.

David's wife had not yet come to a point where she had made a decision to leave her husband. Otherwise, she would have ceased her attendance of the church services and would have filed for divorce. During the time of his initial absence, his wife was comforted almost daily by visits of several members of the church in the evening hours. She was also contacted by phone several times during each day. Rebecca was invited to lunch several times each week, and she was always greeted warmly at services. The outpouring of support from the women in the church was incredible, for they knew nothing of her infidelity. They were honestly concerned for another woman whose husband had given in to the addictive powers of alcohol. Rebecca Clarkston was surprised by the earnest care given by the women of the church. Because of the constant communication by them, she decided to stop seeing the other man for a time. In the beginning she felt the risk was too great of being found absent from the parsonage in the evening hours. She dared not risk him being seen at the parsonage. Part of the excitement experienced by secretly seeing the other man was the risk of being caught, but the risks had now risen beyond her desire to live a life flavored by taboo.

WHEN DAVID RETURNED from the program, he was a much-changed man. No longer did he project himself as the perfect man of God. Gone were the priestly airs. His view of himself, his career, and his family life had been shattered. The lid was off the box and the smell of success had been blown away by the humbling winds of failure. No longer did he demand perfection out of his wife or himself. David and Rebecca began to honestly talk, not as a pastor and a pastor's wife, but as a man and woman. At first, the communication was tense, and the lack of affection was as real as before. They honestly listened to each other in a spirit of kindness and humility. In speech, each gave careful consideration of words spoken.

Within a month she called the other man and broke off further communication with him. During that year she fell in love with the man she had once caught glimpses of before he was ordained. Though no one in the church knew of her infidelity, the couple thought it best to move far away from the man she had earlier entertained. David accepted the ministerial duties of a smaller church in Atlanta, Ga., but he forever remained grateful to the kind people in Ohio. He communicated with them often. David was loyal to his wife, and no one in either church knew of her faults. However, he made no secret of his own. Their struggle in marriage was between them and God. Though they rekindled their relationship, still individual personal moments of pain and remembered sorrow haunted them both. Over time the painful feelings came less frequent.

Though the home life was much improved, David struggled with his desire for alcohol when pressures arose. He openly talked of his addiction, hoping his confession before the church would provide him a source of strength when confronted by the temptation. Some of the sermons preached by David now sprung from his own struggles.

"Our key verse today is found in Hebrews, Chapter 12, verse 1" he said, opening a sermon. "This is a personal favorite of mine."

Wherefore seeing we also are compassed about with so

great a cloud of witnesses, let us lay aside every weight, and the sin which doth so easily beset us, and let us run with patience the race that is set before us.

"Sometimes a hidden weakness has more strength in the dark. Light often tends to cause evil to temporarily shrink back into a dark corner, huddling in a defensive fetal position. Words are spoken out into eternity, and they can never be retrieved. Actions have consequences and things done can never be completely undone. Lamentations 3:22-23 is another personal favorite."

It is of the Lord's mercies that we are not consumed, because his compassions fail not. They are new every morning: great is thy faithfulness.

"When we find that we have tripped and fallen in this race, it's important that we embrace God's immense mercy. With this mercy, we should arise with determination, dust ourselves off, and continue the race. When I struggle daily, I try to put both sets of verses into practice."

DURING THE YEAR, Larry spoke at centers in three different states. He was becoming known among those affiliated with missions for the homeless, and this publicity drew funding for the center from persons outside the Charlotte area. For that reason, the Senior Pastor and the committee on missions encouraged him to accept at least six speaking engagements each year. As summer began to give way to cooler breezes, Larry received a call from a friend in Atlanta.

"Larry, I want you to know that things are looking much better for me," began Dr. David Clarkston.

"That's great to hear!" replied Larry. "Are things better at home?"

"Better than expected and probably better than I deserve," David answered. "Listen, I want you to know how much your friendship has meant to me. Your phone calls over the last few months have been a great source of encouragement. You've helped me so much in climbing back into the pulpit. I owe you a great deal. Your advice for me has been tremendously sound, both for my ministry and in my home. I want you to come to Atlanta and speak at my church next month. The church has a budget for guest speakers, and we can pay your way. The congregation will donate an offering to your mission. I really hope you can fit it into your schedule."

IT BEGAN TO rain as Larry moved up the steps to the front door of the Senior Pastor parsonage. The door opened before he even knocked.

"Come in before you get wet," said Dr. Stevens' wife Gracie. "I was looking out the window when you pulled up. I have sandwiches in the den, but I won't be joining you. I'm meeting some women from the church for lunch. I do this every Wednesday. I hope you won't mind my not being here."

"Not at all, Mrs. Stevens," replied Larry.

"I told you to call me Gracie," she scolded. "I know you're from the Deep South, and I know that I'm 20 years older than you – but I really want you to call me by my first name. We are friends, aren't we?"

"Certainly, we are friends," he said. "Old habits are hard to break, Gracie."

"Now that's better," she replied, as she stretched upwards and gave him a kiss on the cheek. "Come on into the den."

"Harold, Larry is here!" Gracie shouted, as she escorted the younger man into the den.

"I could have heard you scolding him about calling you Mrs. Stevens a block away, Gracie," Dr. Stevens replied. "The young man was brought up correctly, to show respect for his elders."

Larry took his place on the couch beside Dr. Stevens, and Gracie excused herself to have lunch with the church women. Ham and cheese sandwiches and lemonade had been placed on the coffee table along with a bowl of chips. The older man asked God's blessing on the food, before they began to eat.

"I want to talk with you about your speaking engagements this year," Dr. Stevens began.

"Great!" Larry replied. "Actually, I wanted to tell you that I have been invited to speak in Atlanta next month. It came about through the talk you arranged for me at that abuse recovery center last year. I know that I already have six trips scheduled, but the pastor is a friend of mine, and he says that they will take up an offering for the mission."

"Next month?" asked Dr. Stevens. "I expected invitations to come in. Are you prepared to have someone handle the mission during your absence?"

"I wanted to talk to you before accepting the speaking engagement and making any arrangements," Larry responded. "This pastor in Atlanta was one of the men at the center, and he seems to be doing well now. His church graciously waited for his return from the rehabilitation center, and they have afforded him tremendous support. He and I have been communicating over the past few months and we've become friends."

"He must be a very special minister and loved by those whom he serves," said Dr. Stevens. "If you feel that your staff can provide adequate coverage at the mission in your absence, I don't see why you couldn't add this engagement. I leave it to your discretion."

"Thank you, Dr. Stevens," Larry replied.

"Gracie's right, young man," said the older pastor. "You've known us long enough to call us by first names. When we are among those of the congregation, you should still call me Dr. Stevens. However, when in private conversations you can call me Howard. I'm old enough to be your father, but I'm not your father. I know that your father has passed away. I hope you would look on me as someone who might, on occasion, give you fatherly advice in spiritual matters."

"I would be honored to have your advice, Dr. Stevens," Larry replied.

"Howard... you can call me Howard," Dr. Stevens reminded him.

"Okay," Larry said. "Howard, I would be honored."

"I want to share with you a true story of a young pastor," Dr. Stevens began. "I tell you this in confidence because he was an assistant pastor under me at another church. Most do not know why he and I parted ways, and I want you to tell no one of what I am about to share."

"I'll hold this in confidence between only the two of us," Larry promised.

"He was an excellent speaker and a very handsome young man. Being a charismatic figure can be both a blessing and a curse. For a younger man, he had a particular gift for counseling those with difficult personal situations. He had a knack for making people feel better about themselves and the situations they faced.

However, he failed to seek the counsel of others when it came to situations in his own life. A beautiful young woman in the congregation was having marital problems with her non-churched husband. She and her two young daughters attended church, but her husband would have no part of it. Early in their marriage her husband rose to a position that gave him a large salary with an annual bonus. The company later experienced a merger, and he found himself on the losing end. Some leadership positions within two companies are done away with during a merger, and often it falls to politics rather than the skill sets of those retained in positions. He was an honest individual who had attained his position through hard work. Nevertheless, he was forced to take a lower paying position at another company. He was also forced to seriously draw out of his savings to make the house payments of a luxurious home; one that he could no longer afford. The financial pressures took a toll on the marriage. They often do.

The attractive wife dropped by this assistant pastor's office one day to seek counsel regarding her marital struggles. This young minister was smart enough at first to leave his door open to the receptionist area during the counseling sessions, as to make sure they were not alone. But soon one thing led to another. Personal eye contact was the first of several dangerous doors of communication. A lot can be said through the eyes, and she was a woman feeling lonely and hungry for a kind glance from a handsome man. Over time the glances grew to sensual gazes of desire. Hands began to touch, and then whispers were spoken that were beyond the listening ears of the receptionist. They began meeting for private talks in isolated places. Once lips met, it was too late. They began having sex in her car in a remote place outside of town.

To make a long story short, the young minister left his wife and children for her. Her husband was unable to deal with the loss. He shot himself. Needless to say, this young and promising pastor also left the ministry. The ex-minister's wife and children moved to be near her mother and father, and it was probably a wise thing to do.

Small things often lead to larger things, and it can happen much sooner than one would think. He married the woman. Together with her children, they moved to another city. The newly formed family began to attend a church of another denomination, and the man became a lay speaker in that church. He was a gifted orator. Eventually the pastor of that church suggested that he give the ministry a second try. The pastor stood with him before the administrative leadership of that denomination and asked that he be given license to preach as his assistant pastor. The minister reminded the church leadership of how in the Bible David had made the mistake of infidelity with another man's wife. He reminded them that God continued to use David in a mighty way. The pastor was respected, and the leadership granted the younger man license to preach and to hold the position of assistant pastor under the authority of the older man.

The younger man excelled in the position, and his preaching inspired those in the congregation. Over time, many gravitated to his speaking over that of the senior pastor. Unknown to the senior pastor, the younger man had voiced concerns over the direction of the church to a few chosen men of the congregation. In time the church split. The younger minister took over half the congregation from the pastor who had shown kindness and had given this younger man a second chance. I won't tell you his name because he still pastors a congregation in another town. I doubt any in that congregation know the whole story of what this man did and the carnage he left in his wake.

I want you to be open and honest with me in the situations that come before you. Specifically, I know that you've taken a very beautiful woman and her child into the mission. I commend you for your effort, but I want you to be particularly mindful of what can happen. I know you love your wife, Patsy. I'm not accusing you of anything, in any way. I just know the nature of men and women, and I want you to take great care. This woman may come to you for advice and counsel, and you need to be wise. I hope you don't take this advice in a bad way or question my confidence in you. Just be careful."

"I understand," Larry replied. "No offense taken. She is an attractive woman, and to be honest, I wish my wife could be around during times of counsel. I've been careful to invite Evelyn to be present during conversations I have with Tiffany in the office. Evelyn has been a gift from God. She's a widow of a minister and she has a lot of insight. I think this will work."

Chapter 5

A CLOUDLESS SKY offered no omen of things to come. As Chad Maddox stepped from a towering downtown Atlanta office building, the fall breeze carried no warning that he was only moments away from a brutal life-altering event. He heard only the beckoning of his empty stomach. Chad made a point of regularly walking to the park at Five Points before proceeding to a nearby café for lunch. A certain haggard and homeless fellow had a habit of sleeping on a particular park bench during the same hour. The practice of established personal routines was not the only thing the two men had in common.

"There he is – as disgusting as ever," thought Chad, as he approached the park.

Chad was always mindful of this fellow when enroute to the café. He became unusually concerned on this occasion, for there appeared to be no distinguishable signs of life in the homeless man. The stillness of this ragged form caused Chad to momentarily stop directly in front of the occupied bench. In an act of tying his shoe, Chad placed his right foot on the bench. He purposefully made sure his pristinely shined shoe solidly bumped against one belonging to the weathered individual. Semi-conscious eyes briefly opened. Shadowed under a heavy brow, the man's piercing light gray eyes momentarily blazed from sunken sockets. Haunting pale eyes framed by weathered brown skin and unkempt graying hair would be somewhat mesmerizing to most. However, Chad had seen those eyes before.

"Well, that ragged piece of filth has a beating heart, after all."

He wasn't sure whether the man had actually awakened enough to be conscious of him, but he had no intention of waiting around to strike up a conversation. Chad left the man and hurriedly continued his route. Nearing the café on the other side of the small park, he glanced back to find that the park bench was now empty. He quickly spotted him heading south from the park.

No longer mindful of lunch, he headed in the direction of the homeless man. Chad followed him south for several blocks. He had never ventured past this point on foot. As his pace quickened, a cold chill began to run down the back of his neck. Businessmen in suits were replaced by ragged individuals who smelled of body odor and alcohol. He couldn't help feeling disgusted as he passed them. These were stark forms of those not yet dead. They walked upright, but it was as though death had already taken a firm hold on each. Many suffered severe mental illnesses, some due to heavy substance abuse and others due to unspeakable life experiences. They breathed in the same invigorating cool air as Chad, but exhaled little life.

Fear began to squeeze adrenaline throughout his body. Chad continued. His course of action was set, as though every part of his being had been programmed to do this very thing. He was driven - possessed by an uncontrollable force. Chad was within a half block of him when a car stopped near the man. At once three teens bolted from the vehicle and attacked the indigent fellow. They immediately knocked him to the ground and began to violently kick his face and head. At first the man attempted to cover himself with his hands and the bedroll he carried, but soon one of the blows left him unconscious. To Chad's amazement, the kicking continued. Without thinking, he found himself running in the direction of the downed man.

He screamed out at the young men, "Hey! Stop it! The man is down. Back off!"

The kicking ended, and the three started towards him. Chad had witnessed a crime, and now their full attention was on him. He glanced at the still body on the sidewalk.

"Is he dead? Maybe he's just hurt really bad."

Overcome by emotion, he continued on a collision course with those approaching. Chad slowed as he reached the three. Quickly, the fist of one youth struck him squarely on the left side of his head. He was dazed for a split second. Chad then struck back, sending the teen reeling backwards from the blow. The other two pounced on Chad. One grabbed his arms from behind, while the other began to lay blow after blow against his abdomen. Suddenly the fist of the first young man smashed against his nose. A sharp pain seemed to split his face in half. Chad's vision began to blur as he continued to struggle to free himself from the hold of the one behind him. He heard the sound of a whistle, and then everything went black.

EARLIER THAT MORNING, Chad met the pastor of his church Dr. David Clarkston for breakfast. Immediately after coffee was served, the minister informed him of an upcoming event at the church.

"You might want to consider coming to hear this man," the minister said, while placing a letter on the table.

Chad picked up the letter and quickly reviewed it. It was from a pastor of a church in Charlotte, NC, and it contained a biographical summary of someone on his staff. The minister waited silently for a few seconds before continuing.

"This man will soon be a guest speaker, and I wanted to share this letter with you."

"Dr. Clarkston, he sounds like a very interesting guy," Chad replied after finishing his quick review. "I plan to be there."

After breakfast Chad attempted to concentrate on his morning's work, but he found the conversation about the letter running through his mind. Since moving to Atlanta from Boston two years prior, he had become remarkably close to his pastor. The more he got to know the minister on a personal level, the better he liked him. He was a genuine soul; one who could be trusted. The pastor practiced no pretense, and he put on no false airs. In fact, at the beginning of one service this man of God requested prayer from church members for a personal problem. The minister stopped the order of service until he received prayers of the associate ministers, lay leaders, and church elders. Immediately after stating the need, he proceeded to move down to the altar. There he knelt for prayer just as anyone else in the church. For about five minutes, those called out formed a circle around the kneeling pastor and began to pray. Some prayed with a hand placed on his shoulder, and others just stood nearby with heads bowed. Afterwards he confessed before the entire congregation his problems with alcohol. This honesty made a serious impression on Chad, for he had grown up in the household of an alcoholic.

It was the minister's true humility and honesty that caused Chad Maddox to trust him. Over time David began to allow himself to return this trust with genuine friendship. This pastor was the first man Chad had ever known to gain victory over a personal problem of alcohol abuse.

This weakness had robbed Chad's father of his career as an accountant, and eventually contributed to his mother's divorce from the man. At first, Chad's father worked odd jobs and maintained contact with his children. Eventually, the addiction to alcohol overshadowed any hopes of employment. It drowned natural desires to be a part of the lives of those he helped bring into the world. Charles Maddox moved from town to town. By the time Chad left home for college, Charles was totally absent from the lives of his children. At one point, he spent three months at a mission for the homeless in Boston, but he was kicked out after angrily striking a staff member. He had earlier spent time in jail for beating several fellow homeless individuals, but the attack on the staff was the last straw at the mission. He was arrested again. After being released from jail for this violent action he made his way to Atlanta. There, all hope left him. He ceased all efforts of living in missions, and all thoughts of returning to a productive life vanished. He lived on the streets, ate out of dumpsters, and used any money donated to him to purchase cheap alcohol. At this point, the only contact he had with a mission was when staff would take food into the streets to those sleeping on sidewalks and in parks. He was now among the living dead.

For years Chad didn't know what had become of his father. After finishing a degree in accounting, and later an MBA, he decided to make attempts to locate him. While traveling on various business trips, he often contacted local shelters. He contacted several missions for the homeless before finding one in Atlanta that knew of his father.

The following month he returned to Atlanta and visited the area where the mission staff had seen him. The effort was in vain, for he didn't recognize his father to be either of the two homeless men present in Woodruff Park. Chad made another attempt. He walked streets surrounding the park for a half hour before heading to a nearby café for lunch. Chad knew very little about downtown Atlanta, and he was hesitant to venture far from areas populated by well-dressed professionals. While eating at the café, he asked the waitress if there were any other parks within walking distance.

"There's Hurt Park," the waitress answered.

She gave him the directions to the park, and he headed in that direction immediately after finishing lunch. The population on the sidewalks thinned somewhat as he approached his destination. As he entered the park, he took note of a handful of sleeping men. Most were resting on the ground in dirty bedrolls, but he spotted a man on a park bench. He anxiously approached the bench and slowed as he neared. Standing directly before the sleeping man, he nervously searched for familiar characteristics in the features of the fellow. Suddenly, he heard a rough voice from behind.

"Hey, are you one of those prissy guys who like watching men sleep?"

Turning around, he found himself staring directly into a pair of stunning clear gray eyes. He knew those eyes. They seemed to pierce him, as though they were a pair of focused lasers. Chad felt claws of fear begin to grip his soul; fear he had not sensed since childhood. He remembered himself, and purposefully shoved his emotions aside.

"Are you Charles Maddox?" he asked, in a confrontational tone.

"What's it to you, sissy man?" replied the indigent fellow.

By this time Chad had become angry for allowing this familiar fear to be experienced again. He calmed himself. Summoning strength from somewhere deep within, Chad questioned the man again.

"You don't know me, do you?"

"No, I don't know you," the indigent fellow quietly answered. "Hey, maybe I do".

A slight glimmer of hope touched Chad, and he took a step closer to the man. He quickly scanned the form before him. Chad found the oily and matted graying hair disgusting; and when the breeze shifted, he caught the stench of alcohol mixed with body odor.

"You're my old buddy, aren't you?" the man asked. "Don't you want to buy your old buddy a drink?"

Chad said nothing. He just quietly continued to scan the

foul man for other familiar signs. He then turned and walked away.

"Cat got your tongue?" a voice called out, from behind.

Chad stopped and turned back to face the man. "I think you were right the first time," he replied. "I don't think you know me."

This time the indigent man remained silent as the younger man slowly turned again to walk away. Chad Maddox no longer felt the fear of a child standing before a violent man consumed by alcohol, a man who could suddenly turn from making jokes to being totally absent of mercy and kindness.

"This was a mistake," Chad thought. *"I should have left him to rot. He is a maggot, just a stinking maggot. He is doing exactly what he has always wanted to do; just be drunk and rot away. Maybe that is what he deserves. With cheap booze, that drunken heap of trash has burned away every brain cell he ever had. He didn't even recognize his own son. What a piece of work! What a piece of useless trash. I was better off without him. Mom was better off without him. All of us were better off without him. Maybe the world will be better off when that jerk finally rots away and dies."*

Chad was angry with his father for being such a useless waste, and he was angry with himself for making the effort to find his father. However, his heart ached.

"I shouldn't have put myself out for him, but at least I now know," he thought. *"I won't tell Mom. I will leave her out of this; it will just hurt her again. He doesn't have the right to hurt her again."*

The old man watched, as Chad traveled farther down the street. At last, he was out of sight. The ragged fellow quietly dropped his bedroll on a bench and took a seat. Looking down at the sidewalk before him, he then raised his eyes to see if the visitor was coming back. Memories of a distant past flooded his mind, as though the events occurred just yesterday. Charles Maddox placed his weather hardened hands over his face and wept bitterly.

FOR MONTHS AFTER finding his father in a park in Atlanta, Chad Maddox was consumed with thoughts of the aging homeless man. He was disgusted by the wretched appearance of his father, and the smell was probably the worst of it. The older man's face was worn, and his clothes torn. Chad doubted whether the indigent man's thinking fell into the range of sanity, but this was the only father he had. Charles Maddox had not always been this way.

Thinking back to his childhood, Chad remembered both enjoyable occasions and those where this man inflicted pain on family members during drunken tirades. Charles Maddox was exceptionally brutal to Chad's mother, and on occasions the man would toss her to the floor as if she were a dirty pair of socks. For some unexplainable reason, the woman showed no fear of these abuses. She would immediately leap back to her feet and begin pounding her slight fists against her drunken husband. Normally he would let out a string of foul curses and leave the house.

When Chad reached the age of thirteen, male hormones began to stir within him. He sometimes became aggressive with other boys at school. After participating in a couple of fights, most males of his age understood that it was best to leave him alone when his anger rose to the surface.

Shaun Hall was not well liked, but he was respected by those who viewed violence as an acceptable means of expressing one's point of view. He was the worst of the school bullies, and everyone was afraid of him. Chad had walked past Shaun and a group of teens behind the school building while a drug exchange was taking place after hours. Shaun immediately accused Chad of being the type who would inform someone of the illegal activity. In an effort to discourage him from talking, the larger boy began to shove

Chad around. As a last demonstration of what the smaller teen could expect if he told anyone, Shaun sent a powerful open hand slap across Chad's face.

Without hesitation, Chad stepped into the face of his oppressor. It was as if he was on autopilot and couldn't help himself. Immediately noting the sign of disrespect and challenge, Shaun sent a quick blow to the gut. Being so close to his intended victim, his fist fell far short of maximum extension and the impact was somewhat less effective than if it had reached its full capacity. Chad pressed on. Shaun felt that he had no choice than to strike him in the face and did so several times. Chad slowly walked directly into punch after punch. To those observing, the fight appeared to take on a metaphysical air. Eerily, Chad seemed unaffected by the blows. It seemed as if he had gone into some sort of trance, for it was obvious that the fists of the other lad were connecting at their intended points of destination. Blood could be seen from a split lip. However, within the time it took to absorb three licks Chad had managed to turn the table on his challenger. To Shaun's surprise, the smaller male's adrenaline filled pair of hands took hold of his shirt. Chad threw the larger boy to the ground and began to pound him repeatedly. Within seconds Shaun lost consciousness from the blows he received.

Even after the youth on the ground passed out, Chad continued to beat him. Those observing the fight refused to step in until they heard the distinct sound of a nose violently breaking and witnessed blood gushing from the damaged face. Four of them grabbed Chad and pulled him from his victim. His eyes, wild with rage, shifted their attention to those who dared to interfere. Though the four had him in a firm hold, each boy sensed fear.

"Chad, stop now!" one of them shouted. "Are you trying to kill him? Chad, Chad, Chad!"

It was as if the shouts had awakened him from a dream. Somewhat unaware of the entire situation, Chad began looking around to see what the excitement was all about. Seeing the other boy lying with his face covered in blood, he realized what he had just done. He began to shake with an overwhelming sense of dread.

"Did I kill him?"

Panic set in as he looked for answers in the faces of those around him. At last, he saw movement in the injured form lying on the ground, and then he heard moaning. It was the sound coming from the boy that caused chills to run through Chad. He was relieved that the boy was alive, but thoughts of brain damage or other permanent afflictions coursed through his mind.

Two of those holding him loosened their grip and began to attend the injured boy. After several minutes, they were able to help him sit up. Though Shaun's mental alertness was minimal for some time, they determined that the only real damage was the broken nose. By this time, Chad was sitting alone on the ground intently watching Shaun's every movement. He was relieved to witness signs of normalcy returning to him. As the others helped the dazed boy to his feet, Chad jumped to his. With his head now clearing, Shaun gingerly pushed his helpers aside and walked toward Chad. The darkening blood on his face was beginning to dry, and his steps began to be more controlled. Reaching Chad, he held out his hand.

"Okay," he mumbled, in a deep adolescent voice. His eyes acknowledged a newfound respect for Chad, and the hands of the two young men clasped in the most powerful grip each could muster. As he turned to make his way home, Shaun answered each inquiry as to his health with, "I'm all right".

Once out of sight, one of the boys stepped over to Chad and said "Well, I doubt you will have any more trouble with him."

Cautious smiles began to emerge on the faces of some as they began to leave the place of battle, but concern showed in the eyes of most. They had just witnessed a teenage boy totally lose control of himself. Some discussed whether they would have witnessed a killing if they had not pulled Chad off. Some shared a blow-by-blow recap of the match. Others thought Shaun Hall had it coming to him. The rest was history. After this incident, no one challenged Chad. He had the respect of some and was looked on with apprehension and fear by others at school.

Home was an entirely different environment for Chad. Charles Maddox had no fear of this young man and showed little respect to anyone after several drinks were consumed. On one occasion, after throwing his wife to the floor, the situation escalated. Infuriated by her normal reaction of rising back up against him, he slapped her to the ground and then began to beat her. Chad stepped in with a blow to the side of his father's face, and then chaos erupted.

Ignoring his hurting wife, Charles focused his attention on Chad. At first the father seemed somewhat hurt that his son would strike him. However, this wore off quickly and intense rage took hold. He firmly grabbed Chad by the neck, almost to the point of choking the life out of him. The older man slammed his son to the floor and began to slap him intensely across the face. By this time, Chad's mother grabbed a convenient item and desperately began to pound her husband with it. It happened to be a brass candlestick from the mantle above the fireplace, and apparently it was just the tool needed. After a couple of blows to the head, Charles released his hold on Chad and staggered out of the front door of the house.

This time, Mary Maddox called the police. She banned Charles from the house, had a judge issue a restraining order, and began divorce proceedings. Her own physical abuse was one thing, but this was the last straw. She had no intention of allowing his drunken rampages to endanger her children. This was the deciding factor, and it caused the end of the marriage. Over the next couple of years Charles attempted to stop drinking and made attempts to reconcile, but each time he was unable to stay away from the bottle. Each failure resulted in isolation from the rest of the family, and by the time Chad entered college Charles had moved to another town and stopped all contact with his children.

Unlike his younger brother, Chad had fond memories of what his father was like before he succumbed to alcohol. He often thought back to when he was an eight-year-old Cub Scout, and of his experiences with his father at that time. Though Charles had already begun to drink on a regular basis, he had established a positive relationship with his oldest son. Chad remembered how his father patiently spent hours helping him build a winning pinewood derby racing car. He remembered the joy of success they shared when Chad was presented with the First-Place trophy. In fact, he still had that car and trophy tucked away in an old shoebox. He hung on to them, even after his father stopped being an active part of his life. They were a source of stability for him. Although he rarely took the car and trophy out of that shoebox, he always knew they were there. Their existence served as confirmation that normal family life was possible. The physical presence of the objects proved that those "good times" were not just the false products of a child's rich imagination.

Chapter 6

PRIOR TO BEING BEATEN by the teens, Chad had a few successes in reaching out to his father. He was driven by childhood memories that seemed to be permanently etched in the back of his mind, and particular events would trigger actions of reconciliation with his father.

Rarely did anyone accompany Chad during lunch. On one occasion while eating alone, he saw another man of his age having lunch with someone who appeared to be the man's father. This caused him to think about his own father. Reflections of a distant past filled his mind with vivid memories of his father and his heart began to yearn for a father-son relationship. Though he was now a grown man, he realized that something was missing. In his imagination, he saw himself having lunch with a sober and caring father. Chad pictured himself sharing his professional accomplishments in his career. He also imagined discussing personal aspects of his life and asking for advice. He closed his eyes and imagined wise words being spoken by a kind and experienced man. He envisioned a proud smile from a father. At that moment, he made the decision to make another attempt to re-establish that relationship. During his next business trip to Atlanta, he made a point to walk to a nearby downtown park. He had seen his father before in a downtown park, so he considered the chances of finding him again might be good. To his surprise, he immediately spotted Charles Maddox sitting on a bench. Chad cautiously made his way toward his father and stopped about ten feet directly in front of him. He said nothing; the two men quietly examined one another.

"You came back," stated Charles.

"You recognized me?" Chad asked, almost startled by the change in his father's composure.

"You're probably better off without me," replied the older man. "I really haven't done you any favors."

"You may be partly right about that," answered Chad. "You look better than the last time I saw you."

"Well, looks can be deceiving," said his father. "I'm not really much different....just not as cranky today. Come back tomorrow, and I will be my usual butthole self. Why are you here?"

"Business," answered the son. "I come to Atlanta on business every so often."

Chad moved closer and took a seat beside his father. As he told Charles about college and work, the older man listened intently. His stunning light gray eyes danced as he took in each detail.

"Hey, I'm about to go get something to eat," Chad said. "Are you hungry?"

"They wouldn't want me in any of the restaurants around here," he replied. "I don't want to hold you from eating."

"How does a hot shower sound?" Chad asked. "My hotel is just a couple of blocks away. Come on and take a shower. I'm a little heavier than you, but I have some clothes that would do."

"I appreciate it, son, but you shouldn't go to that trouble," answered the older man. "Go get yourself something to eat."

"Are you going to be here long?" asked Chad. "I mean, would you still be here when I get back?"

"It's hard to say," he replied. "Sometimes the police run me off; sometimes things just happen. Don't worry about me, just go get something to eat."

"It will be dark soon," the younger man observed.

"Does that every evening," replied the older man, with a slight smile.

"I guess so," he responded. "Okay, I hope I will see you again."

As he began to make his way toward the café, he heard his father call out his name. He turned and took a couple of steps in his father's direction.

"You're a good man, Chad," stated Charles, his eyes looking away from his son. "Your mother did a good job."

"Thank you," Chad replied.

The younger Maddox made his way to a nearby café, where he quickly consumed diner. He also ordered a sandwich and cookies to go. Chad spent no more than fifteen minutes in the café, and with great anticipation he left the small establishment. The brown paper bag containing the sandwich and cookies swung freely in his left hand as he hurried back to the park. Anticipation turned to disappointment when he found no one on the park bench. He scanned the people he passed as he made a quick tour of the park, but his father had vanished.

Emotions within him stirred like the tempest at the bottom of Niagara Falls. He initially felt guilt, but he could think of nothing he had done to cause his father to leave the park. Guilt changed to anger as he considered the fact that his father had not waited even fifteen minutes for his return. Claws of fear eventually tore into his chest, fearing the possibility that his father had suffered a heart attack. Thoughts of calling nearby hospitals gave way to reason. Violent emotional reactions to his father's erratic behavior had colored Chad's teen years. Most of the time he had been extremely unsettled while being around his father. He calmed himself.

Things can wait until tomorrow morning. The sandwich and cookies should keep in the small hotel refrigerator until that time. I'll visit the park one last time before departing for my flight.

SLEEP NEVER TRULY settled on Chad until the early morning hours, and the unwelcome wake-up call left him feeling exhausted. Check out time was 11:00 AM, and his flight wasn't scheduled until 1:00 PM. Around 10:00 AM he took his bag containing the sandwich and cookies for a short walk to the park. He felt a welcome relief in finding his father seated on the same park bench.

"I brought you a lunch before leaving to go back home," Chad said in his greeting for this father.

Charles Maddox made no acknowledgement of the presence of his son, not even lifting his eyes to make contact. Chad stepped closer and noticed that those clear and striking gray pair of eyes where shielded from view by wrinkled eyelids.

"Dad!" the younger man shouted.

This time the haggard form on the bench moved in response to the call. It took a second for Charles to move from the realm of the unconscious to the actual world in which he resided. At last, he focused on the man standing before him.

"Hey, you're still…," he whispered.

His speech was interrupted by an attack of coughing. Within a minute, he continued.

"So you haven't left yet?" he asked.

"I'll check out in an hour," Chad replied. "I brought you some lunch. Are you hungry?"

"I can eat," Charles answered.

Taking the brown bag and looking inside, the older man brought out the contents and placed them in his lap. He slowly examined each item as though they were rare and fragile gifts, unwrapping them with care.

"Cookies!" he exclaimed. "Been awhile since I had nicely baked cookies. I'll save them until later. The sandwich will do for now."

Chad took a seat beside his father and the two talked more that morning than Chad could remember doing in many years. As the younger Maddox departed to check out of the hotel and catch his flight, he felt like a completed puzzle. There was a sense of satisfaction that could not be expressed in words. As he boarded the plane, he carried an inner peace that he had not experienced since being a small child.

DURING THE FOLLOWING two months Chad eagerly anticipated a return trip to Atlanta. On his next visit, he was pleased to find his father asleep on the same bench as before. With a deep sense of belonging, he quickly walked over to the sleeping form.

"Dad," he called out as he stood directly in front of the bench.

There wasn't a stir. He searched the older man for signs of life, and he felt a relief as he detected shallow breathing. This time he made a greater effort to wake the man.

"Dad!" he called out in a louder voice, as he gave his father's shoulder a slight shake.

This time the man took a deep breath and rolled from his side onto his back. A weathered left hand rose to cover his face, and a deep gurgling sound could be heard as he cleared his throat. The breathing returned to the original shallow state, and the only movement was the slight rising and falling of Charles's chest.

Chad had looked forward to this visit too much to let the effort go. He was intent on gaining his father's attention.

"Hey, Dad!" he shouted.

His call was accompanied by a rough shaking of the

older man's shoulders. The more aggressive effort resulted in a string of foul curses stammering through drunken lips. As the obscenities were angrily pronounced, a set of furious pale gray eyes glared at the person responsible for waking him.

"It's me, Dad," Chad explained. "Are you okay?"

His attempted explanation was met with another string of curses. The younger Maddox caught the sickening smell of chronic intoxication, and suddenly Chad realized that this visit would not be like the previous. He slowly stepped back away from the bench and examined the situation.

"*There will be no waking him,*" Chad thought. "*Maybe next time. Maybe things will be different next time.*"

He walked to a nearby café and ordered a sandwich and cookies to go. As he approached the bench with the bag containing the lunch, he found his father still fast asleep. He took a pad and pen from his coat pocket and scribbled a note.

Dropped by to see you, Dad – but you were sleeping pretty hard. See you next time. Chad.

Chad placed the note in the bag, unzipped his father's coat, and placed it between the coat and his father's flannel shirt. After zipping the coat, he scanned the sky for clouds. Spring had begun, and dry weather no longer resulted in temperature cold enough to pose his father a serious health risk. However, a cold rain could negatively impact a heavily drunken man who would be oblivious to his surroundings until the alcohol wore off. Everything appeared to be relatively safe for the time being. Disappointed, Chad returned to check out from the hotel and make his flight.

OVER THE NEXT SIX MONTHS, Chad was able to return to Atlanta two more times. He began to realize how special that earlier conversation with his father had been. A visit that afforded meaningful communication with his father was very much out of the ordinary. As the colder winds of fall settled into the Atlanta area, he became concerned for his father's life. That one good visit with his father changed everything. Prior to that encounter, several years had passed since Chad felt deep concern for Charles Maddox. He began to search the corporate job postings for jobs in the Atlanta office. Before long, he found a suitable position there and requested a transfer. That December he made the move.

He sold his home and invested in a downtown condo. At first, his visits to the park were done on a random basis. Because of Chad's efforts to look after his father, Charles survived brutal winter nights by staying at a downtown mission.

One cold and wet day, Chad found his father asleep on a park bench in a drunken stupor. He took one look at the pale blue tint of the old man's face, and panic viciously latched on to his soul.

"Oh, God – he's dead!" Chad's mind silently screamed in horror.

He vigorously rubbed his father's cold clammy skin, and he began to feel movement. Within seconds, those stunning gray eyes peered up at him.

"What the hell are you doing?" Charles blurted out, in a half stammering manner.

"You're freezing to death, you drunken fool!" Chad screamed out at his father.

Pulling his father into a seated position, the younger man asked, "Why aren't you at the mission?"

"I'm going," Charles mumbled. "I just wanted to take a nap first."

"I'm taking you to the mission, and I don't want to hear any crap out of you," Chad said.

"All right – don't get your panties in a wad!" Charles blurted.

Chad helped his father to his feet and steadied the old

man's balance. The walk was only eight blocks, but it seemed like hundreds of miles. It had been some time since he had experienced such close physical contact with the man. He stank. His father's sour body odor was flavored by the additional smell caused by large quantities of cheap booze consumed over a long period of time. Each pore of his body produced a rank combination of sickening smells, which permeated his clothing.

"I just hope he doesn't have to throw up," Chad thought. *"I think it would be impossible to keep breakfast down, if that started."*

It was all he could do to keep from getting sick, just at the thoughts of it. It was after that event that Chad began his daily ritual of checking on his father during his lunch hour. On rare occasions he would find the old man alert and sitting on the bench. Chad and Charles would talk for a few minutes before Chad headed to a café. The younger Maddox always brought his father a take-out lunch on the way back to the office.

During the winter he was sometimes able to talk with his father by calling the mission. However, as is common with many of the homeless, the summer months allowed the desire for alcohol to surpass the desire for shelter. Charles Maddox again distanced himself from his son. Often, he pretended to be drunken to the state of unconsciousness, and other times he would greet his son with vulgar expressions and derogatory curses. Chad had changed jobs and moved to Atlanta in hope of restoring a relationship with his father. Discouraged and frustrated, he began to become angry with himself for making the effort. Again, his heart began to harden against his father.

I've let that jerk screw me over again! Why do I do this to myself? The only love that man knows is for the contents of a bottle. He's intent on destroying his life, and I must have the same tendency. For some stupid reason I continue to latch on to him. It's a little like getting into the car with a guy that you know will soon kill himself in a high-speed crash. What is wrong with me?

Still, he couldn't bring himself to leave Atlanta and go back to a life absent from his father. Those few pleasant encounters with the man were like winning at gambling. Even after continued losses, he was drawn back to the table. Yet, deep inside, he sensed there was more to it. Reflections of those childhood experiences with his father remained fresh in his mind. He felt there was a reason he had been able to locate Charles Maddox.

It's like a miracle that found him after all these years, and I'm amazed that he is still alive. I'm not a psychologist or a preacher. I don't know what makes people do what they do, and I don't know what will cause him to break out of this. I found him. I just don't know what to do. I think I need some help figuring all this out.

Chad began to attend the church pastored by David Clarkston. As the cold weather began to set in, he began seeking the council of his pastor regarding his father.

ROB WILLIAMS

Chapter 7

LARRY ARRIVED IN ATLANTA and was immediately informed of an incident involving a member of David Clarkston's church.

"Chad Maddox, a member of my congregation and his father received injuries during a mugging," David said. "I'm on my way to the hospital to visit them. Would you care to come along?"

"Sure," Larry replied. "Are they badly hurt?"

"Chad will probably be released tomorrow, but the older man was injured more severely," David answered. "This occurred under unusual circumstances."

"Most muggings are unusual circumstances," Larry replied.

"No, I mean the relationship between father and son is unusual," said David. "The younger man is a successful businessman, but the father is a homeless alcoholic. In fact, the son moved to Atlanta in hopes to keep a closer eye on his father."

As they drove, David explained how Chad attempted to protect his father as youths were giving the old man a terrible beating.

"Frustrated people sometimes strike out at others," David said. "Sometimes teens act out in an attempt to feel that they have some measure of control in their lives. Some treat strangers in a manner that they would never treat an acquaintance. It's more common for some to purposely cut people off in traffic, but others may resort to more violence."

"I understand what you are saying, but some people are simply mean -- ruthless and cruel," replied Larry. "I continually run into people who have managed to alienate every soul with whom come in contact. Some people take pleasure in inflicting pain and suffering on those close to them. There are those who beat the daylights out of family members, but treat those outside the home graciously. Then there are those who are just plain mean. Beating an old and haggard man is inexcusable. He was nothing to them. To them, the old guy wasn't even a human being. Beating him was like pounding a punching bag. He was simply an object. Unfortunately, I've seen it before."

As David parked his car in the hospital parking deck, Larry attempted to understand more about the two men.

"So, is Chad close to his father?"

"I wouldn't say they are close," David responded. "I think Chad has attempted to re-establish a relationship, but a relationship with an alcoholic is usually rather limited and one-sided."

"True words," replied Larry. "The Bible says that there is no greater love than to lay down one's life for someone else. It sounds like Chad did just that. Putting oneself in harm's way for someone else, shows more than words can say. It's obvious that he cares about his father, but he is really in a tough spot with him."

David and Larry were surprised to find Chad dressed and seated in a chair, while watching TV.

"You don't look so bad," David observed as he entered the room from the right side of the patient.

As Chad turned towards his visitors, David immediately saw that he had underestimated the damage done by the youths. The left eye was blackened and swollen shut and dark stitches replaced the shaved left eyebrow.

"One side of my face isn't so bad," Chad replied. "I really hope the swelling goes down before I go back to the office."

"I hear that your father is in far worse shape, and that you may have saved his life," David said.

"That butthole probably hasn't felt the first ounce of pain!" exclaimed Chad. "He was drunk on his sorry butt when the beating began, and the staff has him drugged up in this hospital. He's probably taking a vacation from what is left of his pickled brain."

"My name is Larry Chatterson," Larry said, introducing himself. "I've been invited to speak at your church tomorrow morning."

"I had planned to hear you speak, but I was somewhat sidetracked," Chad explained. "I am supposed to get out of the hospital tomorrow, but I don't want to go to church looking like this."

"I would call getting your head beat in, certainly being sidetracked," Larry replied with a smile.

"I'm sorry," the wounded man said. "I shouldn't have greeted you by mouthing off about my old man. You probably didn't have such a screwed-up family."

"My father wasn't homeless, but he made life hell for everyone in the home," replied Larry. "He was somewhat of a functioning drunk, but he beat the crap out of every member of the family."

"I guess maybe you do understand -- to a degree," apologized Chad. "I hate what booze does to a lot of people. A man does the booze, then the booze does the man, and then the man does everyone he comes in contact with."

"That pretty much sums it up," Larry chuckled. "Can I borrow that analogy from you? I run a center for homeless people in Charlotte."

"Are you out of your mind?" asked Chad. "What in God's name made you want to do that after putting up with your Dad? Are you nuts?"

"Probably," answered Larry. "I would have to say that it had to be God putting me in this line of work, and He's the One who helps me handle each day. I think it helps me stay close to Him. Without God's help I would probably find myself running down the street screaming like a lunatic."

"Actually, Larry helped me get some things together in my life," David piped in. "He's become a real friend."

"I think this was the last straw with my father," stated the battered man as he stood and gingerly made his way to the hospital bed. "I'm done. He made life hell for me when I was growing up, but I hoped things could be different now. I can't go around taking beatings like this, just because he wants to live the life of a sorry bum. I was an idiot to think that I could help him. I'm afraid he'll never change. This is what he is, but I don't have to hang around and watch him do it. I shouldn't have left a promising position in Boston to come down here for this job. I did it for him. I tend to allow him to screw my life up."

"I spent some time in Boston," Larry said. "North End has really good restaurants."

"I wouldn't figure that a pastor of a homeless shelter could afford to eat in the North End very often," said Chad.

"I wasn't a minister then," Larry explained. "I was a financial consultant at a brokerage."

"Man, your life has taken a downhill plunge!" exclaimed Chad. 'You must have made some serious mistakes and lost a lot of money for some rich fat cat. Did they kick you out?"

"No," Larry answered. "I left a very promising career to go into the ministry."

"You're scaring me, man!" said Chad with a somewhat twisted grin. It was obvious to Larry that his mouth was tender and that it was painful to smile. "Maybe I had better stop praying. I sure don't want God to do something like that to me."

"No, don't do that!" Larry replied. "I think God probably already has His quota of financial consultants turned preachers."

The three men talked for about an hour before Larry asked Chad if it would be all right for him to visit his father.

"Visit that old drunk as much as you would like," Chad said. "Knock yourself out. In fact, why don't you just take him back with you to your center in Charlotte? My old man would be a real challenge for you. I warn you; he would be the one to send you running down the street screaming like a lunatic."

"I might just do that," Larry told him before leaving the room.

David and Larry moved on to visit Chad's father. They found Charles Maddox sleeping and decided not to bother him.

AFTER SPEAKING AT the church on the following day, Larry again visited Chad, who was now recovering at his home. Chad was still very angry with his father. He repeated his earlier statement about it being a mistake to move to Atlanta to reconcile with the old man. After leaving Chad Larry visited the older Maddox at the hospital.

"My name is Larry Chatterson and I'm a minister in Charlotte," Larry said as he introduced himself. "I was invited to speak at your son's church, and I've been visiting with him since yesterday."

It was obvious to Larry that the beaten man was in pain. Chad's father was slow to answer.

"I guess you know that my name is Charles Maddox," the older man slowly mouthed from a severely battered and weatherworn face.

He was missing a couple of bottom front teeth, and multiple stitches appeared to hold his face together. The swelling was such that it looked as if his face would pop like a balloon if a couple of stitches gave way. Still, those cold light gray eyes leapt from swollen eyelids as he glared at

Larry.

"I'm sure that you don't feel like a long conversation, so I won't stay long," Larry explained.

"They tell me that Chad saved me, and that he took a beating in the process," Charles said.

"That's right," Larry confirmed.

"I guess I am really lucky he happened along," replied the old man.

"Well, your son didn't just happen along," explained Larry. "He left a promising career in Boston to come down here with you. Chad hoped that you two would re-establish some kind of relationship, and he made some efforts to look after you. Of course, you haven't made that very easy. He and I talked for some time."

"It's really none of your stinking business," Charles slowly spat out with a glare.

"True," Larry replied. "I sometimes butt in when I am not invited. Life is short and I came to make you an offer.'

"Offer?" the old man stammered. "Get the hell out of here, before I call a nurse!"

"Go for it, you twisted shell of a man!" Larry replied.

"What kind of preacher are you, some snake oil seller?" barked Charles through swollen lips.

"Nope, I run a shelter in Charlotte," Larry answered. "I'm offering to take you back with me."

"I am here with my boy!" the old man exclaimed, in a somewhat muffled voice. Facial swelling prevented his words from being carried with the normal volume of expression. "You aren't taking me anywhere."

"You may be here, but you aren't here with your boy," said Larry. "Your boy has had enough of your bull crap, and he told me that I should take you back with me."

"If that was the case, he would tell me that to my face," Charles angrily stated.

"I'm telling you," began Larry. "He isn't going to tell you anything to your face, because he has had his fill of your garbage life. Here, I'll dial his number for you. Maybe he will tell you over the phone. Maybe he'll tell you how he was following you and looking out for you when those kids jumped you and beat the daylights out of you. He stepped in and all he got from helping you was a beating by those kids. You both would've been beaten to death if a couple of cops hadn't shown up. If he stays around you, you are liable to get him killed. Is that what you want? Your son has had it with your drunken lousy life."

"Put him on that phone!" exclaimed Charles.

His bloated face reddened. His eyes burned. Larry dialed the number and asked Chad to explain to his father his wishes for him to go to the shelter in Charlotte. As Chad began to curse and state that he had nothing to say to his father, Larry quickly put the phone to the ear of the old man. As Charles heard his son go on about being through with his father, the reddening of his face and the glare from those gray eyes diminished. He slowly handed the phone back to Larry.

"You need to leave," the old man slowly said in a soft tone.

"I'm leaving, but my offer stands," Larry said. "If you have any love for that boy of yours, you will come with me to Charlotte."

Charles rolled onto his side and turned his silent face away from his visitor. As Larry left for the airport, he called David to let him know of the visit with the older man and the offer made to him. He neglected to reveal the heated nature of the visit.

TWO DAYS LATER, David paid Charles a visit in the hospital.

"How are you, Charlie?" David asked.

"I am doing much better, thanks," Charles told the minister.

"Your son has offered to take care of your bill, but he doesn't want to see you," explained David.

"I know he is tired of my garbage, but he didn't need to pay the bill," Charles said. "Hospitals take care of indigents like me."

"Actually, the hospitals have to charge other patients more to cover the loss from taking care of indigent people," David explained. "Your son didn't want that."

"Chad turned out to be a good man, and I'm proud of him," Charles quietly answered. "He really deserved a better father. I think he needs a break from me. That preacher from Charlotte invited me to come to his center. I don't have any money. Would your church spot me a bus ride to Charlotte?"

"I'll do better than that," David answered. "I would be glad to see my friend again. I can give you a ride up there."

"I get out of the hospital tomorrow," Charles said. "When were you planning on going to Charlotte?"

"That's a coincidence," replied David. "I was planning to visit Larry tomorrow. That would be perfect."

Both men knew that an extra day on the street meant that Charles would never see Charlotte. He would be drunk and wasting away in a park somewhere in Atlanta. David called his friend Larry and informed him of the upcoming trip with Charles.

"Tomorrow, I will be bringing Charles Maddox to your center in Charlotte. Yeah, the hospital has assured me that they've dried him out, and I expect this may be his only chance at staying off the stuff."

LARRY GREETED THE TWO TRAVELERS from Atlanta at the front door of the mission. After escorting them to his office, he made sure Charles understood the rules perfectly. The center allowed no booze, he was to attend a service at the mission once a week, and he must be available each day for work. Classes at night were available, but not required. Larry introduced Charles to George, who escorted him to be given a bunk and a hygiene kit. The kit contained a bar of soap, disposable razor, shaving cream, toothbrush, toothpaste, bath rag, hairbrush, and a comb. Now that the two ministers were alone, Larry asked David for an update regarding his status.

"Okay, how's he been?" quizzed Larry. "Assuming responsibility for indigent men, who are often unstable, can be hard enough. Those duties can become exceptionally difficult when the person's status is unknown."

"Charles had little opportunity to find liquor recently," replied David. "I was at the hospital before he was released this morning, and he hasn't been out of my sight except to use the restroom at a gas station."

"I mean, how is his attitude?" Larry asked. "I understand that Charles Maddox has a history of displaying anger when confronted about aspects of his abusive life. Did he really want to come here, or is he just looking for a change in scenery?"

"I'm not sure, as I don't have your experience with men in his situation," Dr. Clarkston answered.

"I hope you don't think I'm badgering you, but it helps if I obtain as much information on a fellow before I am left to find out on my own," Larry explained. "What does his son Chad think about his coming to Charlotte?"

"Chad wants nothing to do with his father," David replied. "I think his patience has run its course for now. He tried for so long to be there for the old man. The beating did more to him than just the physical damage. It's like it turned off the family button or something. He doesn't even want to talk about his father. I told him that I was going to bring Charles here, but he dropped the subject quickly."

"I understand," responded Larry. "I really understand. He may care more than he wants to admit to even himself, and I'm sure it's a relief to him to have his father in someone else's care for a time. Let him bring the subject of his father up when he wants to talk about it. Just leave it alone and let him kick back a little and get some rest. Just wait him out and stay quiet about it."

Dr. David Clarkston was more academically educated in ministerial study than Larry, but he was also wise enough to know when practical experience needed to lead the way. He agreed to leave the matter alone concerning the younger Maddox.

"Is Chad still attending church?" Larry asked.

"Yes, he still attends," answered David. "However, he hasn't called me as did before his ordeal. I thought we had become close, but he is keeping his distance other than the services. I called him a couple of times, but he didn't want to talk very long. I have to say that I'm a little worried about him. He doesn't seem to be himself."

"Just wait him out and make sure you make yourself available if he does want to talk," Larry said. "The fact that he is still attending church is a good sign. Continue to be warm when you see him, but give him space. Let me know if he ceases to attend the services."

"What would that mean?" David asked. "What if he stops attending?"

"It could mean a number of things, or it could mean nothing," Larry replied.

Larry knew that some children of alcoholics tend to also become alcoholics. He was also aware that some have thoughts of suicide.

Chapter 8

LARRY WAS NOW READY TO CHANGE THE GAME. Three months had passed since Charles Maddox arrived at the mission. He had done what he was told and had become a model client. He attended the one service per week, was never found to have alcohol, and he was always available for work – even when he had a fever one morning.

"Charles, I have a question for you. I understand that you were once an accountant."

"That was a lifetime ago," replied Charles.

"I'm off in my books, and I can't seem to find the error," explained Larry. "Would you mind taking a look?"

"You've got to be kidding, Reverend Chatterson," replied Charles.

"I doubt that I'll be audited any time soon, so there is no pressure for the error to be found quickly. I am sick of looking for the screw-up, and I would really appreciate a second pair of eyes. Would you be willing?"

"Okay, but don't get your hopes up," promised Charles.

"I ACTUALLY FOUND SOMETHING in your books," Charles began. "I'm sorry that it took me two days to notice it. I told you not to expect much."

"Come on into the office; let's take a look," Larry offered.

The older man entered Larry's office, holding a copy of the mission's accounting records. A couple of pages were neatly folded. Charles placed the copy on Larry's desk and opened it to the first folded page. Neatly written in the margin was a correction to a noted mistake.

"I'm not sure who made this entry, but this is not really an asset," Charles explained.

Larry glanced over it, and then quietly chuckled. "You are exactly right, Charles," he said. "So, have found another mistake? I see you have a second page turned down."

Charles turned to the other folded page and explained the second mistake. The two discussed this entry for a few minutes, and it soon became obvious that a second mistake had been made.

"You really helped me out on this one," Larry said. "Charles, you're better than you gave yourself credit. I had been looking at these entries for several days. With my schedule, I really can't do a proper job of reviewing the accounting entries."

"I could imagine," Charles replied. "You come to the mission early, and you leave it late at night. You certainly have a lot on your hands, taking on the responsibility of so many troubled people."

"I have a proposal for you," began Larry. "I told you that I want you to be available for work each day, and you have certainly been faithful in that area. I would like to take you off the physical work detail and assign you specific duties regarding your expertise. I want you to help me in the office with the business aspects of the mission. Non-profits have to be very careful with bookkeeping, and we must maintain the status of truly being a non-profit organization. Mistakes like the ones you caught could jeopardize this entire effort. I'm simply too busy to do it all. I would like to take you off the work crews and keep you in the office. You technically wouldn't be on staff because I can't afford to pay you. However, you would be attending the mission staff meeting each week to explain our books. Would you do it?"

"Hey, I think I just lucked out on finding those mistakes," answered Charles. "I'm not so sure that I should be counted on."

"You did a better job than I, didn't you?" Larry asked. "I wouldn't extend this offer if I didn't need your help."

"I'm sure you're swamped with work," Charles replied. "Maybe I should begin on a trial basis, sort of like taking a probationary shot at it."

"Sounds reasonable," Larry said, as he rose from his chair.

He extended his hand to the older man before Charles had time for second thoughts. The two shook hands, and immediately Larry escorted him to Evelyn's reception area.

"Evelyn, I plan to move a second desk into your area for Charles. This man has a background in accounting, and I want a second pair of eyes on these books."

Wearing a curious smile, Evelyn extended her hand. "Charles, it will be nice to have some company," she offered.

The aging man took her hand. His eyes shifted between the administrative assistant and the minister.

"My friends call me Charlie."

"Welcome aboard, Charlie," Evelyn replied.

Larry left the office to have lunch with his wife. Patsy and Larry were rarely able to eat lunch together, as he usually had some sort of crisis going on during the day that demanded his attention. During the lunch he explained to Patsy how Charlie had found the mistakes.

"He has accepted the duty of reviewing the accounting practices of the mission," Larry explained. "He insisted that it be on a trial basis, but I'm sure he can handle it."

"Seems like I remember you being something of a

financial genius prior to going into the ministry," she chided.

"I just don't have the time anymore," Larry said with a slight grin.

"You knew those mistakes were in the books, didn't you?" she spoke.

"I really don't have the time," Larry insisted, as the grin grew into a larger smile.

Larry and Patsy had connected from the time they met, and they naturally understood each other as no one else. Larry quickly changed the subject.

OVER THE NEXT two months Charlie threw himself into accounting regulations and laws governing non-profits. He maintained the books and met with the staff weekly to discuss options regarding expenditures for the mission. He entered the office early each morning, and he and Larry regularly began work long before Evelyn came in. Charlie ate in the cafeteria with the other men, but in the evenings, he stayed in the office long after the work crews came in from physical tasks.

TIFFANY AND HER DAUGHTER BRANDY entered Larry's office for their monthly status session. As usual, the door was left open between Larry's office and the area that served Evelyn and Charlie. During the session curious little Brandy strolled from Larry's office into the next room. She first caught the eye of Evelyn and flashed a big grin her way. She turned to see an older gray-haired man concentrating on accounting figures. Brandy waved her little hand at him, but he didn't see her. Not deterred from her pursuit of his attention, she quickly moved beside him. Still, he didn't lift his eyes from the duty at hand. She persistently gave his pants leg a big tug. He glanced in her direction and gave her a polite nod. She was captivated by the worn old fellow.

Brandy gave the pants leg another tug. Charlie lifted his eyes again, and this time she presented him with a smile that began deep within her little soul and made its way to her face. He couldn't help but return the smile.

Brandy accepted this act as an invitation, and she threw up both arms as a request to be taken into his lap. Her innocent charm was irresistible. Brandy's sweet pleading eyes moved Charlie to abandon his work and take her into his lap. She wrapped her little arms around his neck and held him as if she had always belonged there. She placed her soft little face against his weather-worn countenance. Suddenly, long-dormant memories poured into his mind and heart. He remembered holding his little son in his lap and recounted more promising days from his past. Regret filled his heart. His eyes began to blur as they filled with tears of sorrow and pain. Sensing his sorrow Brandy held even tighter to his neck, and then she softly kissed his face. Charlie gingerly placed her back onto the floor. Standing, he excused himself.

"I've got to go to the restroom, Evelyn; I'll be right back," Charlie explained as he left the room.

His heart pounded as made his way to the restroom. Once entering a stall, he sat down on a toilet and placed both hands over his face. He began to wail as one who had just received word that a loved one had perished. It was uncontrollable once it began. His body shook as tears streamed down his face and uncontrollable moans leaked from deep within. Remembrance of wasted years punished him as never before. Long suppressed memories of inflecting drunken-inspired pain on his wife and son pummeled him over and over. There was no escape. It was unrelenting. He called out to God.

"Oh, God!" Charlie uttered. "Help me. Help them. I am such a worthless piece of crap! What was wrong with me? Oh, God! Please. I am so sorry, so stupid, so worthless. Dear God, help my son Chad. I've robbed him of a father, and I've wasted a lifetime. I'm so sorry…I am so sorry. Help him and help me. Help this beautiful little girl…Oh, God!"

Inexplicably, he felt a warm sensation bathe him in peace and love. For the first time in his life, he sensed the presence of his Creator. It would be nothing he could explain to anyone else because it was something much deeper than the intellect. The Spirit of God had reached into his soul and communed with his spirit. There were no words, but he understood. Charlie dedicated the rest of his remaining days on this earth to making life better for those around him. It wasn't because of the inspirational preaching of a minister or due to a rational challenge to his intelligence – it was the innocent love of a little girl that drew him and exposed his heart before God. It was a matter of the soul. Charlie experienced a touch from God, which words cannot express. His wasted life was laid bare before him by his Creator, yet he did not now feel condemned. He left the restroom with a peace that was beyond logic, and with purpose and hope.

When Charlie returned to his desk, he found that Brandy had rejoined her mother in Larry's office. A half hour later, the little girl caught Charlie's eye as the mother and daughter exited the area. Larry addressed both Evelyn and Charlie regarding a pressing matter.

"I've found Tiffany a job as a stock clerk in a local grocery store. Would you two be willing to care for Brandy while her mother is away at work?"

"I think I would like to give it a shot," answered Evelyn. "We can set up a play area in the corner of the office and stock it with toys, children's coloring books, and a few reading books. We could use a little life in this place."

EACH DAY, EVELYN set aside a few minutes to read to the little girl. It quickly became apparent to her that Brandy was a fast learner and insightful. The young girl became mindful of when it was acceptable to interrupt Evelyn's work and when it wasn't. A couple of months into the arrangement, Evelyn called in sick, She asked Charlie to care for Brandy and to do the daily reading. When Evelyn later returned to work, she found that she had lost her reading duties to the older man. Brandy had basically given the job to Charlie.

When Brandy began kindergarten, a small desk was placed in the corner of the reception area for her. After school she still requested that a story be read by Charlie. However, he always insisted that she finish assigned homework and study prior to the reading session. Charlie purposely picked books which were slightly above her reading level to read to her. In doing so, her ability to read and comprehend grew rapidly. Her vocabulary was far more advanced than the other children at school.

Larry maintained a close friendship with David Clarkston and regularly updated him regarding Charlie. Both Larry and David periodically provided Chad Maddox with a status on his father. Without warning, one morning Chad Maddox walked into the mission office and found his father busily reviewing the books. The older man hardly appeared to be the same fellow who had been beaten so severely in Atlanta.

"Hi, Dad," said Chad as he entered the office.

"Well, hello, Chad," Charlie replied. "This is a surprise. Is everything okay?"

"I got your letters, and I guess I finally decided to come up to Charlotte to see how you are doing," Charlie answered. "It's 11:30 AM, do you have lunch plans?"

"I normally eat in the cafeteria, but I have a little money on me," Charlie said.

"It's on me, if that's all right," the younger man said while glancing in Evelyn's direction.

"I'm Evelyn Reynolds," she said, introducing herself. "I work as the administrative assistant here."

"It's nice to meet you," replied Chad, a bit embarrassed that he failed to introduce himself when entering the room. "My name is Chad Maddox. I'm this man's son."

"Pleased to meet you," she responded. "I'm sure you both have a lot to talk about. If you'll excuse me, I have to take care of a few things in another part of the building. I'll be back in a little while."

"There's no need for you to leave," replied Chad. "I just wanted to see if my father had time for lunch."

"Go on, Charlie," stated Evelyn, giving Charlie a gentle push. "I'll tell Larry when he comes by."

"Tell him that I will be back in about an hour," said Charlie nervously.

"Stay as long as you wish," she replied with a wink. "I'm sure Larry won't dock your pay."

After the ride to the restaurant, the initial tension between father and son subsided. Charlie told his son how Larry had been invited to speak at several places and was beginning to be known in mission circles throughout the United States.

"In fact, in some cities he's given presentations in large auditoriums," explained Charlie.

"I came to hear about you, not Larry Chatterson," Chad explained. "I read your letters, and it seems you're doing well."

"I'm doing better than I have for most of my life," Charlie said. "Certainly better than during most of yours. There is absolutely nothing I can do to undo the damage I've done to you, and there's no way I can reclaim years that should have been lived differently. I can only determine how the rest of my life goes and try to be a much better person. I've apologized in my letters to you, but that doesn't bring back those years. It is so good to see you. Tell me about what you have been doing."

The two talked for an hour and a half before noticing the time. When Chad dropped his father off at the mission, they each felt refreshed.

THE FOLLOWING MONTH Larry spoke at an old closed high school in New York that had been converted into a shelter. The speech was held in the auditorium, and more than forty people came down to pray with him after the closing invitation. Larry was shocked. Prior to that night, he felt successful if one or two people immediately responded at the end of a speaking engagement. Over the next six months similar responses occurred. Almost overnight, Larry became nationally known.

"Charlie, please come to my office when you are finished with the books this morning," Larry requested.

About an hour later, Charlie excused himself from Evelyn's presence and lightly knocked on Larry's door. Glancing back over his shoulder, he found the elderly administrative assistant giving him a sly smile.

"Charlie, come on in," invited Larry. "Please close the door and have a seat."

"What can I do for you?" Charlie asked.

"You've been doing volunteer work here at the center for some time," Larry began. "I can't tell you how relieved I have been to find someone who could handle our accounting. As you know, funding for the mission has consistently been pretty good. I talked this over with the Committee on Missions and they have allowed me to offer you a full-time staff position here. You wouldn't make much, and you are welcome to still live here. What do you think?"

"What about George?" Charlie asked. "He's been here longer than I have."

"I've had a conversation with George, and he has accepted a similar offer," Larry replied. "What about it? Would you accept this position as being our accountant? You are already attending the staff meetings, but now you would be officially on staff. One of your duties will be to present our finances to the church council. I plan to turn that duty completely over to you. Do you want to think about it awhile?"

"No, I don't need more time," Charlie responded. "I would be honored to be on your staff. Thank you. When do I start?"

"Sign this form and you'll start today."

With his signature, Charlie became a full-time staff member of the mission. As he walked into the administrative area, he was immediately confronted by Evelyn.

"Well, are you on the team or not?" she quizzed.

"Of course, I took the position," Charlie answered.

Evelyn rose from her chair and gave him a sincere and loving hug. It took Charlie by surprise, but he returned the hug.

"I'm so glad," said Evelyn.

"I've got to go," Charlie said. "That morning cup of coffee is screaming to leave my body."

As Charlie made his way to the restroom he beamed from ear to ear. He thought about how much his life had changed over the last two years. As he stood in front of the urinal, pictures from his past flashed through his mind. Those wasted years spent in self-destructive behavior now seemed like a bad dream. His mind was now clear. Charlie wasn't as sharp as he had been as a younger man. Years of intoxication had taken its toll. However, he was certainly able to handle the simple accounts of the mission. As soon as he returned to his desk, he was given permission to place a call to his son to give him the news.

OVER TIME, TIFFANY'S DAUGHTER began to view Charlie as a type of grandfather figure. Each weekday afternoon, she was left in the office with Charlie and Evelyn while Tiffany worked her grocery job. Brandy loved to sit in his lap as he read to her and told her stories. Evelyn was always a distant second choice for her. There was a natural connection between the old man and the little girl. Brandy was remarkably compassionate and insightful for a child who had dealt with so many difficulties so early in life. When she was in his lap, Charlie held her as if he was holding his own. He often reflected on his failures as a father. Charlie's silent personal sorrow drew Brandy, but she also sensed his genuine love for her.

Tiffany had adapted quickly to the mission program, and eventually she entered phase three. She and Brandy moved out of the center and into a nearby apartment. Larry and Charlie agreed to allow Brandy to continue to stay with Charlie at the center while her mother was away at work. The old man and the little girl became almost inseparable. On Saturdays Tiffany would sometimes invite Charlie to the apartment for lunch. One Wednesday afternoon Tiffany found her daughter Brandy sitting on Charlie's lap. He was seated on a couch in the reception area, reading a story book to her. The little girl was captivated until she noticed her mother enter the room.

"Mom!" Brandy shouted, as she quickly leaped from his lap.

She wrapped her arms around her mother's waist in a strong embrace. Then she took her mother by the hand and led her over to the old man.

"Listen to the end of the story," she commanded.

Brandy jumped back up onto Charlie's lap, and Tiffany took a seat beside him. The little girl clapped her small hands when the book was closed at the conclusion of the story. She immediately dropped off his lap.

"I need to go tinkle," she scouted, as she quickly scurried out of the reception area.

"Charlie, I sometimes feel absolutely worn out," Tiffany spoke. "I love my daughter, but I sometimes feel so exhausted by the time I go to bed at night. In prison I had very few responsibilities. Now, I am on the go from the time I wake up until my head drops onto the pillow at night."

"Is it worth it?" he asked.

"What do you mean?" she questioned.

"Is an honest life with your daughter worth all the stress and effort?" he asked.

"Of course, it is," she replied. "It's just a little hard to get used to – that's all, This morning I noticed dark circles under my eyes. I have never been like this."

"For years I abused my body with alcohol and exposure to the weather" he said. "I wasted years being away from my children, and I accomplished very little along the lines of work and the fulfillment it brings. I enjoy my work now. Like you, I'm pretty tired at night."

"I don't see how you do it, Charlie," Tiffany spoke. "I know you're in poor health, and sometimes I feel bad about you keeping my daughter all day while you're doing the other work here at the center. How do you keep going?"

"God has given me a second chance at life, and I want to make better use of the days I have left on the earth," he said as he reached for a bowl on the end table. He took an orange from the bowl and placed it on his lap. Slipping his right hand into his pants pocket he pulled out a pocketknife. Though his hands were worn from years of abuse he was able to flip the blade out quickly with his thumb. He scored the peeling of the orange with the knife and soon separated the peeling from the meat of the orange. He placed the peelings back in the bowl.

He cleaned the blade with his handkerchief and slipped the pocketknife back into his pocket. Charlie broke the meat of the large navel orange in half with his thumb and handed Tiffany one of the halves.

"This is a really nice-looking orange," she said while separating a slice. "Where did you get it?"

"People sometimes just drop things off here, but Evelyn brought this one to me today."

"This is so good," Tiffany raved as she licked the sticky juice from her fingers.

"Ever tasted the peeling of an orange?" he asked.

"One time, as a child" she replied. "That was all it took."

Looking down at the peeling in the bowl, Charlie spoke. "You have to remove the peeling to get to the good part. One day, someone will find this old body lying somewhere. When they do, they will be seeing only the peeling that is left. The good part will have gone somewhere else. We all have to be peeled at some point to let the good part of us out. God touched me a while back and He refreshed the inside of this old man. The outside is still wasting away. The damage has been done. But the inside is an entirely different matter."

"Do you really think people go to heaven when they die?" Tiffany questioned.

"Have you ever seen a dead body?" he asked.

"Yeah, I saw my aunt when she died in the hospital," she answered.

"Did you know her very well?" he asked.

"Oh yeah, I loved her very much," she replied. "I was as close to her as I was with my own mother."

"Did her body look empty?" Charlie asked. "Morticians do a fine job, but did her dead body really look like your aunt?"

"It was different," she answered. "I can't put my finger on it, but it was much different than watching her while she was asleep."

"That's because she wasn't there anymore," he said. "You're not just what you see in the mirror. The real you is riding around inside your body, seeing through your eyes, hearing through your ears, thinking in your mind, and feeling from the depths of your soul. You know that it's true. What do you think happens to the real you, when the shell that covers you breaks and dies?"

"I don't know," she said. "It's hard to believe in a place

you can't see, like heaven."

"You aren't someone with a soul; you are a soul existing in this world by being encased in a body," Charlie explained. "The world, as we know it, is a foreign environment for a soul. It's a lot like an astronaut having to wear a space suit in space. We can't exist here without this suit, this body. If the body breaks down beyond repair, our soul has to depart to a more suitable environment. Death is simply our soul leaving a suit."

Brandy entered the room, skipping. She seemed to never be short of energy. Taking her daughter by the hand, the mother leaned over and kissed Charlie on the head. As Tiffany left the older man, she had no idea how soon his illustration with the orange would become real.

Chapter 9

CHARLIE MADDOX NERVOUSLY

dialed a number on the hotel phone.

"Hi Chad, it's your father. I wanted to let you know that Larry and I are in Atlanta. He is to speak at Dr. Clarkston's church on Sunday, and I've been invited to speak at the old mission Monday evening. This is the first time Larry has taken me with him on one of his speaking engagements."

Cautiously, Charlie waited for a response. Although it came within a couple of seconds, it seemed to be an agonizingly long wait of the old man.

"Dad, that's absolutely great!" exclaimed Chad. "Where are you staying? I want to pick you up and take you to dinner."

The two talked for half an hour. After Charlie ended the call, he sat motionless on the hotel bed for a couple of minutes. Slowly he slid his knees to the floor and buried his face in the comforter that covered the bed. He thanked God repeatedly for the opportunity to be with his son, and he prayed fervently for both his and Larry's upcoming speaking engagements. By the time he pulled himself from the floor and onto the bed, his knees were in severe pain. His body normally ached, nonstop, but this time his knees agonized for more than twenty minutes. Years of living in the elements and abusing himself with alcohol had aged his body far beyond the normal wear and tear of someone his age. Though his soul was refreshed by God's mercy and forgiveness, his body still paid the price of intense self-destructive behavior.

His knees were still sore when Chad picked him up for supper, but he was able to walk without a noticeable limp. About halfway through the meal the conversation took on a serious tone.

"For a long time, I doubted whether you would stay sober," Chad began. "I figured you would be back on the street. I expected any day to receive a call from Larry telling me that you had been found dead, alone on a park bench. You really are not the same man I talked with a few years ago in that park. I want you to know that I'm really proud of you."

Charlie replied with words of regret.

"I'm very grateful to have you for a son and I'm truly blessed beyond what I deserve. I've wasted so many years. I caused you and the other members of our family so much pain and there is nothing I can do to undo any of it. I'm very sorry, but being sorry does nothing to bring back those years. They're gone. They can never be relived. I can only determine what kind of person I'll be during the time I have left."

"I haven't seen you like this since I was really young, and my memories of you from those days are a bit foggy," the younger man replied. "I have memories of us working together on my Cub Scout pinewood derby car. In fact, I still have that car."

The two talked for an hour, sharing and laughing. By the time they departed for the evening both felt refreshed.

"This may be the best day of my entire life," Charlie thought.

When he returned to the hotel, he found Larry waiting for him in the lobby. The younger man looked exhausted.

"I need to share bad news with you, and I suggest we

move the conversation to your room," Larry began. "Do you mind?"

"Sure. Is it serious?"

Larry's face looked as though he had been half drained of life.

"I'm afraid it is, but I would rather wait until we are in private before discussing it."

The ride up the elevator began in a deafening silence. Larry broke the dead air just before reaching Charlie's floor.

"How did things go with your son?"

"It was great," Charlie stated with a hesitant smile.

The bell of the elevator sounded, and the door opened. The hall was empty of other guests. The sound of the latch on Charlie's door seemed significantly loud.

"I've received bad news from Charlotte," Larry said. "Let's have a seat."

JUST THE THOUGHT of leaving Charlie for first grade saddened Brandy, but her mother convinced her that it would be fun to spend additional daytime hours with other children. The six-year-old girl comforted herself in remembering that she had a few days before she would have to leave the old man for school. He was her favorite. She waved to him as he and Larry left for the trip to Atlanta. This was a weekend to be spent with her father. Russ Boyd was a hard man. Though she loved her father, Brandy always felt a bit uncomfortable in his world. He seemed to always be busy with adults. He sometimes left her alone for hours in front of the TV.

On that particular Saturday, she overheard her father talking loudly to someone on his cell phone. After the call, he let out a string of curses. Curious, she stepped into the doorway of the room just in time to see him throw a chair across the room. As Boyd turned toward the doorway, he noticed the fear in the eyes of his daughter.

"I'm sorry, Brandy," he said. "I just found out that I have to run an errand, but I will be gone only for about an hour."

Brandy's lip began to quiver. She said nothing. A tear rolled down her left cheek. The moist line expressed everything.

"I guess you can come with me, if you want," Russ offered in a reassuring tone. "But you might need to stay by yourself in the car for just a few minutes. It's not a place for little girls. Can you do that?"

Brandy silently nodded.

"I've got to put something in the car, but I will come back inside to get you," he said. "Collect a couple of your reading books and I will be right back. Okay?"

Brandy silently nodded again.

Soon they were on their way. Seated in her car seat in the back seat, she asked, "Where is the stuff you put in the car?"

"What?" he nervously asked.

"I don't see anything in the car," Brandy stated. "Did you forget to put that stuff in the car?"

"Oh, it's in the trunk," Russ answered. "I'm bringing some groceries to a friend."

"Okay," she sweetly replied.

Boyd's car exited the freeway and onto smaller streets of a densely populated neighborhood. Within a couple of minutes Brandy saw a black sedan swerve in front of her father's car. Russ immediately hit the brakes and came to a screeching stop. He quickly dropped his vehicle into reverse and began to back up. Although he was an extremely able driver, a second car cut off his retreat.

"Brandy!" Russ shouted.

"What, Daddy?"

"Right now; I need for you to unbuckle your car seat, get out of it, and get down on the back floor of the car!" he called out. "Now! Do it, now!"

As soon as she dropped to the floor, she heard the sound

of gun shots. The rear window of the car shattered as her father slammed the car back into drive and hit the accelerator.

"Daddy!" she screamed.

Another car rammed his car on the driver side, and Boyd's car came to a sudden stop.

"Daddy!" she again screamed.

She heard more shots being fired and she leapt up from the floor of the car to a spot between the two front bucket seats. Her tummy was pressed against the console. She wrapped both arms around the muscular right arm of her father and buried her face against his shoulder. More shots rang out, and she felt her father's body shake and jerk. The shots continued and she felt a burning sensation. Suddenly everything went dark. She faintly heard another shot; then everything was completely quiet. All fear left her. It was over.

Two men stood next to her father's car and peered in. The arm of one reached in through the open car window on the driver's side and took the keys from the ignition. After a moment they walked around to the rear of the car. Opening the trunk, they removed the contents.

One man said to the other, "Check him out again – make sure."

The second man used a rag in his hand while opening the driver's side car door. Placing his gun to the head of Brandy's father, he pulled the trigger. The impact of the bullet slammed into the side of his head causing his body to be viciously thrown in the direction of the front passenger seat. At once, Brandy's grip on her father's arm loosened and she fell to the back floor of the car. Spotting the movement, the man raised his gun again. Peering over the dead man's body, his focus fixed on the small form. The man pushed the body of his adult victim, so that it slumped into the passenger front seat. Now, he had a full and unrestricted view. His gun lowered as he looked into the lifeless eyes of the little girl. A bullet had passed through the arm of her father and had blown a large hole in the small chest of this unintended victim. Her heart was instantly shattered. A second bullet had grazed her right shoulder, but she never felt it.

WHEN TIFFANY RECEIVED the news of her daughter she went into hysterics. She came to the mission in search of Larry. Evelyn attempted to console her, but the younger woman screamed curses at God and began throwing things around the office. After a couple of hours of breaking things at the mission she finally collapsed in the corner of Evelyn's reception area. Huddled on the floor, her body shook violently as though she was suffering from Artic cold. Evelyn patiently helped her up and escorted her to the bed in her room at the mission. She covered her with a blanket. As a mother caring for a feverish little girl, she laid down beside her. Eventually the emotionally exhausted Tiffany fell into a deep sleep. Evelyn used the opportunity to call Larry on his cell.

The news about Brandy crushed Charlie like nothing else in his life. He was so deeply hurt by the loss that his soul was almost grieved beyond recovery. He wept uncontrollably for more than an hour. Larry explained to Charlie that he would need to return to Charlotte immediately after speaking the next day at the church. He then asked if he would be able to still speak at the Atlanta mission. The aging and broken-hearted fellow confirmed that he would speak at the mission, as promised. Though exhausted from grief, Charlie stayed awake for a couple of hours after going to bed. Larry was unable to sleep at all that night.

THE NEXT MORNING, David picked up Larry and Charlie

from the hotel and brought them to the church. The conversation in the car was entirely about Brandy's horrible death and the status of Tiffany. Larry began his message with the news of Brandy. Larry explained to those attending his presentation of his need to return to Charlotte immediately after the service. His speech overflowed with emotion and there were very few dry eyes left in the congregation at the conclusion of the message. A large crowd swarmed around Larry at the end of the service, but after a few minutes he excused himself.

David dropped Charlie off at the hotel near the mission before taking Larry to the airport. Charlie's flight was scheduled for the following evening. Exhausted, the older man went to his room and collapsed on the hotel bed. Within minutes he was fast asleep, but his dreams were such that when he awoke, he still felt very tired. Charlie was powerless to change the situation that grieved him so, but he felt he had to do something. Restless, he could not handle staying alone in the hotel room. It was late in the afternoon and the sunlight was beginning to dim. Charlie decided to go for a walk. Almost by instinct he headed in the direction of the Atlanta mission.

Once there, he stood for a few minutes thinking about how different the place seemed. Soon he realized that he was the one who was different. As he began to move past the mission, the late afternoon gave way to evening. Dark inebriated forms passed him as he slowly walked. Their dark avenues and alleys no longer offered anything for him because he was no longer one of them. After a few moments, he returned to the mission. Standing outside the building he could hear muffled voices from within. He didn't need clarity to know what was being said. He had heard it all before. Charlie listened to the faint familiar sound of the mission inhabitants being called for supper. He was about to walk away when he recognized a woman coming out of the front door of the building. He called out as she passed him.

"Nettie!"

She stopped and turned to face him. Charlie remembered a night when he had passed out in sub-freezing weather. This homeless woman wrapped both herself and him in her blankets. She had saved his life. He remembered waking up with her the next morning, realizing what she had done.

"How could I ever forget this woman?"

Her mind was no longer what it was. Years of continued substance abuse had taken it's tool. Nettie found him familiar, but didn't recognize him. He explained to her how thankful he was for the kind care she given to him years before.   She smiled, but he could tell that she didn't remember. Charlie knew why she wasn't staying for supper at the mission. She was in search of alcohol. He tried to get her to stay at the mission, but she refused. Charlie then offered to take her out for supper.   She didn't clearly remember him, but she knew there was something very familiar about Charlie. She trusted him. He took her by the arm and escorted her to a restaurant that featured a piano player and a singer.   He convinced the host to give them a table in the back of the room. He knew she would never be allowed to be seated at a table near the piano. Charlie treated her as if she was the most elegant and lovely woman in the restaurant, and he used the majority of the cash in this wallet to buy her diner.   The meal came with a basket of rolls. He consumed a couple of them, but left the rest at Nettie's disposal.

Afterwards, they parted ways. Charlie knew she would not rest until she found alcohol, but he didn't want to wait around for it. He wanted to think of her as he had left her. Charlie returned to his hotel. He ignored the reality of where she would probably spend the night. Instead, he thought about how much she enjoyed the piano. Charlie pictured her cleaned up and seated at the table in an evening dress.   He thought about how different her life should have been. The experience of giving to the woman somehow lessened his grief for the little girl, and he fell asleep thinking about Nettie.

CHARLIE WAS AWAKENED by a knock on his hotel room door. Sitting up in bed he began to mumble to himself.

"It's probably Nettie, but I am surprised the hotel gave her my room number."

He switched on a nightstand lamp and stumbled to the foot of the bed, where he had earlier hung his pants. Charlie slipped them on and took in a deep yawn. Opening the door, he found a man standing in the hallway.

"Hi, Charlie," the man began. "You've been invited to the dining area. Would you please come with me?"

"I don't think I know this guy, but he seems strangely familiar," Charlie thought. *"There's kindness in his voice, and there is something interesting about his demeanor."*

"Do I know you?" Charlie asked.

"I'm sorry; my name is Jerry," the man explained. "Come with me."

Charlie stepped into the hallway, and it seemed to be longer than he had remembered. Although little conversation passed between the two as they walked the hall, here was something very pleasant and comforting about this fellow. As they neared the end of the hallway Charlie began to hear warm cheerful voices coming from around the corner. He couldn't recall seeing the dining room earlier that evening when he had made his way to his room.

"Maybe I am not fully awake," he thought.

As the two entered the dining room, all faces turned to greet them. Smiles and kind eyes beamed from each person.

"Why are these people looking at me, this way?" Charlie questioned. *"I don't know anyone here; at least, I don't remember meeting them."*

"Here, this is your place," Jerry offered, as he pulled a

chair away from a table.

Though he didn't recognize anyone, Charlie felt oddly at home with those people. He no longer felt sleepy and tired. Wondering about the time, he looked around for a clock. He found none. The dining area appeared bigger than he expected for a hotel of that size. In earlier times, the neighborhood around the hotel had not always been a rough part of town. He thought about the possibility that elaborate gatherings in the past may have been held in that room. He closed his eyes and felt his soul bathed in peace.

Charlie sensed a familiar tap on his arm, and he opened his eyes to see a little girl standing next to him. She reached up for him to take her, and he lifted her into his lap. As she buried her small head in his chest, he returned the embrace. Suddenly, it was as though he had been transported back in time. Everything seemed so familiar. When she lifted her head, he realized why. Sitting in his lap was Brandy. He remembered all the times he kept her while her mother worked, and he remembered how often she fell asleep in his lap during evenings at the mission. She smiled as she looked up into his eyes. He now understood.

His attention moved from the little girl to the room. He found that the dining area had expanded into a huge banquet hall. It seemed to grow larger as he viewed it. Thousands of tables were occupied by many thousands of people. Many of the people in this place were still looking at Charlie.

There may be millions in this ever-growing room.

"It is so good to see you," Brandy whispered. "Everyone is glad to see you."

"Why are they looking at me?" he asked her. "You may not have noticed, but they are looking in our direction."

"You are personally special to some here, and others simply understand that that you are a special person," Brandy replied.

"Believe me, there is absolutely nothing special about me – at least, not in a good sense," he said almost in a whisper.

"You are special to me," she answered. "That's why I'm sitting in your lap."

"No, you are the one who is special!" he countered. "Honey, you are the sweetest little girl in the world. I am just an old man who became a disappointment to himself, and an even worse disappointment to other people. You just don't know."

"Oh, I know a lot," she said. "I know a lot more about things than you realize. You are special. You spent time with me when no one else did. My Mom didn't spend time with me at first because she was in jail; later, she was busy working. My Daddy spent very little time with me. I know he loved me, but he was busy with other people. When I sat on your lap, you read to me and told me stories. It was like I was the only person in the whole world who you thought about. You always made time for me. I watched you even when you didn't know I was watching. Since coming here, I know every unselfish and good thing you ever did. When Mr. Chatterson went out of town, you didn't even take the time to eat."

"You are the special one," Charlie said again. "You're the one who brought refreshment to my heart, each day. I really wasn't all that busy; it just probably seemed that way to you."

"I know why you didn't eat," Brandy answered. "Everyone in this room knows why you didn't eat. It was on purpose. Every weekend that Mr. Chatterson spent away from the mission to go speak to other people, you were fasting and praying for God to touch the hearts of all those people who heard him speak. God was listening. See all these people around you?"

"Yes," he answered.

"Those are the people the Holy Spirit prepared for hearing the words of Mr. Chatterson," she told him. "Your prayers opened their hearts to listen. Those words touched their hearts partly because those people were spiritually prepared to receive his words through your prayers. You didn't know that God was listening, did you?"

"I failed so many people," Charlie stated. "The least I could do was to pray for people."

It was at that point when he noticed that relatives and old friends occupied some of the surrounding tables. Some were indigents he had known in missions, and some were those sleeping near him in parks when he had been on the street. Each was well. No one was sick, cold, or lonely. None was consumed by an overwhelming desire for the next drink.

"Why does it seem that there are more and more tables and people in this room?' he asked. "It seems like the room is expanding."

"These are not only the people who listened to God through the words of Mr. Chatterson," Brandy explained. "The lives of those people have impacted the lives of many others, and those lives continue to impact the lives of even more people. That's why it continues to grow in your perception. They are all here, but you are only seeing part of them as you adjust to your surroundings."

"How much time does it take to adjust to this place?" he asked.

"Time doesn't exist here," the little girl explained. "The adjustment doesn't depend on time; it has to do with leaving an old life. You were transformed when you came here, but you just haven't fully realized it. When you completely adjust and finally leave that world behind, you will see it all. You will see everything as it is, as it always has been, and as it always will be. There is no then and now, or future. You left that world, and your soul has moved into another realm. It's not based on time, it's different."

"It's so good to see you," Charlie said.

"God let me be a part of your arrival," replied Brandy.

"I must be dreaming," Charlie whispered.

"You are just now waking up," she explained.

"How is that?" he asked.

"You know, dreaming is what you do for just a while," she said. "Then you wake up to what is real and what lasts."

He knew it to be true. The life he left behind seemed to be just a dream. As the two shared this realm, the one he left behind became more and more distant. She wrapped her small arms around his neck and gave him a kiss. Charlie's soul was flooded with peace, and the cares of his past life were washed free and carried away. Guilt of past failures and wrongs done were no longer a part of him. Worries left, never to return.

"Everything is as it should be," he whispered.

"Can you see Him yet?" she asked.

"Who?" Charlie asked, in response.

Until then, he had not noticed the fact that the tables surrounded a throne. Gentle light seemed to emit from the general area of the throne, and it consistently provided light so that no shadows were cast. Charlie looked up to find no lights hanging from the ceiling above. In fact, there was no ceiling above. Although the room was huge, no table seemed to be very far from the throne.

Glancing back to Brandy, for the first time he noticed she was wearing a white robe. So were all the others in the room.

"I didn't notice your pretty robe," Charlie commented. "It's really interesting."

The little girl placed her hand over her mouth to contain a sweet tiny giggle. She then poked him in the ribs with her small finger. Glancing down at the finger, he saw that he was also wearing a white robe.

"That was silly, wasn't it?" he asked with a smile.

"I told you that you are just now waking up," Brandy explained.

"How long does it take to fully wake up?" he asked her.

"There isn't any how long; it just is, what it is," she said, still smiling. "You'll see."

Chapter 10

TAKING HIS CELL PHONE from his pocket, Larry punched in a familiar number. Waiting for a response, he paced the floor like a big cat in a zoo. His mind was spinning, his nerves on edge.

"Today was terrible," Larry complained to his best friend Ryan.

"I wouldn't expect things to have settled much," replied Ryan. "Brandy was only buried today, right? Tomorrow, you have another funeral. Charlie had become more than just a client and staff member; he had become a friend to everyone at the center. Still, the death of a child has got to be the worst."

"I'm sick of this!" exclaimed Larry. "I am sick of death, and I am sick of watching people in misery day after day. There's no let up. I wish I could just walk away from everything. I wish I could leave this place and take my family to Brandon Springs. I want to pack up my family and just leave."

"Can you make arrangements to get way for a few days?" asked Ryan.

"No, I can't!" exclaimed Larry. "This entire center is a wreck. Everyone who knew them is hurting in their own way. Evelyn is continually in tears. I can't concentrate on anything that is work related. When I first took that little girl and her mother in, I was super nervous. However, Brandy became sunshine in the lives of so many. She was a bright beam of hope and life in a sea of garbage. Most of these people are consumed with a combination of self-loathing and self-indulgence. Each day I see people who are committing slow suicide through an uncontrollable desire to escape reality through drugs and alcohol. As some of them began to focus on her, she took their minds off their own personal torments. She was like medicine. I honestly think some of them stayed at the mission just to enjoy her hugs. I never knew Freddie had teeth until Brandy forced a smile from him. She would come skipping up to the guys waiting in line to join work crews, and they couldn't help themselves. Smiles just came. Brandy was a great part of why Charlie's life turned around. It certainly wasn't anything that I was doing."

"Okay, hold on there," Ryan scolded. "It was you who convinced Charlie to come to the mission in the first place. Without that invitation, he would have never met Brandy. He would have earlier died on a park bench somewhere in Atlanta, with pigeon crap all over his ragged and stinking clothes. He would have died without ever reconciling with his son. Charlie would have died in misery, and who knows how long he would have laid there until someone noticed that he had not just passed out from cheap booze."

"You are right in pointing out that Charlie could have died in much worse conditions, and it is not so bad when an older person dies. The death of an older person is easier to deal with. Maybe I should have expected it with Charlie. I had noticed that he was moving a little slower. I can't even focus on the accounting books. Charlie left them in perfect order, but I can't focus long enough to put together the financial presentation that is supposed to be given to the church committee next week."

The call between the two friends became silent. Ryan

sensed that more had to be said, so he allowed the gap in the conversation.

"Why did God have to take Brandy?" Larry exploded. "I can't image what she went through while hiding in the back seat of a car during a shoot-out. A kid should never have to experience garbage like that. Why didn't God take that piece of trash, Russ Boyd, and leave her out of that stupid situation?"

"Russ Boyd put her life in danger," Ryan replied. "He was the one who put her in that car, not God. He was deeply involved with really bad people. A girl can't pick her parents, and that irresponsible jerk put her in harm's way. God didn't do this to her."

"What's done is done," Larry whispered. "Now it's over for her. It's all over for her."

"Do you really think it's over for Brandy?" asked Ryan. "This world was not much of a friend to her. Don't you think God has a place for her?"

"I've got to go," answered Larry.

"I'll come to Charlotte this weekend," stated Ryan.

"You've got things to do," replied Larry. "You don't need to come. Things will settle in a few days. I just needed to puke through the phone at someone, and you'll still love me in the morning. Sorry for being such a whiny jerk."

"I'm coming to Charlotte this weekend," repeated Ryan.

After the phone call Larry dropped his head onto his desk and wept.

"*Ryan was right*," Larry thought. "*This world has not been a friend to Brandy.*"

As he prayed, Larry pictured her in heaven with Charlie. She was sitting on his lap, while he told her stories. In his imagination he saw them both filled with God's peace and absent of the cares of this world. They were free, and joy replaced all sadness. A weary Larry closed his eyes and soon fell asleep.

The ringing of the phone awakened him. It was Patsy.

"Hello, Larry Chatterson," he answered, still somewhat in a dreamy haze.

"Are you okay?" asked Patsy. "You don't sound right."

"I guess I fell asleep," replied Larry. "I am really tired."

"It's been a stressful time for a lot of people, and you've been right in the middle of it," said Patsy. "I know it's not Friday, but I would like for you to come home on time tonight. Let's order a pizza and go to a movie."

"What do you want to see?" Larry asked.

"I don't care," she answered. "I just want us to get out. It's all arranged. Evelyn is going to keep Speedy at her apartment tonight."

"Sounds like you've been busy," he replied. "Okay."

After the conversation, Larry thought back to the day Patsy gave birth to their son. Larry wanted to name him Ryan. However, Patsy thought it would be too confusing when they visited their friends in Brandon Springs. Larry told her that he wanted the boy to grow up to be like his best friend.

"I want him to grow up to be like his father," responded Patsy.

They compromised and named the boy Lawrence Ryan Chatterson. During the first eighteen months, they tried calling him "LR". However, once he began to walk, he earned the nickname "Speedy." The kid was fast, really fast. He only had two modes, full speed and off. Speedy was a continual burst of energy during his waking hours, but when he ran out of gas he was totally out. Once he dropped off into a deep sleep, it was almost impossible to wake him before sunrise.

AROUND 6:00 PM, Patsy dropped Speedy off at the center to stay with Evelyn.

"I plan to take him to my apartment in about fifteen minutes," Evelyn explained.

Taking Larry by the arm Patsy physically escorted him out to his car.

"You are leaving right now," she ordered. "The pizza has been ordered and we need to leave immediately."

"Okay," Larry replied, as he opened the door of his car. "You are pretty serious about this, aren't you?"

"We are not going to say another word until we are home," she commanded. "The longer you hang around this place, the more likely someone will need something. We are going home."

"Yes Ma'am," he answered with a smile.

The pizza arrived within a half hour of their arrival at the house, but they never made it to the movies. They had positioned themselves on the couch and in front of the TV. However, the programming on the television was completely ignored. While eating the pizza alone at the house, Patsy made sure his mind was off the center. With each bite of pizza, she removed an item of clothing. If he had not known her for so long and known her profession to be that of a nurse, he would have suspected that she had a history in another profession. Her teasing glances at him were exceptionally provocative. She had his full attention and after he had consumed three slices of pizza, he turned the event into one of making love in the den.

Afterwards, Larry consumed two more slices of pizza. They talked and laughed for about an hour and a half, before remembering the fact that Evelyn would soon need to be relieved of Speedy's care. She was an experienced woman with children, but Speedy was an exceptionally energetic young boy. He constantly asked questions and made suggestions about a host of activities for the two of them. Almost magically he quickly moved from one room of her apartment to another. It was all Evelyn could do to make sure he was not getting into something that he shouldn't.

Patsy decided that she should be the one to pick up her son because she knew how easily her husband could be sucked into conversation with Evelyn about the needs of the center. Speedy jabbered nonstop during the ride home about everything he and Evelyn had done that evening. Upon arrival at the home, the boy was given a bath and was dressed for bed. He continued to run around the house and act out the events of his visit with Evelyn for about an hour. Larry then convinced him to listen to a story. Speedy eagerly hopped into bed, and his father selected a story book from a bookcase in the bedroom. Within twenty minutes a deep sleep overcame the child

"Now that he is asleep, I need to take a shower," Patsy announced.

Seconds after she closed her eyes and placed her head under the running water, she felt a presence behind her. Larry's arms reached around her body and began to caress her.

"I didn't say you could partake of my shower," she jokingly complained.

Larry said nothing. He pressed his aging, but still fit body against hers, and she offered no other comments. As they shared the shower, the cares of the world were swept down the drain with the water. After drying, they dropped into the bed, still caressing each other. Patsy fell asleep first.

"It's been a really long time since we enjoyed hours of intimate time together," Larry thought as he watched her sleeping.

Caring for the mission was always hectic, and having an active little boy around consumed a lot of thought and energy. The loss of Brandy and Charlie was almost unbearable, but grief began to give way to the stress-filled thoughts of adding Charlie's work to his. Larry missed having time with his wife, Speedy, and his friend Ryan. He missed the earlier carefree times in Brandon Springs. As he drifted off to sleep, he imagined standing on the mountain that rose up behind the small simple house in that rural setting. He could almost feel the cool breeze of mountain air.

PATSY AWOKE THE next morning, alone in the bed. She put on a robe and found Larry making breakfast. It had been a long time since he had taken the time to prepare food in the morning. He usually grabbed an apple and a prepackaged cinnamon roll as he headed out for the center.

As he turned two eggs in a skillet, Patsy moved in behind him and wrapped her arms around his waist. She lovingly placed her head against his broad back.

"Hungry?" he asked.

"Yes," she answered. "And you must have worked up an appetite last night. As I recall, you expended a great amount of energy."

"It was your fault," he accused. "You seduced me. You lured me home with the false bait of pizza and a movie, and I never even got to see a movie."

"Maybe on another night," she suggested.

"What gives me any assurance that you won't take advantage of me again?" he joked.

"I guess there are no guarantees in life," she said. "Did you really miss the movie?"

He turned from the skillet and took her into his arms. His hands moved down to her backside, and he gave her a firm squeeze.

"Not really," he answered.

"Don't burn my eggs," she ordered.

Larry released her and finished preparing breakfast. Within minutes of sitting at the table, the muffled sound of quick little feet produced a small boy standing at the table.

"Breakfast!" the boy shouted, throwing both arms into the air.

As Speedy sat down to a bowl of oatmeal, his father gave him a kiss on the top of his head. Without even looking up, the small boy yelled out "Bye, Daddy!" and then crammed a large spoonful of the lumpy stuff into his mouth.

"I've hung around here too long," Larry said to his wife. "Charlie is no longer there to help, and I am sure Evelyn is tired."

With that, Larry finished dressing and left for the mission. Along the drive, his mind was filling with the responsibilities of the morning. As he entered the office, he immediately noticed Evelyn's puffy eyes. Larry eyes then moved to Charlie's now empty chair behind his desk. He stopped for a moment, glancing back at Evelyn. She was now attempting to avoid eye contact. Looking closer, he realized that those were not eyes suffering from weariness, but rather swollen from tears.

Larry took hold of Charlie's old chair and pulled it over beside Evelyn. "I miss him, too," he whispered.

"Both of them!" she blurted. Her mouth quivered, and she held both fists tightly clinched. "One was bad enough, but we have lost them both. I can't seem to shake it."

Larry gave her a hug and then went back to his office to begin looking through the accounting information. He found it difficult to concentrate, so he lay the data aside and began to pray. His nerves were on edge. A strange uneasiness came over him. Larry walked over to the office door that separated his office from the reception area containing Charlie's now empty desk. He closed the door and returned back to his desk. Instead of sitting in the chair, he dropped to his knees and placed his hands and head on the seat of the chair. Larry shut the world out. The deaths of Brandy and Charlie, Evelyn's broken heart, and the review of the accounts dropped from his mind and heart. He concentrated on God and focused his soul upon his Savior. It was worship without words, and he soaked his entire being in the Presence of God's Spirit. Within minutes he felt at peace.

Refreshed, he again sat in the chair and turned his

attention to the accounting figures. Almost immediately, he heard a familiar voice outside his door. It was Tiffany. Opening the office door, he found her standing outside.

"I need to talk with you," Tiffany whispered.

"Come on in," replied Larry, purposefully leaving the office door open. He wanted Evelyn to witness the conversation.

"I would like to talk in private," she stated.

"This is as private as it gets," he answered.

Tiffany's demeanor changed from that of softness to that of being totally vulnerable. The combination of her physical beauty and the change in manner was seductive; he felt deeply drawn to her. Still, the door remained open.

"How are you doing?" he asked, as he motioned for her to take a seat in a guest chair.

"Not very well," she responded.

As she took her seat and looked up at him, her glances were inviting. A stirring within Larry drew him to close the door and be alone with her. It was as if an unseen power was reaching inside him and almost taking control of his arms and hands. It lured him to simply close it. He resisted. The door remained open. He forced his eyes away from the door and onto a picture of his wife that he always kept on his desk. As the temptation began to subside, a soft voice questioned.

"Why did God allow this?" Tiffany asked.

"This place is definitely not Heaven," he replied.

"I have never felt so alone in my life," she spoke. "Brandy is gone; Charlie is gone; even Russ is dead."

"You are always welcome to come back to the center," Larry said.

"I don't need the center."

"I'm just saying…"

"I don't need the center," she softly spoke. "I need you."

"I'm always available," he replied. "If I'm not at the center, you can always call my cell phone."

"I said, I need you," she stated. "I'm alone, and I have

never had someone understand me the way you do. There is a connection. I know you feel it."

"I can't be … connected with you," he answered.

"I need you," she said.

"You need to let God be your strength."

"You understand me like no one else," she said.

"We have a few things in common," Larry attempted to explain. "You are going through an exceptionally hard time, and we have both suffered loss. I violently lost my brother, and you lost Brandy to a violent death. God uses tough experiences to mold us into better people if we let Him. If I had not lost Ronnie, I would probably not be able to relate to your suffering. God uses tough times to chip away at our lives. He wants to make us more like Him. God is like a stone mason chipping everything in the stone that does not look like the intended image. Nobody enjoys …"

"Don't tell me that God is doing something good with this," she interrupted.

"We all die," Larry stated. "Try to look at it in the light that Brandy was just moved up to the front of the line. This life is short for each of us, and it is nowhere as good as Heaven."

"Stop it!" she exclaimed. Her voice then became soft again, almost a whisper. "Don't use that preacher stuff with me. I'm not playing around with you. Don't throw Holy Roller words at me. I am talking to you straight out of my heart, and I need you. I don't need to hear a sermon from you. I need you."

With those words, she rose from the chair and exited the office. Larry's heart pounded within his chest. He was rattled and was a little afraid. He felt a strange power almost draw him from the office to run after her. Still, he remained in his chair.

"She is trouble with a capitol 'T'," he heard Evelyn say as she entered the office. "You have a problem with her, and you had better watch it."

"Tell me about it," Larry replied. "I'm sure she is still grieving for Brandy, and hopefully she will settle down over the next little while and realize what she needs to do."

"Regardless of what she does, you need to make sure you do what you need to do," Evelyn said.

"I have never given her any indication that I am personally interested in her, and I would never do something like that to Patsy," Larry assured.

"I'm not implying that you have," Evelyn explained. "You handled it as well as any red-blooded man could. I am just telling you to be on guard; I doubt she will let it go."

"I'll be on guard," Larry promised.

ON HIS WAY home from work that evening, he placed a call to his friend Ryan using his cell phone. Larry was sick of death, sick of sad situations, and sick of dealing with conflict.

"Hey man, have you got a minute?" he began.

"Sure, what's up?" Ryan asked.

"Can I run away and hide in that Brandon Springs farmhouse?" Larry asked.

"Things are tough for you," stated Ryan. "Having two loved ones die within two days is pretty tough. You know that you're always welcome to use the house in Brandon Springs. How can I help?"

"It's not just Brandy and Charlie dying," Larry responded. "That is bad enough, but I've got Brandy's mom hitting up on me."

"Are you sure she is not just needing comfort because of a dead child?" Ryan asked. "Good grief. The woman just lost a daughter and the child's father in the same violent incident. Are you sure she's hitting on you?"

"Evelyn overheard the conversation that Tiffany and I were having, and she gave me a pretty stiff warning about her," Larry replied.

"Okay, I guess she was coming on to you," Ryan stated. "Evelyn is a no-nonsense practical woman who is well seasoned and experienced. I respect her opinion. Have you talked to Patsy?"

"No, I am on my way home from the center," he explained. "I need to tell her about it."

"You, Patsy, and Speedy are always welcome to spend a few days in Brandon Springs," offered Ryan. "You have a key to the place. Just let me know."

"I wish I could take you up on it, but there is no way I can break loose right now," Larry replied. "I just wanted to let you know about the situation. I really need prayer,"

When Larry arrived at the house, he found Patsy starting supper. Walking over to the kitchen window, he spotted his son kicking a ball in the back yard.

"How was your day?" Patsy asked.

"Well, besides the fact that Evelyn sobbed most of the day and the fact that Tiffany hit up on me, I guess it was all right," he stated in a matter-of-fact expression.

"Wasn't last night good enough for you?" Patsy asked with a wink. "Now, it's gone to your head. I guess women are falling at your feet at the mission."

"Stop it; I'm serious," Larry said.

"I know you have an ego, but Tiffany just lost her daughter," said Patsy. "Aren't you drawing conclusions where you shouldn't? I would think her emotions are still pretty volatile. You probably misread what she said to you."

"You can ask Evelyn," he responded. "I left the door open so she could hear the conversation. Immediately after Tiffany left the center, Evelyn stepped into my office to voice her concerns. Tiffany was hitting up on me."

"What do you mean by 'hitting up on you'?" Patsy quizzed.

"Pretty much like it sounds," Larry replied. "She told me that she needed me, and that I was the only man that understood her. It was the way in which she said it. Evelyn told me to watch out for her. She thinks the woman is trouble. Talk with Evelyn. She can certainly explain it to you."

"How do you plan to handle this?" Patsy asked.

"I want to stay away from her, as far away as I can," replied Larry. "There is a part of me that wishes I could just take you and Speedy and just run away. Brandon Springs would be the perfect place. I'm just talking, I'm not serious. You know me; I have no plans to leave what God has put before me. It's just been a miserable last few days. Death, and now this. I'm just going to have to watch out for her."

Patsy stopped stirring the contents of the pot on the stove and stepped over to her husband. She kissed him and ran her slender hands across his chest. Larry rested his chin on the top of her head and held her tight.

"Maybe tomorrow will be a better day," he suggested.

OVER THE NEXT few days, Larry saw no sign of Tiffany at the center. Nevertheless, she had vividly implanted herself in his thoughts. He expected her return, and he had difficulties concentrating on his work. Mental images of her flashed through his mind. Whenever he realized that she captivated his imagination, he would attempt to shake it off by getting up from his desk and walking into Evelyn's area. It was Friday afternoon, and he was restless.

"Evelyn, is there anything that I can help you with?" he asked.

"I am fine," she replied. "How are you coming with your accounting figures?"

"Nowhere!" he exclaimed. "I still can't seem to concentrate."

"A pretty girl coming on to a man like that can do things to his mind," she stated.

"Is it that obvious?" he asked.

"I wasn't born yesterday," she replied.

"I told Patsy about the situation with Tiffany, but I don't want to tell her that still I have the encounter replaying in my mind. That would cause her to worry, and she has nothing to worry about. I've never loved a woman like I love Patsy. Maybe if Charlie hadn't died, I wouldn't be so volatile. Maybe it wouldn't have impacted me the way it did. I just need to stay busy until I shake this off."

"Good plan," said Evelyn. "That, along with prayer, would be a good idea. I am always here to talk."

Suddenly, the door of the reception area opened. Standing there with a silly grin on his face was an old friend.

"Surprise!" exclaimed Ryan.

"Man, you came out of nowhere!" exclaimed Larry. "What's the occasion?"

"You are," Ryan replied. "I thought it was time to visit my best friend. We don't get to visit very often these days. We both have family, and we both stay busy. I just decided to drop things for a couple of days and come see you."

"It's always good to see you, Ryan," Larry answered.

"Hey, it's eleven-thirty; have you had lunch yet?" Ryan asked.

"I always bring leftovers or a brown bag," Larry stated. "I have a sandwich here in this bag."

"My treat," Ryan offered. "Can you break away? We don't have to spend a whole hour, if you have something that you need to do."

Larry looked over to Evelyn.

"If you don't get out of here and go to lunch with a guy who has driven all this way, I'm going to give you a whipping right here in front of Ryan," Evelyn explained. "Give me those budget figures. I'll look them over and let you know what I find."

"All right," Larry replied. "Let me give Patsy a call and let her know that Ryan is in town – and that we're going to lunch."

"You can call as I drive," offered Ryan.

The two left the office and made their way to Larry's favorite Mexican restaurant. After the call to Patsy was completed, Larry dropped his head and gave a sigh.

"How bad is it?" asked Ryan.

"How bad is what?" asked Larry.

"Cut it out!" Ryan threatened. "This is me sitting here in this car with you. How bad is this situation with Tiffany? I remember her when she and her daughter came out to the house in Brandon Springs. That woman is hot, and I would guess that she can be trouble. How bad is it?"

"She rattled me, man," stated Larry. "It's been some time since a beautiful woman really came on to me. Okay, you know, besides Patsy. But it's not just that. She is scary. It's more like she makes me scared of myself. I feel like a big fish who has taken a hook, and I can't shake it loose. I can't stop thinking about her. I mean I would never cheat on Patsy, but I hate the fact that I think about this woman so much. It's not good. How did she do that to me?"

The question hung in the air as Ryan parked his car in front of the restaurant. Switching off the engine, he turned and gave Larry his full attention.

"She has probably spent a lifetime reeling in men, and she probably started when she was really young," Ryan answered. "Open the glove box, take out my Bible, and turn to Proverbs 7. I know that you are the minister, but I read this last night and it is what prompted me to come see you."

Larry took Ryan's Bible from the glove box, and he opened it as instructed. As he scanned the first few verses, he said, "I've read this."

"Read it again!" commanded Ryan. "And read it out loud."

My son, keep my words, and lay up my commandments with thee. Keep my commandments, and live; and my law as the apple of thine eye. Bind them upon thy fingers, write them upon the table of thine heart. Say unto wisdom, Thou art my sister; and call understanding thy kinswoman: That they may keep thee from the strange woman, from the stranger which flattereth with her words.

For at the window of my house I looked through my casement, And beheld among the simple ones, I discerned among the youths, a young man void of understanding, Passing through the street near her corner; and he went the way to her house, In the twilight, in the evening, in the black and dark night: And, behold, there met him a woman with the attire of an harlot, and subtle of heart. (She is loud and stubborn; her feet abide not in her house. Now is she without, now in the streets, and lieth in wait at every corner.)

So she caught him, and kissed him, and with an impudent face said unto him, I have peace offerings with me; this day have I paid my vows. Therefore came I forth to meet thee, diligently to seek thy face, and I have found thee. I have decked my bed with coverings of tapestry, with carved works, with fine linen of Egypt. I have perfumed my bed with myrrh, aloes, and cinnamon. Come, let us take our fill of love until the morning: let us solace ourselves with loves. For the goodman is not at home, he is gone a long journey: He hath taken a bag of money with him, and will come home at the day appointed.

With her much fair speech she caused him to yield, with the flattering of her lips she forced him. He goeth after her straightway, as an ox goeth to the slaughter, or as a fool to the correction of the stocks; Till a dart strike through his liver; as a bird hasteth to the snare, and knoweth not that it is for his life. Hearken unto me now therefore, O ye children, and attend to the words of my mouth. Let not thine heart decline to her ways, go not astray in her paths. For she hath cast down many wounded: yea, many strong men have been slain by her. Her house is the way to hell, going down to the chambers of death.

As Larry finished the passage, he shook his head and his

eyes stared intensely through the windshield. It was as if something had caught his eye, and he was fixed upon it. Truth had taken hold of his heart, and he was locked in on it. For a couple of minutes neither man said a word, and then Larry broke the silence.

"Thank you," Larry whispered. "Thank you. As I read those verses something happened inside. These words were meant for me, and God sent you. There is no question about it. God sent you to me with these words. Man! This thing has been lifted off me. It feels as if someone took an eighty-pound sack of potatoes off my shoulders."

"Are you hungry?" Ryan asked.

"I could eat the entire restaurant!" exclaimed Larry.

ROB WILLIAMS

Chapter 11

LARRY STRUGGLED while giving the eulogy at Charlie's funeral. Afterwards, in private he presented Chad with his father's journal. Larry understood that the book offered intimate insight into the remarkable transformation of the man, and he believed several notations would result in questions from Chad. He was right. From time-to-time Chad dropped by the center to ask Larry about entries in the journal. Although the initial visits were somewhat rare, Chad became a regular financial donor to the mission.

Chad was not Larry's only visitor. Tiffany still dropped by the mission on occasion to talk with him. She made no overt passes at him during the visits, but he still made sure to leave the door open between his office and Evelyn's reception area. He no longer felt powerfully drawn to her, but he was never sure about the motives of this beautiful and seductive woman.

AFTER A LATE night at the mission, Larry dropped into a neighborhood convenience store. As he peered through the glass door of a soft drink cooler, he felt a familiar light touch on his shoulder. Turning, he found himself looking into the clear blue eyes of Tiffany. They talked for about a half hour. She assured him that she was fine, but he wasn't sure she was telling the truth. As Larry was about to leave the store, she asked him for a ride to her apartment.

At first the conversation was light. However, as he parked his car in front of her apartment, the mood changed. Tiffany began to cry. She reached for his hand and held it tightly. Without saying another word, she kissed him on his neck and left the car. When he arrived at his home, he told Patsy that he had seen Tiffany, but he decided not to mention the kiss. Larry told himself that it probably meant nothing. He thought perhaps his conversation with her stirred memories of her daughter. He saw no reason to concern Patsy with that detail.

TWO WEEKS LATER, leaving the center again after working late into the night, he was surprised to find Tiffany waiting beside his car. They talked for a few minutes before Larry excused himself to go home. As he started the ignition, she dropped into the passenger seat and asked for a ride home. She told him that he was the only man who understood her. He ignored her statements and attempted to change the subject. Although he was a little apprehensive, he decided to do her the favor. Feeling a bit awkward, Larry attempted to initiate small talk.

"Still living in that lousy apartment?" asked Larry.

She ignored his question.

"I guess that was a little crude," he said. "Do you still work at the store?"

"I'm in love with you," she whispered.

Larry raised his right hand in protest. "We're not going to have that conversation," he replied.

For blocks the two said nothing. The noise of the engine provided the only welcome interruption of the tense silence. Just as he began to feel more relaxed, he heard her whisper again.

"I love you, and I need you," she said. "I would do anything you want."

Her voice was soft and seductive, just above the level of breathing. Larry glanced over to see her begin to slide her dress up her thighs. Tiffany's hungry eyes began to take hold of his. He turned his attention back to the road ahead.

"Stop it," he quietly warned.

"I mean it," she whispered again. "I would do anything that you could imagine, and I would love every minute of it."

Glancing in her direction, he quickly took note that the dress had been pulled up to just above her waist. She was wearing no underwear, and he couldn't help scanning her beautiful thighs, hips, and tiny waist as the vehicle passed under streetlights. He forced Patsy into his mind, and he shouted.

"I said, stop it!" Larry exclaimed. "I'm serious; you stop it right now."

In silence, she spoke invitation to him with her eyes. She tucked the bottom of her skirt under her bra, leaving her hands free. She ran her hands up her thighs and across her waist. Her eyes still begged. Closing her eyes, she then reached over her head and placed her hands on the ceiling of his car, while arching her back.

Opening her eyes, she slid her hands over her breasts and down to her thighs. Larry began to sweat. Silently he called out to God. *Oh God, please help me!*

With her skirt still trapped under her bra, she began to make even stronger advances. She placed her hand seductively on his thigh and began to slowly move it up between his legs.

"Stop it!" Larry stated, as he took hold of her hand and removed it from his leg.

Larry immediately pulled the vehicle to the curb and brought the car to a stop. Purposefully, he reached for the key and cut the ignition. For a moment, the two sat in silence. He was sweating and searching for words. Tiffany still sat quietly, nude from her breast area down. Larry stepped from the car and ordered the bewitching woman to exit from the passenger side. Nerves still on edge, he stood beside the car. A couple of uneventful minutes went by. Fear and apprehension filled his mind with several scenarios of dread. Larry nervously looked down at his right hand to confirm that he had taken the keys from the ignition. He was so relieved to realize that he still had possession of the keys, but he feared the keys were the only aspects in his control.

"At least I have that much control of the situation."

Larry comforted himself in the realization that Tiffany would not be unable to drive off with his car, leaving him stranded. They were now five blocks from her apartment, and Larry considered it to be a perfectly reasonable distance for her to walk.

Suddenly, the passenger door opened. Tiffany emerged; her dress brought down to its proper place. There was hurt in her eyes. "I love you," she whispered as she turned from him and began to walk away.

Larry found himself shaking as he sat back down behind the wheel. His trembling hand slid the key into the ignition switch. As he started the car, Larry nervously looked up to see if she had turned back toward him. The headlights of the vehicle bathed Tiffany's form in light, as though she was the only object in a sea of darkness. His mind was conflicted as he watched those hips move down the street. Larry knew there was nothing but enticing flesh under that skirt, and he found it difficult to think of anything else. He watched the light material seductively slide over each hip as she walked.

"Should I offer her a ride to her apartment? This is not the best of neighborhoods."

Again, he forced a mental picture of Patsy into his imagination, and he immediately knew the answer. It would be spiritual suicide to entertain anything other than immediately making his way home to his loving wife. Driving away, he considered himself fortunate to be out of the situation. He had escaped. *God answered my prayer.*

Still shaking, Larry immediately called Ryan on his cell phone. He told his best friend about every detail. In earlier years, he would have been bragging to a buddy. In earlier years, he would have taken her up on the invitation without hesitation. Things were different now. God had captured his soul and provided him with wisdom and strength. He was now a married man and a father. This was no manly tale of conquest. This was not an opportunity for bragging. He had escaped a moment of temptation, which would have certainly led to tragedy.

Ryan listened to the entire story and advised his friend to share each aspect of the event with Patsy. He told him to tell her about "every single thing" that had gone on in that car.

"Patsy doesn't deserve secrets; she deserves to know that you love her above all women," Ryan told Larry.

The two friends made plans to spend the weekend at the cabin in the mountains of Virgina. Too much time had passed since the two families had enjoyed a weekend there. This time Larry made no objections. This weekend, he would not place the mission above his family.

They also discussed what to do with the last of the money that had been stored away at the cabin. For some time, Larry and Ryan had been the primary handlers of a large amount of cash. The money was the source of anonymous ventures of charity, and it was time to make another donation to a worthy cause. Ever since a group of elderly men had passed this responsibility to Larry and Ryan, it became the source of major complications in the lives of the younger men. The older men had obtained the money illegally. For this reason, the existence and handling of the cash had to be kept secret. For decades the elderly men and their wives were the only persons with knowledge of the large stash of cash, and they alone had handled the charitable gifts. Knowing their time on earth was coming to an end, they cleverly pulled Larry and Ryan into their circle. The responsibilities associated with the money were passed to the two younger men and their wives.

Due to a misuse of that money, and other contributing factors, Larry's younger brother had been murdered. Larry's brother, Ronnie, should never have known about the money. Once he became aware of it, he threatened to publicize the operation unless the two gave him a significant "donation". Refusing to heed Larry's warnings, the younger brother flaunted his newfound wealth. As a drug dealer, Ronnie had relationships with very bad individuals. These people thought little of killing someone suspected of pocketing money made from drug deals, and for this reason Ronnie was killed. Only Ryan, Larry, their wives, and one elderly woman now knew of the cash. On a monthly basis they would have discussions about worthy candidates in need and then "make the drop" to the location of the selected individual. Packages of $10,000 in cash were the normal donations. Initially the two couples found the secret charitable work to be exciting. Now the responsibilities of parenthood put the risk of handling of these funds in a new perspective. The two men wished to be through with it. As he drove, Larry discussed with Ryan the option of selecting a worthy recipient and donating the rest of the money in one large gift rather than giving the normal amount to several people.

Larry felt better after the long talk with his friend. As he continued the drive home, he analyzed the situation that he experienced with Tiffany. Larry determined that he would never, for any reason, allow himself to be alone at night with any woman who wasn't his wife or wasn't old enough to be his mother. He had been moments away from losing everything. Larry thought about the scripture that Ryan shared with him the last time he had experienced pressure from Tiffany.

Let not thine heart decline to her ways, go not astray in her paths. For she hath cast down many wounded: yea, many strong men have been slain by her. Her house is the way to hell, going down to the chambers of death.

If he had given in to his lust for her, he would have crushed his relationship with the only woman who had ever really shown him the love that a wife should have for her husband. He would have failed his son, and he would have failed his Heavenly Father. Larry would have cast aside the life God had given him. He would have made mockery of Christ's brutal beatings and death on a cross. Larry would have failed the leadership in the church who had placed their trust in him. He would have failed each of those wounded souls that God had placed in his care at the mission.

As soon as he arrived home, he held Patsy in his arms and told her everything. He told her to make plans for a trip to the small cabin in the mountains two weekends away.

"The staff can hold down the fort this weekend," Larry told his wife.

Early planning would give him time to help make the preparations. He needed a quiet weekend with his family.

THE FOLLOWING WEEKEND, Ryan drove alone to the rustic cabin to prepare it for inhabitation of the wives and children. It was one thing for Larry and Ryan to hang out for a weekend in this primitive setting, but it was a different story when the women and children were present. Also, he was to take all the money from where it was stored in a gun safe and count it. Ryan opened the safe, placed all the remaining cash on the kitchen table, and began the count. There were five large envelopes, each containing $10,000. These had been prepared earlier to facilitate the donations. However, there were several stacks of loose bills on one of the shelves. When the count was finished, the loose bills amounted to $5,260. This made the total add up to $55, 260.

He carefully placed the loose bills in envelopes and wrote the amounts on the outside of each envelope.

The cabin was in no shape for the inhabitation of family members, so he began to clean the place of cobwebs and dust. He scanned the cabin for insects and found it to be relatively free of them. Opening each cabinet, he took inventory of needed supplies. Ryan chopped wood and kindling for the fireplace.

"It isn't really cold enough to require its warmth, but a nice fire always made visits seem complete," Ryan thought.

Just as he finished writing the inventory of needed items on the small piece of paper, Ryan realized that the Mexican dinner he had consumed the night before had made its journey through his system. He could wait no longer. The contents of his lower bowels were now screaming to be released!

The primitive cabin only had one facility to accommodate his need, and it was the marginally repaired outhouse that stood some distance away. Ryan quickly snatched a can of insect spray that he had brought and made a quick getaway to the small rustic island of relief. Opening the door of the outhouse, he lifted the toilet seat and blasted the area with the spray. He had no intentions of allowing his backside to suffer the abuse of a black widow spider. On another occasion he had seen one stationed under that toilet seat. Turning his attention to a wasp nest attached to the ceiling, he blasted that also. Needless to say, the wasps were none too happy about the treatment and they began to swarm. While flexing his buttocks to avoid an early release of what was building within, Ryan scurried away from the angry wasps.

He had made it out without a single sting, but his bowels immediately reminded him of the original purpose for going to the outhouse. Ryan stood very still, butt muscles clinched tightly, tensely waiting for the swarm to subside. It seemed as if the timing could not have been more perfect. For as the last of the wasps struggled in the grass from the effects of the spray, his disciplined rear muscles had begun to weaken their guard. He had to go, and quickly.

Ignoring the irritating stench of the bug spray, he entered the outhouse. He was happy to see that no wasp remained, and he began to scan the inside of the facility for toilet paper. To his dismay, the search was in vain. He suddenly realized the importance of placing this item first on the inventory list of needed supplies.

"Oh God, what am I going to do?" he loudly shouted to the heavens.

He began to panic. There was nothing for this use in the car or the cabin. The only sheet of paper was the tiny inventory list, but he doubted that he would make it all the way to the cabin and back in time. Glancing at the surrounding trees, he believed he had his answer.

"Leaves!" he shouted victoriously.

Lots and lots of leaves covered the trees that shaded the outhouse. Before he found himself in a situation where the "train was leaving the station", he quickly gathered as many as he could safely pluck,

Immediately upon dropping his exhausted buttocks on the toilet seat, a tremendous explosion rocked the small outhouse. It was as if every bean burrito in Mexico passed through him all at once. Smaller explosions followed, much like tremors after an initial earthquake. Leaves in hand, he chuckled in relief.

"Man, this will be a good story for the coming weekend," he thought.

"Layla will be embarrassed, but the kids will love this story!" he shouted out loud.

Feeling assured that the emptying of his bowels had completed, he began to apply the leaves. He found that they were not as comfortable as toilet paper, but they seemed to work.

"After all, man did something for thousands of years

prior to the invention of toilet paper," he reminded himself. He sensed a kinship with his ancestors. If they could do it, so could he. Rising from the seated position, he took two scoops of ashes from a bucket that always remained in the outbuilding. He lifted the toilet lid and dutifully dumped them both onto the waste below.

As Ryan stepped from the outhouse, his eyes caught one of the most beautiful sunsets he ever beheld. He took in a deep breath and sensed total peace. As darkness began to fall, he made his way back to the cabin. Ryan remembered the two burgers and soft drink he purchased while earlier traveling to the cabin. He found and lit a white gas lantern, and then started for his prepared meal that awaited inside his car. Crickets began to sing, and stars began to shine. Listening to the chorus of happy crickets, he consumed the meal by the light of the dimming lantern. Ryan pumped the lantern until the mantels glowed white hot. He considered making a fire with the firewood that he chopped earlier, but he decided to save it all for the fellowship of the two families.

He brought the lantern over to the sleeping area and slid the handle over a hook mounted on a nearby wall. Ryan found bedding items residing in a small makeshift closet. He quickly arranged the bedding and gathered a novel he had brought along. Within an hour his eyes became heavy. Ryan placed a flashlight beside the bed and turned off the lantern.

AS THE AMBER glow of sunshine pierced the heart of the cabin, he was quickly awakened by a fierce burning sensation in the anal area of his body.

"Ants!" he shouted, as he leapt from the bed. "Ants! Where did ants come from?"

With amazing speed, he stripped himself down to a state of total nakedness. He examined his body, and then his underwear. There was no sign of any type of insect. Ryan went through the bedding, and again there was no sign of ants.

As he stood naked with his anus burning, the cloud of mystery began to lift. He remembered a childhood story that Larry once told of him and his little brother Ronnie. Ronnie was four and Larry was seven. The summer heat of the Deep South created such a suffocating condition that only the shade of the forest provided relief. There, the two young boys played out the story of Daniel Boone. All at once, Ronnie announced that he needed a bowel movement. Though the two were only about a hundred yards from their home, Ronnie refused to leave the woods.

"I want to do it out in the woods, like Daniel Boone did it," argued Ronnie.

"Okay, I give up!" exclaimed the older Larry. "Just go somewhere behind a tree - where I don't have to see you."

Grinning, Ronnie scampered off behind a group of trees. After a few minutes, Larry heard his brother calling for help. Finding him broken down in a squatting position, he inquired of the need.

"I need someone to wipe me," requested Ronnie.

"No way!" yelled Larry.

All at once a terrible truth fell on the older brother. If he refused to do this deed, there would be no way of explaining to his parents why he left his little brother alone in the forest in this condition. He was trapped. His parents would kill him if he refused this request.

"Well, what am I supposed to wipe you with?" Larry asked.

"Leaves, just like Daniel Boone did it," explained Ronnie.

Dutifully, Larry plucked several leaves from a nearby tree. Gritting his teeth with disgust, he accomplished the task. Happily, Ronnie arose from the previous stance and the two played for two more hours. As the story goes, the next morning Ronnie was in agony. His rectum was on fire. Larry had not realized that a poison ivy vine had grown up the tree, and those leaves had been mixed with those of the oak. Ronnie was in the hospital for more than a week.

It was the remembrance of the childhood experience shared by Larry that caused Ryan to fully understand his current condition. Overcome with dread of things to come, he verbally expressed his despair.

"Oh, dear God!" Ryan cried out. "What have I done?"

Chapter 12

IN THE PARKING LOT of an upscale shopping center, Larry spotted her stepping out of an expensive European sports car. Almost two years had passed since Larry last saw Tiffany. He had to take a second look to make sure it was really her. It was as if destiny had placed their two cars within twenty feet of each other, and within a heartbeat's time their eyes locked on one another.

"Larry?" questioned Tiffany.

"I see you must be doing well," Larry said.

"Don't believe everything you see," Tiffany replied. "I'm okay. Do you live nearby?"

"Oh, no. I wouldn't be able to afford a place in this neighborhood. I spoke to a group at a nearby church this morning, and I stopped here to pick up some coffee. How about you?"

"I'm married now, and the house is about a mile away. We have the house to ourselves. My husband's first wife passed away, and his adult son now lives out of state."

"Congratulations. I hope you're happy. You've had too many difficult years."

"I guess life is what you make it," she replied.

"That's very true," Larry said, as he glanced down at the large diamond ring on her left hand. "It's good to see you.

153

I'm glad things have worked out for you,"

It was then that he noticed how well she was dressed. Larry studied the expensive styling of her hair and how perfectly her nails were manicured. As their eyes met again, he noticed a hint of sadness in hers.

"I have another appointment in a little while, so I had better move on," Larry stated. "It was good to see you."

"You, too, Larry," she said in almost a whisper.

She watched Larry drop down into the driver's seat of his car, and then she turned to walk away. Tiffany listened as he started the engine, and her ears seemed to lock on to it as though his was the only car in the massive parking lot. As the sounds of his departure died away, she stopped as if to take something out of her purse. She needed nothing. Looking back, she watched his car until it passed from her field of vision.

"*He doesn't know, and there is no way of telling him*," Tiffany thought.

If she truthfully told him about her life, she would be in unimaginable danger…and so could he.

Larry had a duty to present an annual update to each church that made sizable donations to the center. As he made his way to his next appointment, his thoughts were not on his message about the status of the mission. His mind was absorbed by thoughts of Tiffany.

"*Those sad eyes*," he thought. "*What was going on behind them? Maybe she still has feelings for me. That's not it. There's something else. She isn't happy. Tiffany probably has every material thing she could have imagined in earlier years, but those were not the eyes of peace and contentment.*"

Taking out his cell phone, he placed a call to Patsy. "Hey!" he began. "You would never guess who I ran into a few minutes ago. – No, it wasn't Chad. I ran into Tiffany. – Of course, she had her clothes on! She was stepping out of a Mercedes, a really high dollar one, at that. – Yeah, she said she is married now. – Maybe so…. Maybe she is happy, now. I hope so. See you tonight."

Talking with Patsy always brought his mind down to where it needed to be. It didn't matter what she said. She didn't need to say anything profound, and the conversation didn't need to be intimate in nature. He always found healing in her voice.

After the second speaking event in this prestigious area outside of town, he made his way back to a more familiar and less desirable neighborhood. Larry couldn't help noticing the profound difference in dress and manner of the people residing in the two places.

"The working poor in the United States seem to be far more genuine, and they seem to have more unique personalities than the wealthy," he thought. *"Their apparel is usually more authentic, as well. They don't have the money to spend in attempts to mimic those portrayed in movies, on TV, or in magazines. If they want to stand out, it takes a little more creativity. I remember a guy who placed a new pair of jeans on the sidewalk, stepped barefooted in a pan of bleach, and then walked on the jeans. After the bleach set in, he had a unique pair of jeans with bleached footprints. It only cost him the pair of jeans and a bottle of bleach."*

TIFFANY SIPPED HER coffee and moved her left hand over the elegant granite kitchen countertop. As the sun rose outside the window, she thought of how her life had changed. No longer was she working long hours and living in a rundown apartment in a crime-ridden part of town.

I wonder what my life would have been if Larry had left Patsy for me. I doubt it would have been as I imagined. It would have changed both of us.

As she closed her eyes and took another sip of coffee, she felt a familiar hand on her shoulder.

"I want you to be at the *Wormhole* at 8:00 PM tonight,"

he began. "I have a special client to be entertained."

Tiffany thought back to how her dream of a lifetime turned into an incredible nightmare. She remembered the evening she met her future husband. Tiffany was working at the store when John Molato came in to buy a pack of gum and a paper. There was no one else in line behind him, so they talked for a while. It was obvious to her that this was a man of power and influence, and she saw in his glances that he was attracted to her.

He returned the next day and offered her a hostess job at his bar/restaurant. She was now off probation, and no longer did she have to report where she lived or worked. Immediately, she went to work for him. Over time a romantic relationship formed. After the restaurant closed for the night on one occasion, he took her to his massive home on the outskirts of town. Within three months they were married, and she felt her dreams had come true. He often brought "special clients" to the home to entertain them during business deals. These discussions were off limits to her, and she would retire for the evening when he gave her the signal.

One evening she returned to the kitchen for a glass of water, and she overheard a portion of the conversation that was meant to be in private. She had never seen his eyes take on such a cold glassy stare. The following night he took her for a drive to a warehouse. He placed her in a side room, where a one-way soundproof window allowed her to see into the next room. As she watched a man being tortured in that room, she got the message. No explanation had to be made, and she made sure she never interrupted another "business deal." She understood now that her life of ease had huge risk, and that she had married someone who had many dark and dangerous secrets. Tiffany was afraid.

THREE MONTHS AFTER seeing Larry in that parking lot,

Tiffany ran into him again at a café. They talked, and she confided in him. Without thinking it through, she began to tell him everything. Tiffany knew no one else in the world she trusted more. Her life was in his hands. If word ever got back to her husband, she would be in real danger.

When she returned home, she was surprised to find her husband waiting for her. He asked her where she had been and why she had been gone for so long. She was terrified to mention Larry, so she made up a story about running into an old girlfriend. He smiled, finished his drink, and kissed her on the forehead.

"I've got work to do," he stated as he left the house. "Don't wait up for me."

EARLY THE NEXT morning, she awoke to the sounds of her husband leaving the house for the day. Tiffany had not remembered him coming to bed the night before, but she didn't think anything of it. His hours were never regular. The evening before, she had experienced difficulties falling asleep. This morning her eyes were extremely heavy. About 10 minutes after falling back to sleep, she was awakened at the sound of the closing of the front door of the house. Hearing footsteps in the kitchen downstairs, she decided that her husband must have returned for something he left. Exhausted, Tiffany immediately fell back asleep. She was awakened by the touch of a man, and she quickly realized that he was not her husband.

"Don't make a sound, or I'll kill you right where you lay, Baby Doll."

She was petrified with fear. The man was huge, and he was naked. He threw the covers off her, in a single motion. The stranger glared down at her nude body, bathed in the soft early dawn light coming through the window.

"I think you might even like this," he said.

She tried to fight him, but his huge hand almost choked

the air from her windpipe. She could tell that he wasn't going to hit her, but he didn't need to. His powerful hands made sure he had total control of her. He raped her, and then sodomized her. Once he was finished, his eyes were fixed on her as he slowly put his clothes back on. The man looked at Tiffany as if she were a slain deer that he was about to bring home for mounting on a den wall.

"Did you enjoy that, Baby Doll?" he asked, as he dressed. "I know I did. Good God, Honey! You were made to order. I might even want to come back for seconds some time - but only if the boss gives the word. You wouldn't mind, would you?"

Before leaving he took her hair in a firm grip and placed his other huge hand on her neck. His eyes became crazed.

"If the boss ever finds out you are lying to him, I can assure you that you will not enjoy it as much as you did this time," he warned.

A STRANGER WITH cold eyes entered the house that evening. His stature and build were identical to that of Tiffany's husband, but his manner was not that of the man she married.

"We are going for a ride," he instructed.

From that moment on, the special entertainment of clients at the house stopped. Tiffany's husband was involved heavily in black market activity; gun running to cartels in Mexico, shipments to the middle-east, and countless areas of crime that Tiffany wished desperately to know nothing about. That evening he introduced her to *Wormhole*. This was a special club, with extremely limited customers. It was located in the basement under a bar that he owned. The only access to it was in the rear of the building. This was where he would bring his "special clients," those he intended giving special treatment. As a wormhole is thought to draw matter from one part of the universe and transport it to another, this was the place where Molato drew certain clients in. There, everything was "on the house." Tiffany became an item on the menu.

From that moment on, the dream became a nightmare. The man she married never again showed romance, tenderness, or even kindness. The mask was off, it was no longer needed. She was now only another tool in his trade. Tiffany had never known such terror and despair. Within six months, absolute fear had dissipated into a state of numbness. Despair became the order of life. Day after day, she breathed, ate, drank, slept, and woke – but she wished for death. Still, she could not bring herself to suicide.

HER THOUGHTS OF LARRY produced a small seed of life within her. As those thoughts began to germinate, something deep within her awakened. As she relived her days at his center for the homeless, she remembered the words of an old man.

"You have to take the peeling off to get to the good part. One day, someone will find this old body lying somewhere. When they do, they will be seeing only the peeling that is left. The good part will have gone somewhere else. We all have to be peeled at some point, to let the good part of us out. God touched me a while back, and He refreshed the inside of this old man. The outside is still wasting away. The damage has been done. But the inside is something else."

Charlie's words returned to her, and they reminded her of God's love. She closed her eyes and remembered the peace she always felt in the presence of the old man. Tiffany recalled how her daughter had loved him. Something warmed within her, and relief spread over her soul like a hot bath taken in chilled air. She had little choice than to obey her husband's cruel orders. Other than suicide, her world as a captive offered no escape. Tiffany did the deeds required by him. Her situation had not changed, but remembrance of

Charlie kindled an unexplainable hope that began to take hold of her spirit.

OVER THE NEXT two months Larry spoke at centers in three different states. It was unusual that he would be given such frequent opportunities to be away from the center, but he was becoming nationally known. It was during that time that the senior pastor, Dr. Stevens, brought Milton Holloway to the center to meet Larry. Milton was an accountant working for the FBI and was a new member of the church. It turned out to be a short visit, for within minutes of the introduction a call on his cell phone resulted in Mr. Holloway's departure. Before leaving, the accountant spoke directly to Larry.

"I am considering making a donation to your center," Holloway expressed, as he handed Larry a business card. "I think you possibly do as much good in stopping crime as the FBI. I would like to meet with you again and talk."

THAT SECOND MEETING occurred two weeks later.

"I'm going to be honest with you, Reverend Chatterson," Holloway began. "You and I have a mutual acquaintance and without saying much more, she is in grave danger. In fact, I believe you and your family may be in danger as well."

"Tiffany!" Larry blurted out.

Holloway gave him a slight wink. Larry now saw a different side to the man who was earlier introduced as an accountant.

"You're not really an accountant with the FBI, are you?" Larry asked.

"Sure, I'm an accountant," stated Holloway. "I have several career interests, but I am an accountant. However, this meeting is not really about me. This meeting is about a very evil individual, who needs to be removed from a position of power and influence. This meeting is about a woman who may lose her life; and this meeting is about the fact that an evil individual has observers in a lot of places. The FBI has done some observing of its own, and your relationship with this woman has come to our attention. My family enjoys attending the church associated with this mission. I would have to say that my family's participation at this church came about at my suggestion. I enjoy listening to Dr. Stevens' sermons, and I have very much enjoyed meeting you. You're a fine person, Reverend Chatterson. However, you and I both know that not everyone in this city is a fine person."

"What do you want with me?" Larry nervously asked.

"I want to point out the obvious. I understand that you have a brilliant mind regarding finances. As an accountant, I can appreciate that. As a truly smart and gifted individual, you certainly must realize that employees of the FBI can't be the only ones observing you. I believe the FBI can help you in that matter and can also help your old acquaintance in her situation."

"What do you want me to do?" Larry questioned.

"For now, I just want you to listen and to do a little thinking," Holloway answered. "I want to have another conversation in two days. Would you be willing to have me drop by again?"

"I think a return visit from you would be more welcome than a visit by some other people who come to mind," Larry replied.

"Good," Holloway said. "I'll see you in a couple of days. Oh, I almost forgot. I do want to make a contribution to your center."

Holloway rose from his chair and handed the minister an envelope before slowly walking out of the office. Larry sat behind his desk and stared at the envelope. Within a minute, a familiar face stood at the door.

"What was that meeting all about?" asked Evelyn. "You know me, I am about as nosy as the next person. I've never seen that fellow before, and you usually don't close your door unless you are counseling someone. That man didn't look like someone who was here for counseling."

"Oh, he is a new member of Dr. Stevens' congregation," Larry explained. "Dr. Stevens brought him by a couple of days ago when I was making the rounds here at the mission. I believe he gave us a donation."

"Well, open the envelope," she advised. "We could certainly use a few more bucks around here."

She moved beside Larry and stood eagerly waiting for the envelope to be opened.

"You really are nosy," Larry chided. "Maybe I should open this in private."

"Don't make an old lady stand and wait," she scolded. "Open the silly thing."

Larry nervously took the letter opener from the desk drawer. He had no clue what Holloway had really put in the envelope, and he was a bit cautious about Evelyn seeing it. A hundred scenarios raced through his mind, as his hand slowly brought the letter opener near the envelope.

It could possibly be pictures of me and Tiffany at the café, or maybe it was a picture of Tiffany being threatened, or maybe it was a note from her....

"Open it!" Evelyn demanded. "Where are you? You must be really tired or something. I've been worried about you, lately. You haven't looked well. Are you coming down with something, or do you just need sleep?"

"I have been a little tired," he responded, as he ran the opener across the envelope.

Reaching inside, he found it to contain only a check. The check was for $3,000.

"I knew that fellow looked like someone of means," Evelyn stated. "He probably was a stockbroker who lives simply, but is rolling in money. I've known the type."

"You're close," Larry replied. "He is an accountant."

LARRY ALMOST DREADED talking with Patsy. Enroute home, he called his friend Ryan.

"Ryan, I have problem," Larry began.

"When do you not have a problem?" asked Ryan. "You are surrounded by people who are problems for themselves and everyone around them."

"I'm not talking about someone here at the mission," Larry replied.

"Okay, I'll shut up and listen," Ryan answered. "What's going on?"

"This is more serious than our acts of charity. When would you be able to come to Charlotte? I want to talk with you face to face."

"Layla and I will be there Friday night," promised Ryan.

That evening, as he helped Patsy wash the dishes after supper, Larry reached into the dish water and took hold of his wife's hand.

"We have to talk," he stated.

"What's wrong?" Patsy questioned.

Larry walked over to the kitchen door and peered into the den. Satisfied that their son's attention was captivated by a TV show, he quietly closed the door. He told Patsy of his conversations with Mr. Holloway, the situations involving Tiffany, and of the danger his family faced. As Patsy stood almost breathless, the kitchen door burst open.

"Mama, can I have my bedtime snack now?" a little voice asked.

"Sure, Honey," Patsy replied, as she wrapped two cookies in a paper napkin and placed them in his small hands.

"Thanks, Mama," her son said.

Speedy immediately gave her a hug and scampered

back to the den. The exchange of words, the granting of the cookies, and the resulting hug gave little relief to the tense situation. It only drove home the seriousness of allowing the FBI to intervene in the handling of the threat. The conversation shook her to the core.

"I want to get away from here," Pasty sighed. "Can you ask for a few days off, so that we can go to that cabin in the woods? It is away from everything."

"What about the place in Brandon Springs?" Larry asked.

"People know that Ryan and Layla own that property there, and the last thing I would want to do is to drag that family into this mess," she responded. "The cabin in Virginia is really remote."

"I'll ask Dr. Stevens for a few days of vacation," promised Larry. "Sounds like the cabin is the place to go. We don't even have to notify Ryan about going there, since he and I are joint owners. Would you want Ryan and Layla to come along?"

"I would love to be able to talk about this with another woman, but I just don't want to put them in danger."

"We would be coming from different directions," replied Larry. "I seriously doubt any of those goons would follow us there, and we would be aware of it if they did. That road leading to the cabin never has any traffic. If any vehicle followed us for any distance on that road, it would be obvious. If we were being followed, we would call Ryan on his cell and warn them not to show up. We would drive on past the gravel road leading up to the cabin and go on to the next town. I would find the Sheriff's office there and park the car in the parking lot. From that parking lot, I would call Holloway at the FBI. We should be okay. What do you think?"

"I think we would be safer there than we are here, right now," Patsy stated with dread in her voice.

Patsy was normally the even tempered one in the

family, but she was almost shaking with fear. Just the thought of someone hurting her little boy sent her into panic. Larry pulled her close, and he quickly noted the tension in her body.

"All right, I'll make it happen," Larry whispered in her ear. "I'll talk with Dr. Stevens tomorrow, and I will immediately tell Holloway. He needs to know where we are. I can trust him."

"Okay," she answered. "Thank you."

Larry gave his wife a hug, but Patsy was still so tense that her body was almost stiff. He squeezed her hand, and then called his friend Ryan.

"Don't come to Charlotte," he began. "I shouldn't have even asked you to come. I don't want to go into it on the phone, but we would much rather meet you and Layla at the cabin. Would you be willing?"

"Of course," replied Ryan. "We will meet you there Friday."

"One last thing," said Larry.

"Yeah?"

"This time make sure you bring toilet paper," chided Larry. He heard a groan on the other end of the conversation.

"Sure you don't want to try the leaves?" offered Ryan.

"I'll leave that up to the wilderness survival expert."

"I've stocked the place with TP, and I always include a pack in the trunk of my car each time I go. Once is enough."

"On a serious note, it's important that you keep your cell on while traveling to the cabin this time," explained Larry. "I may need to call this off at the last minute."

No one, not even Patsy, could read Larry as well as Ryan. He quickly assessed there was much concern in his voice.

"Something big is up, and whatever it is has seriously shaken Larry."

ROB WILLIAMS

Chapter 13

LARRY CHATTERSON HAD AN UNCANNY ABILITY to read men, even men who normally stimulated no interest in the minds of most. From his youth he found it easy to pick up on the personal subtleties of those he met. As a minister to the homeless, he now viewed these unique characteristics in people as part of God's overall design.

"Every man has a soul," Larry once told his best friend Ryan. "Like a living puzzle, every man is a piece created by God to fill a particular spot in creation. The vast majority of those abandoned by society once held a place in someone's life. Events have taken place in the lives of each individual served by the mission which either caused the person to want separation from the lives of others or caused others to want to separate from them. The people we see at the mission weren't always in their current state. I have hope that, with God's help, some may become more of who they were intended to be."

Larry often picked up on subtle hints of significance. A particular dialect offered a clue as to the origin of a person. Even the homeless have preferences in the clothing they retain. Men with prior military history sometimes select clothing that reflects that past.

Melvin was an unusual man whose mental challenges soon became apparent after entering the mission. The first problem was that Melvin probably wasn't really Melvin. No one at the mission knew his real name, where he was from, or much about the life he lived prior to being in his current state. In the world of the homeless, not every person offered his or her actual name. Some chose not to give the correct name and others were incapable of giving the information. When an unidentified indigent person came to the center for help, that client was given a temporary name by the mission staff based on an alphabetized ordered list. That morning this nameless newcomer was given the name "Melvin" for the letter "M".

Because this man's mind was severely out of sync with reality, Larry found him all but impossible to read. If the morning had gone differently, Larry might have had more time to unfold those mysteries. Unfortunately, Melvin's presence was the cause of a disturbance at the mission. It had taken the staff an hour to calm everyone down.

As usual with new entries to the mission, the center first attended to his most immediate need. This man was hungry. He was escorted to the crowded dining area, where most clients stood in a long line. The tables were just beginning to fill. Melvin was seated at an empty table, and Larry motioned to the staff for food to be placed before the man. Melvin was fully capable of standing in the line, but there was a reason for placing him away from those awaiting meals. This man was absolutely rank from weeks of accumulated oily body odor; and the stain on his pants leg gave off the sourness of dried crusty vomit. The man's clothes spoke loudly of every filthy environment where he had recently found rest. Though he had been seated alone at a table, the stench was strong. Those attempting to eat at surrounding tables didn't appreciate his presence. Within minutes one client approached the table and loudly demanded that he be removed. Melvin rose from the table and straightened himself in a regal position of attention. In Napoleonic fashion, he slid his right hand between the buttons on his shirt and began making weird sounds.

"Berrrp – wooly worm, wooly worm!"

As Melvin loudly recited this phrase repeatedly, several in the dining hall began shouting at him. Enduring the filth, Larry took him by his free arm and escorted him to another area of the center. Leaving Melvin in the care of two staff members, Larry issued a new policy for the mission.

"Next time a hungry man with such foul personal hygiene enters the mission, food is to be brought to him in a separate room," Larry whispered to staff members. "I will rewrite our policies before the end of the day."

Larry immediately washed foul residue from hands used to guide Melvin to safety. He then retreated to his office to find a more suitable environment for Melvin. Exhausted from the stressful situation, he tried to determine which social agency would be the best fit for this man. A tap at his door interrupted the weary minister.

"Mr. Holloway is here to see you," sang Evelyn, his receptionist.

When Larry first met this accountant for the FBI, Larry thought there was more to the man than met the eye. The difficulty in reading Holloway was not the same as that of reading a mental case like Melvin. Milton Holloway was trained professionally in masking his activities and motives.

"I suggest that you and I go for a little ride in my car," Holloway quietly spoke.

Larry immediately obeyed. This was not the first unannounced visit by the FBI accountant, but on this occasion, there was something unsettling in the tone of his voice. Little was said until both were seated in the car.

"I have good news, and I have bad news," Holloway proclaimed as he guided the car into the flow of traffic.

"I want to hear the good news first," said Larry. "So far, the morning hasn't gone so well. I could use some good news."

"Tiffany has decided to fully cooperate with the FBI, and she is willing to do anything to get out of her situation," said Holloway. "She's made a deal with us to help bring down Molato. In turn we will help her."

"I have a feeling that I'm not going to like the bad news," said Larry. "We're sitting in this car for a reason. Tiffany must be in real trouble. For you to pay me a private visit, I'm thinking that I must be facing trouble as well."

"I want to focus on Tiffany for the moment. Normally, we work with people who are willing to testify in court to a major crime. In this case, Tiffany is intimately knowledgeable about serious criminal operations. When I say intimate, I mean it. She heard details of conversations between her husband and some his "special clients" in a place called *The Wormhole*. Molato thinks he has total control of her, and he's been careless with what has been said around her. He had her roughed up some, and he thinks she is so petrified of crossing him that he doesn't have to worry about her. Plus, he has a standing order for her to be dealt with if she is found to have close ties to anyone who is not in his inner circle. For example, if she was found to be having an affair with someone outside of his control, she would be as good as dead."

"I would guess that person she was seeing would suffer the same fate," stated Larry. "What about close friends?"

"A close friend outside that circle would never be permitted," explained Holloway. "Molato can't risk her slipping up and spilling information. She has knowledge about his relationships with some of the worst domestic and foreign criminals and is privy to dates and places. Tiffany knows them personally. She is in a position to lead us directly into the heart of major operations. Things being as they are, she is willing to take great risks to herself in this deal. Her giving testimony in court is not the kind of deal we are willing to make. If it only involved Molato, it would be different. We want to take down a major part of the network, and Molato is only a piece. A big piece, but only a piece. If we were to only arrest him and have her testify in court, it would be extremely difficult to protect her from other elements of this massive organization. We need to take down the network, and she can't be seen as working with us. That would blow everything. She has the ability to give us insight into ongoing activity that would allow us to catch them in multiple acts. We can get her into a witness protection plan, but it's complicated. We don't have the goods on this organization yet, and the effort will be ongoing. At this time, I can't go into details of how we plan to take them down. You don't need that information."

"So, why are you telling me what you have?" questioned Larry.

"What I am telling you is that she'll never be safe unless certain people believe she has passed away," explained Holloway. "She is known by several of his high-level associates, and they would have their people crawling all over to find her. The only way she's going to escape her situation alive is to be seen as dead."

"So, why do you think I need that piece of information?" asked Larry. "Why is it important for me to know that she needs to be viewed as dead?"

"That's one of the many reasons I like you," stated Holloway. "It is really refreshing to work with an intelligent man. Not only are you intelligent, but you're a no-nonsense guy that appreciates getting to the point."

"Cut the crap!" spouted Larry.

"That doesn't sound very preacher-like," stated Holloway. "Cut the crap?"

"Get on with it, but without the smoozing," said Larry.

"Just as I was saying, you want the facts straight up – no nonsense. All right, here it is. Once the FBI comes up with a way to make Tiffany appear dead, and after we are able to put the clamps on Molato and a number of his high-level associates, we will give her a new identity and move her through the US Marshals Service Witness Security program. We can do that. Once Tiffany is relocated and given a new identity, she will be able to live a different life. What we can't do is provide a temporary source of income for her until we are able to take these people down. I don't trust her to continue to give us information after she has been granted witness protection funding and is formally in our program. She will not be granted funding until she has helped us bring these people down, and she will need an outside source of income during this time. She should not pull money from any Molato account prior to turning up deceased. It would trigger suspicion if that money came up missing. She needs a source of income for a period of time between her apparent death and our stopping Molato and his people. That's the deal. She will only enter the witness security program after we take them down. Until then, we will only hide her by moving her to various locations. She will not yet be able to work a job and live in the open under a new identity. That is the deal. Over time, she will help us put the pieces together. This could take some time and she'll need money."

"Why would you come to a minister to the homeless with a request for money?" asked Larry.

"I believe in you," Holloway said, with a grin. "You might say that I have faith in you. I'm a man with a financial background, just as you. I believe you to be a very resourceful individual who would be able to come up with some funding for a needy former client. I bet you have sources of funding that most ministers to the homeless just don't have. What do you say?"

Larry became uncomfortable.

"Has Holloway found out about the secret pool of money Ryan and I use for charitable causes?"

"What kind of money are we talking about?" Larry asked.

"Fifty thousand dollars would go a long way towards

REST IN BRANDON SPRINGS

putting Tiffany on a new path," Holloway spoke, grinning.

"Are you nuts?" Larry blurted. "Fifty thousand dollars? What makes you think I could come up with anything close to that amount of money?"

"It doesn't have to be fifty grand," explained Milton Holloway. "Just see what you can do. The FBI can set up an express account for her. Anyone would be able to deposit money just by using the account number. She would make withdrawals from the account using an ATM, and she will pay cash for everything she needs. We've done this before. We'll relocate her, but she will not be given a new identity until after we take down her husband. Are you ready for the bad news?"

"I thought the fifty thousand dollars was the bad news!" Larry exclaimed. "What other bad news do you have?"

"Your buddy, Chad, has been following Tiffany around since she came to meet with you," replied Holloway.

"Oh no," moaned Larry. "Chad must be thinking with what's in his pants instead of what's under his hat."

"I don't think I've ever heard a preacher say that about a friend," Holloway chuckled. "If the FBI is seeing this activity, Molato's people are probably aware of Chad. He may soon need someone to step in, but we may not be able to do much to protect him."

Clarity of the situation had now become more apparent to Larry. Whether by FBI design or by Chad's stumbling, the minister was being squeezed.

"All right, I'll see if I can come up with some funding for her," Larry promised. "Please do what you can to protect Chad. He's really a good guy, but I can't imagine him having any street sense. Tiffany can make men crazy; you know. Chad has a career in marketing. I doubt he's been around many women like Tiffany. He must be goo-goo eyed over her. Maybe if I had explained a few things about her to him, he would have decided to stay away from her. I didn't think she would go so low as to use Chad. She must be desperate."

"This isn't her doing," said Holloway. "He is doing this on his own. It isn't all bad. The FBI could work his presence to our advantage. We've considered planting a bug in his car. If he picks her up, we will have a way of gaining information from her conversations with him about Molato. He would think she is confiding in him, but she would be passing tips to us."

"She has a way of luring men," stated Larry. "You would probably just have an earful of Chad blubbering over her."

"I think this is different," replied Holloway. "This is not a game of teasing a dazzled naïve boy. We ran a thorough background check on Chad. I don't believe him to be as naïve as you think. Regardless of Chad's motives, or even his hormones, I believe he really thinks he can help her. She thoroughly understands the danger, but I doubt he knows what he is walking into. He's lacking information that might have made him think twice about being involved with her. However, he's hip deep in it now."

"What about Chad? Will he need protection?"

"Possibly," answered Milton Holloway. "He's on our radar, but he doesn't offer the FBI much in the way of getting Molato. We will do what we can to look out for him, but we can't currently justify the expense of witness security for him. Doesn't sound very compassionate, but that's the honest truth."

"If you are going to use Chad, then you should make sure he's protected," Larry sternly stated.

"We are talking about high level witness protection, because Molato is an extremely dangerous man. This is going to take a very big effort on the part of the FBI, involving a very big target for the agency. Make no mistake, Tiffany is in real danger. She will be in real danger for some time, and Chad has stepped in the circle. We aren't funded to place everyone in this type of program, but we will do what we can for him. I hope the plan works."

Milton Holloway parked the car in front of the mission. He ended the conversation with a reminder of the funding needed for Tiffany.

"Good luck in your efforts to come up with that money," Holloway told Larry, giving him a wink.

The FBI agent indicated with a hand motion that it was time for Larry to depart the vehicle. As the car moved down the street, Larry watched it and considered the last statement made by Holloway.

It's possible he knows about the money, but Holloway doesn't have a clue as to how much Ryan and I have left. Fifty thousand dollars! I guess he was shooting high just to see my reaction. This guy is a master. He is dangling both Tiffany and Chad, to pull me into this – and at the same time he is using this as a means to look into the money used for the charity. He is trying to scare the crap out of me, and he's doing a good job.

Larry called his best friend on his cell phone, but he was reluctant to go into detail with Ryan about the situation he and his family faced. He only told him that their lives had become complicated and that it had a lot to do with a certain woman who had lived at the mission. Ryan understood without Larry revealing the name of the woman, and he could tell the seriousness of the situation by the tone of Larry's voice.

"Don't ask me questions until we meet face to face," Larry cautioned his friend.

He was sure the FBI was listening to his calls, and he was deathly afraid Molato might be doing the same. Anticipation and tension grew in both households, as each ached for an opportunity to share details of the situation in a safe setting.

LARRY, PATSY, AND Speedy were almost there. It had taken hours, but the cabin was only minutes away.

"I've got to pee!" Speedy announced from his booster seat.

"Can you hold it another ten minutes?" Patsy asked.

"I have to pee!" the small boy warned.

Hearing the desperation in the shrill high-pitched voice, Larry quickly pulled the car onto the rough shoulder of the road. Patsy knew the drill. As soon as the car stopped, she immediately exited and began to unhitch the boy from the booster seat. By the time she succeeded in freeing him, Larry was at her side. Just as smoothly as a well drilled quarterback hands a football off to a tailback, she shoved the boy into the waiting arms of her husband. Tucking the child snugly against his chest, Larry sprinted into a nearby stand of trees. Once there, he lowered Speedy to the ground and in one motion quickly pulled both pants and underwear down to the chubby knees of the child.

The timing was perfect. Immediately a stream of urine shot out from the little boy. At first, he let it flow without any secondary purpose, but within seconds he was taking aim at several targets in the area. He blasted a small sapling, before spotting a toad. He couldn't resist. With uncanny accuracy the reptile suffered a direct hit. Speedy squealed with delight as the toad made a hasty escape.

"I peed on a frog!" exclaimed Speedy.

He giggled as only a little boy could from such an exhilarating experience. It was almost uncontrollable. His eyes closed and his little body shook from the laughter. As he laughed, the stream of urine bounced in concert with each giggle. This made the experience even more hilarious for the child. As the stream diminished into a series of squirts, Speedy looked up at his father. Larry couldn't contain himself. His laughter caused the little boy to launch into a second round of giggling. The two laughed all the way back to the car.

"What is so funny?" questioned Patsy. "What in the world have you two been up to?"

"I peed on a frog!" shouted Speedy.

Father and son immediately broke into laughter. Over the next few miles, Larry and Patsy heard the little boy chuckle from time to time. As soon as they arrived and placed Speedy on the ground beside the car, he ran toward the cabin yelling at the top of his little lungs.

"I peed on a frog!"

Kaylee and Joseph gathered around to hear of the event, and Speedy shared the experience with great enthusiasm. The others erupted into laughter as he expressed his joy in continued giggling.

Towards evening, Ryan started the grill and reminded them all of his experience with the poison ivy. More laughter ensued as he tried to explain this particular situation of torment without being overly graphic. If a doctor had not given him a regimen of steroids and antihistamines, Ryan would have been miserable for a couple of weeks.

As the laughter from that story died down, Speedy again shouted "I peed on a frog!" The timing and manner in which Speedy proudly proclaimed his accomplishment resulted in each person laughing until abdomens hurt and tears ran. Speedy's story and expressions were funny, but the heartfelt laughter also had to do with the release of tension the adults had been experiencing over the past few days. The little cabin in the woods served as a type of haven from the dreaded situation at hand. As the laughter subsided, Larry was reminded of Proverbs 17:22 in the Bible.

"A merry heart doeth good like a medicine: but a broken spirit drieth the bones."

Immediately after consuming grilled burgers, the children played in blissful innocence and the adults settled down to more serious matters. In this remote setting, where trees were filled with the songs of birds, it seemed almost impossible that the lives of everyone in the Chatterson family were in danger. Gentle fresh breezes drifting through the site carried no warning of lurking terror. The soothing warmth from rays of sun, slipping through openings in the leafy canopy above the cabin, offered a misleading sense of peace and safety.

"Because of my public conversation with Tiffany, I have placed my family in real danger," began Larry. "She didn't know when she married him, but her husband is heavily involved in organized crime – even murder. Tiffany is suffering unbelievable abuse by her husband and his associates, but she knows that he'll have her killed if she leaves. She is being watched. Because I spoke with her in public, I'm now being watched. My family is in real danger. I've been approached by the FBI, who has been watching everyone. They know John Molato, and they have enough on him to put him away for a while. However, they want to completely destroy his organization, and they want enough on him to put him away for good. They know Tiffany is in grave danger and they have a plan to enable her to get away."

As Ryan and Layla listened to Larry explain the FBI warning, that he had managed to unknowingly gain the attention of a ruthless leader in organized crime, they understood that their family could not risk falling under the sweep of that same radar. Whatever support the couple could offer had to be carefully executed.

As Ryan studied Larry's young son at play, he remembered the devastating sadness of losing a child. Between the adoption of Layla's lovely daughter Kaylee and the birth of his own young son Joseph, he and Layla had lost a baby daughter through a late term miscarriage. They gave the unborn infant the name Brittany. Ryan reflected on the frantic call to 911 and the amount of blood loss. Terrified, he carried his wife to the car and sped toward the hospital. Ryan and Layla spoke no words along the route. His only thoughts were hopes of saving both Layla and the child. Though it only took ten minutes, the trip to the hospital seemed like an eternity. A fortunate aspect of the situation was the fact that Kaylee was in school at the time and a neighbor volunteered to wait at the house for her to come home. Ryan remembered when he and Layla returned home from the hospital to face the dismantling of the nursery they had prepared. Ryan purchased three burial plots near the grave of his Aunt Sally in Brandon Springs for Layla, himself, and Brittany. Larry presided over the private funeral.

Kaylee was old enough to understand that she had lost her sister. Ryan and Layla struggled for an explanation that made sense. It was only in his attempt to explain it to Kaylee, did Ryan find an element of peace during this period of grieving.

"We're all going to die and go to see God," he told her. "It's like a race, and God let little Brittany come in first. God doesn't want us to kill ourselves in order to make it to Heaven sooner, because that would be cheating."

"If God wants to give us a shortcut – well, that would be all right," offered Kaylee. "Little Brittany is already with God in Heaven because she was given a shortcut. When we get there and see her, she will probably ask us what took us so long. She might even call us a bunch of slow pokes."

The idea made perfect sense to the little girl, and Ryan was rewarded by a smile from her. When Kaylee later explained the idea of a "shortcut" to her mother, Layla took her daughter in her arms and held her long and tight. Since the loss of her baby, Layla had cried herself to sleep each night. That night, she reflected on her daughter's simple explanation of the "shortcut to Heaven." An unexplainable peace took hold in her heart and her sleep that night was deep and refreshing.

Ryan thoughts returned to the conversation with Larry and Patsy, and he sensed the deep anxiety felt by his friends. The more Ryan heard, the more willing he became to help. He now feared for his best friend's family.

"Someone needs to get Tiffany out of that situation, and this guy has to be put in prison," Ryan stated. "Your family has to be relieved from the danger you face. You've told us about the FBI warning, and that they have a plan. So, what is the plan?"

"I understand the general plan, but I am unsure of all the details and of everyone involved," explained Larry. "The general plan may involve a donation from our private charity, and that is what I first want to discuss with you in detail. If Tiffany is to get away, she will need money from an outside source – a source that is unknown to her husband. I don't want you or Layla to be seen as having anything to do with this. We have the money in the charity funds, but we have to be very careful. All I want from you is an agreement to use the remainder of the funds for this purpose. What do you think?"

Ryan glanced at his wife, and then gave his answer.

"We would like to be done with the charity as soon as possible, and we would be glad to use the rest of the money for this effort. Before going through with giving the rest of the funds, I suggest that you and I pay a visit to an old friend in Boston."

"I think that would be an excellent idea," Larry replied. "I've been thinking about her lately. She's in a nursing home, and I hope her mind is still strong enough to remember us."

The remainder of the waking hours that evening was spent playing cards on the kitchen table, and the four of them found the time together refreshing. In highly stressful times, it is often comforting to experience uneventful activities of normal life. Each was reminded of the simple joys shared in years gone by, of quiet evenings where the sounds of the night were composed of the shuffling of cards, soft voices, and dogs barking in the distance. Most of those evenings were spent at the farmhouse in Brandon Springs. The only stress during those visits involved the excitement of selecting worthy recipients of packages of cash and planning how to carry out the drops in secret. Larry wanted to embrace as much of this peaceful setting as possible. He didn't want to share too much with his friends, as he didn't want the horrors of his own peril to ruin the reunion. He made sure not to go into graphic details regarding the evil Molato was capable of committing. Larry's main objective to accomplish this evening was to obtain an agreement from the others to invest the last of the charitable funds in this single last cause. If Tiffany could begin a new life in safety, he believed it would be worth the effort. However, Larry wanted to minimize the danger to this family, He could not afford to raise suspicion. He needed to maintain a picture of normalcy at the center.

"I had no problem obtaining permission from Dr. Stevens to get away from the center for these few days," Larry told his friends. "However, this is a rare opportunity. George and Evelyn can hold down the fort for a few days, but it would be too much of a burden to ask them to carry the full burdens of the mission for long periods of time. I'm squarely in the middle of this, but I have no intention of discussing this with my senior pastor. If I obtain permission to travel to Boston to visit Mrs. Thompson, it may be my last time away from the mission for a while."

By the end of the visit, Larry and Ryan agreed to notify Mrs. Thompson of the plan. She was the last surviving original member of the secret charitable effort. That evening, they planned the trip to Boston.

EVEN THOUGH THIS was one of the finest nursing homes in the Boston area, the place carried a faint smell of ammonia. This, combined with the overly heated environment in the facility, made Ryan feel as if he was walking through an abandoned chicken house in the south, tainted with stale diseased air.

While walking down a hallway, Larry was detained by an ancient fellow who mistook him for a buddy who had been killed during the Korean War.

"*Alzheimer's is a terrible sickness*," Larry thought.

He realized the old man would forget the conversation within five minutes, so he played along. He assured the veteran that the enemy had not captured him; that they had only been separated for a time, and that he was very much alive. As Larry hurried to catch up with Ryan, he glanced back to see the elderly man still smiling.

Ryan found Mrs. Thompson's doorway slightly ajar. He hoped she would recognize him. He pushed the door open and found a nurse pulling the covers up around the old woman's neck.

"Mrs. Thompson, you seem to have a couple of visitors," the nurse announced. "Do you know these two?"

"Of course, I know them," she replied. "I don't know why they would be paying me a visit, but of course I know them."

"I'll leave you with your company," the nurse stated as she left the room.

"So, how's the charitable venture coming along?" Mary Thompson asked.

"We would like to bring that endeavor to an end, and that is the primary reason we are here," explained Larry.

"Everything in this world eventually comes to an end," Mrs. Thompson replied. "I'm approaching mine. But let's focus on the charity. God has chosen you. Wouldn't you say that God's hand has been on your life throughout this endeavor? Think about where he has taken you over the past few years."

"I know that your husband and his friends chose me, but I am a little reluctant to say that God selected me to do things which were somewhat illegal," Larry stated.

"Acquiring the money and bringing it into the United States was illegal," replied Mary. "Putting the money to good use doing charitable ventures was a much different story. Do you think God would have wanted the money confiscated by the government and used to fund a pet project of a member of Congress or a lobbyist, or do you think He would rather have the money used to meet the needs of worthy individuals? Think about it. Jesus taught us to pay our taxes and abide by the laws of the land, but He also wanted us to minister to those in need."

"I think it is apparent that we felt better about using the money to help people in need," stated Ryan. "Otherwise, we would have taken a much different course. We didn't turn the money over to the government. But in not doing so, we stepped outside the law. The government wastes billions, and we chose to make sure the money was used for deserving people who were in need. Our actions speak for our hearts and minds, but the IRS might not see it that way."

"You have a point regarding the IRS,' the elderly woman firmly stated.

"We have a special situation, and we believe that it warrants the use of the remainder of the funds," said Ryan. "It is best that you don't know the details, because lives might be at risk if the wrong people got wind of it. We have prayed about…"

"I trust you," interrupted Mary, as she placed her aging fingers to his mouth. "No explanation is needed. I have total and complete trust in the both of you."

Her eyes confirmed that she was speaking the truth, and this said more to Ryan than additional words she could have spoken. Larry took her hand in his and gave it a slight squeeze. Slightly trembling with exhaustion, she brought his hand to her face and kissed it. Releasing it, she gave a weary sigh.

Larry bent forward and kissed her forehead, a forehead now painted with age spots and gently plowed with wrinkles. Noting how tired she appeared, Larry and Ryan excused themselves.

As they stepped into the glow of setting sunlight, Ryan glanced at his friend and said, "Well, I guess everything is officially in motion."

"With the blessing of Mary Thompson, it is," Larry replied. "I love that old woman."

AS MILTON HOLLOWAY LEFT THE ROOM, Larry felt exceptionally tense. Moments before, he nervously confirmed that the money was available for Tiffany's use and was surprised that Holloway asked no questions regarding the source of the funds. It was apparent the accountant's focus was on taking down a very brutal man and critically damaging the underground operations of his associates.

Finally, alone in his office, Larry placed his hands over his eyes and began to pray. He had neglected to close his office door when Holloway departed, and soon voices in Evelyn's office disturbed the peaceful moment of spirituality.

"Reverend Chatterson's door is open, so he should be available to see you,'" Evelyn spoke as she stepped into the doorway to address her boss. "Larry, a Russell Wells would like to see you. He believes you knew his father."

As Larry lifted his head, his exhaustion was evident to Evelyn. He forced a smile and nodded approval of the visit. With a gesture she silently invited the man to enter the office. Larry stood to greet him. As the two men's hands clasped, he sensed something familiar.

"I believe you knew my father, Sam Wells," the visitor stated bluntly.

"Yes, I was acquainted with Sam Wells. Please take a

seat."

"My father was a secretive fellow, and I guess his line of work called for it," began Russell. "Police work can put an awful strain on a person. I'm going to come straight to the point."

"Please do," answered Larry, as he motioned for him to take a seat.

"I overheard a phone conversation of my father's, where he discussed having access to hundreds of thousands of dollars. I don't believe he was talking about police money. It was clear that he was talking about private funds in his possession, or funds that he had access to personally. My father never lived like he had money. As expected, there was only a very small amount in his bank account when he passed away. I hoped maybe you knew something about these additional funds."

"What makes you think that I would know more of your father's finances than you?" asked Larry.

"I've checked into a few things!" the visitor snapped back. "For example; I know that you have a background in finance. I know that you had a successful career in that line of work before you got religion. I also know that the cabin on the mountain now belongs to you. It had belonged to my father for a number of years. It stands to reason that you paid my father a pretty penny for that place, but there is no record of a financial transaction for that purchase. I figure that you must have paid my father in cash under the table. There are two things that I haven't figured out. One, where did that money go? Two, where would a preacher, who runs a homeless shelter, get that kind of cash?"

Larry was stunned. He had never thought his ownership of the cabin would become public knowledge. On the inside he was kicking himself.

Of course, the deed would be public knowledge. All anyone has to do is call the county tax assessor in Virginia.

Trying not to show weakness, Larry attempted to dismiss

the reasoning of his visitor.

"Your father gave me that land and that cabin," Larry stated in a slow and deliberate manner.

"Bull crap!" shouted Russell. "That is pure bull crap, and you know it! My father loved that place. It was really special to him, and he certainly wasn't the giving kind of man... at least, on matters like that. He would have never given that place to someone outside the family unless that person had something on him. Did he give that to you so that you would keep quiet about something? Is that what went down? Just tell me. He's dead now, so no one can hurt him now. What did you have on him?"

"It was nothing like that," answered Larry. "He and I were friends, that's all."

"That is total crap!" shouted Russell. His eyes narrowed and tension filled his face. "My father never mentioned you, ever, in any conversation. He loved that place, and so did I. It was special to both of us. While growing up, he took me hunting there for years. It was the one place where he and I could be at peace with one another. We butted heads all the time, but not there. We both loved to hunt, and ..."

The room became deathly still and quiet. Larry had certainly hit a raw nerve with his comment, and it was entirely unintended. He felt he had to avoid any conversation that led to the sharing of money between himself and Sam Wells, and he felt he needed to stop Russell's line of reasoning. Larry realized that he had opened up an entirely new can of worms. Sensing he had aggravated the situation almost beyond reason, his tired mind raced to find a way to calm the situation.

"I'm sorry," whispered Larry.

By that time Evelyn had come to the doorway of the office, and she was staring wildly at Larry.

"It's okay, Evelyn," he assured her. "Everything is okay."

She slowly moved back into her receptionist area, but

Larry knew she would later be ripe with curiosity. He would have to deal with those questions in time. Currently, an angry young man sat in front of him.

"I'm sorry," Larry began again. "I didn't know that members of Sam's family had any interest in the place. I was somewhat surprised that your father gave that property to me. I don't really know what to say."

Larry caught a glimpse of the true source of rage. Besides confusion, there was an element of deep hurt in Russell Wells. It became clear that this property was dear to him, and he was deeply disturbed at the thought of his father giving it away to a stranger.

"That is about the weirdest thing imaginable," Russell quietly spoke. "I heard the talk about having a lot of money, and I learned that you owned the property. I figured my father needed the money for something, and that he spent it. I certainly didn't find any money in his house. Just before he died, I searched the house for it. The house was empty for some time while he was dying. Periodically, I checked on the place. On one occasion, I noticed that a few things had been moved around. So, I considered robbery to be a possibility. I'm not a cop, but it was evident that someone had been in the house."

Larry recalled the time when Sam instructed him to enter the home in secret to retrieve an item from a desk. He remembered someone coming in while he and Ryan were in the house. Hiding in the hall closet, the two nervously feared they would be found. As the sound of footsteps came from various parts of the home, it became clear to them that someone was in search of something.

Looking squarely into Larry's eyes, Russell questioned him. "Why would my father GIVE that property to you? You have to have some explanation. I can't imagine him doing a thing like that for no reason."

Larry inwardly ached to tell him the truth. He wanted so much to ease Russell's pain with a clear explanation. He couldn't. Anyone with knowledge of what that cabin had been used for could be in real danger. Larry had just closed the door on that charitable venture by committing the last of the funds to Tiffany's situation. The FBI plan was risky. There was no way he could pull Russell Wells into the inner circle. He could not allow himself to further complicate the matter. Larry was an honest person, but he decided to make an exception for the sake of protecting Russell. He attempted to mislead the younger man with hypothetical language. He hoped it might offer some degree of comfort.

"Maybe Sam was slipping in his last days," Larry said. "Maybe the pain was getting to him more than people knew. I can tell you this; Sam loved you. He talked about you. He told me about how you played football, and he was proud of you. I can't give you a good explanation about the cabin property, but it's possible that the stress of his terminal illness impaired his thinking. It happens."

Russell nodded his head and rose to his feet.

"I know my way out," he said, as he moved toward the door.

Once the man departed the center, Evelyn peeked into Larry's office. She found him with his head resting on crossed arms upon his desk. She decided that her questions could wait, and she quietly returned to her reception area.

Larry's attempt to shut the world out was interrupted by the ringing of his phone.

"Hello, Larry Chatterson here," he answered dutifully.

"Man, what is wrong with you?' asked Ryan. "You sound terrible. Is everything set?"

"Pretty much," replied Larry. "I was just visited by the son of Sam Wells, and he wanted to know why his father gave the Virginia property to me."

"How did he connect it to you?"

"Tax assessor's office would be my guess," answered Larry.

"That makes sense. Well, what did you tell him?

"I told him that I didn't have a good answer," replied Larry. "I told him that it was possible that Sam was slipping during his last days, and that was possible that he acted irrationally in some matters. It really caught me off guard and there was no way that I could tell him the truth. He doesn't need to get sucked into this."

"Agreed," stated Ryan. "I want to keep my family removed from it, as much as possible. I realize that I can't completely avoid it, but I have to be careful."

"I'll be glad when it is all over," said Larry. "Russell Wells has fond memories of the Virginia cabin and property. He and Sam hunted there for years. I am sure that he expected the property to be left to him in his father's will, and he is really bewildered about the entire thing."

Larry glanced over to the door of his office and found Evelyn there. She gave him a wide-eyed glare. Holding her hand close to her stomach, she secretly motioned that there was a visitor in her reception area.

"Ryan, I have a visitor," Larry informed. "There has absolutely been a steady stream of them today. I'll call you later. This seems to be a day of visitors."

"Okay, we can talk later," Ryan replied.

As Larry ended the call, Evelyn whispered "You have a familiar female visitor."

Larry clearly understood that she meant the visitor to be Tiffany. He remembered the conversation with Holloway and his warning that any close associate of Tiffany could be in grave danger. Dread filled his mind, and he suddenly felt drained of energy.

"Leave the door open," he whispered, in return.

Evelyn gave him a quick wink, and invited the visitor in.

"I had to come," began Tiffany. "My mother passed away. I'm on my way home from the funeral home."

"I'm very sorry to hear about your mother," said Larry. "Why would you come here to tell me that?" he whispered.

"My husband is acting really strange, and I'm scared to

death," confessed Tiffany, in a quivering whisper. "I'm afraid to go home."

Her hands were shaking as if she had the chills from a high fever.

"I don't know what to say," whispered Larry. "I would offer a room at the center, but I really don't want to endanger anyone here. Have you talked to Milton Holloway? Maybe he has something."

"I contacted him first," she explained. "He said that he didn't want to jeopardize the plan that he is setting up. My husband is the primary concern, and my safety seems to be secondary."

As the conversation continued, anxiety filled the office. The two of them became less conscious of their setting. Emotion replaced reason, and their voices became louder. Tears streamed down the cheeks of the beautiful woman and her body began to tremor with frustration and fear. Finally, she blurted out, "I've got to find a place to live!"

Instantly, another familiar voice answered from the doorway. "I can help," offered Chad.

He had been waiting in Evelyn's reception area for his turn to meet with Larry. When Tiffany cried out, Chad rushed to the doorway before Evelyn could stop him. The older woman stepped into the office and attempted to escort him out.

"Hold on, Evelyn," said Chad. Looking directly into the eyes of Tiffany, he stated, "I could have picked out your voice if I had been blindfolded in a room filled with one hundred women. I can help. Just let me know what you need."

Larry saw a look in Tiffany's tear swollen eyes that he had never seen before. Her hand briefly rose to her mouth, and then dropped back into her trim lap.

"No, I can't do that," she softly spoke. "I can't do that."

"She is right, Chad," Larry said. "We can't explain the situation, but that would be a very bad idea."

"Since when is it a bad idea to offer help to someone in need?" asked Chad. "Isn't that what this mission is all about? What's going on here?"

Larry had not been in the habit of purposely hiding things from Chad, but he felt this situation should be an exception. Because Charlie had been almost like family, his son Chad was given similar standing. Besides that, Chad had become a very generous contributor to the mission. Charlie's son considered himself to be an insider. Chad stiffened with resentment. The beautiful woman seated in front of him immediately noticed this change in demeanor. Tiffany rose from her chair and took Chad's hand in hers. Wiping her tears with her free hand, she stepped close to him.

"I can't tell you how much your offer means to me," she began. "I wish I could explain, but I can't put you in a position that would put you in real danger. You have to believe me. Listen to Larry. This is a bad situation, and he is trying to look out for you."

Chad's eyes softened. "Okay, I know when I don't belong in a conversation."

Evelyn watched him exit the office and proceed through her reception area. Once she felt assured that he was outside the range of her voice, she turned to Larry.

"I hope you know what you are doing," she stated firmly. "Chad's a fine man, and he deserves your friendship and honesty."

Giving Tiffany a suspicious woman-to-woman glare, she turned away and went back to her desk in the next room.

"I need to make a phone call," Larry said.

Larry's call to Milton Holloway was short. He quickly informed him of Tiffany's perceived danger, and immediately handed the phone to her. Holloway told Tiffany to return home or there would be no deal, there would be no FBI protection. Staring straight ahead with eyes much like those of a dead person, she responded.

"Okay, I'll go home."

"Did you really lose your mother?" asked Larry.

"She's dead," replied Tiffany. "Seeing her body brought this all home. Even though we weren't close after I got out of prison, it was comforting just to know she was around. You know, she and my sister kept Brandy while I served time. I haven't been much of a daughter, but I know she loved me. I really feel alone, and I am scared. I know it was a mistake to come here, and I'll go. I just wanted to see the face of someone who cares."

Once she was clear of the reception area, Evelyn appeared at Larry's door.

"What in the world are you doing?" she asked.

"This is serious, Evelyn," he began. "I really can't tell you, and I wish I could. I have always respected your wisdom, and I need your stable and practical advice on matters. All I can say is that I am dealing with very bad people, and I am afraid for my family. I probably shouldn't even tell you that much. Because of Tiffany's visit today, I am now even afraid for the safety of those on my staff. I'm sorry. I really am. The least involvement you have, the better. I'm truly afraid. I really need your prayers. My family needs your prayers, and everyone at this center needs them."

"I knew she would be trouble; and I mean with a capital T," Evelyn replied. "If you have a choice, I would side with Chad over her – in a heartbeat. She has caused enough trouble, and Chad is a good man. He sees you as a friend. At least, he did prior to today."

"I don't have a choice," he assured her. "I will be glad when this is all over."

"Will you be able to talk about it then?" Evelyn asked.

"I doubt I will ever be able to talk about it, and I hate it," he replied. "I lost my brother to a slimy jerk, and this is just as dangerous – maybe worse. It could turn out very badly. This is different. I need to be careful about what I say, even to you. I love and respect you, and I hate not being able to talk with you about this. I've said too much already."

CHAD MOVED HIS car down the street and waited for Tiffany to leave the mission. He followed her to her side of town. As she stopped at a coffee shop, he slowed his vehicle and watched until she entered the place. As if it was by design, a parking place opened in front of the establishment. He slid his car into the opening and watched as Tiffany carried a cup of coffee to an empty table. Within a minute he found himself seated in front of her.

"What are you doing?" she asked.

"I want an explanation," he demanded.

Nervously, Tiffany glanced out the window. "You really don't need this," she stated.

"I need an explanation," he said.

"You need to get as far away from me as you possibly can," she began. "You have no idea. The longer you hang out here, the more dangerous things could be for you. I'm not kidding. I am asking you to leave."

It was clear that her eyes didn't match her words. Chad told her that he had no intention of leaving until she gave him an explanation. Tiffany was flooded with mixed emotions. She was fearful for herself and for Chad, but she welcomed his company. She felt so alone. She also felt guilty for not getting up and leaving, but she was afraid to go home.

"*He will never drop this until I talk with him*," she thought. "*I have no choice. He has forced my hand.*"

"There is a good chance my husband will kill me or have me killed," she whispered. "I had no clue what he was when I married him, and it is impossible for me to leave him."

She was silent for a moment, as she watched a car move slowly past the coffee shop.

"Unfortunately, Larry has been dragged into this and I'm afraid for him," she explained. "Now, I am afraid for you."

"If you need me, give me a call," Chad offered, as he placed his business card in front of her.

Tiffany refused his card, sliding it back to his hand. Noticing his cell number printed on the card, she quickly memorized it. Giving his hand a squeeze, she excused herself and left the shop. As she drove home, her eyes filled with tears. She felt overwhelmed at the thought of pulling Chad into her personal danger. Even as a very young girl, she developed the ability to use males to accommodate her wishes. However, this was not the same. Chad's involvement was not her doing. She began to weep almost uncontrollably. Tiffany was genuinely afraid for him, and this was not like her. In those short minutes in the coffee shop, she finally saw Chad for who he really was. This was an honest man, willing to place himself in the pathway of real danger for her – and he did this on his own volition. She had not seduced him for favors. She knew him well enough to know that he was not the type to be shallow enough to fall for a woman's glance or touch. This was a disciplined man with a stable future. Chad was an intelligent thinker. He had weighed the odds and made a calculated decision to risk himself for her.

The thoughts of placing him in danger overtook personal terrors threatening her life. Her mind raced, and her tears began to dry. For the first time since the death of her daughter, she deeply cared for the welfare of another person. Tiffany had to think of a way to keep him safe.

"Chad doesn't deserve to be dragged into my horrible life. John wouldn't hesitate to have him killed...or worse. I have to make sure he stays away."

Chapter 15

TIFFANY'S CAR WAS NOT HARD TO SPOT as Chad drove past the coffee shop. Her life was spinning out of control. She grasped for normalcy wherever she could find it. In that coffee shop she was just another customer. In that place she was not someone trapped by a monstrous husband who pimped her out to clients just as easily as the worst of dog owners inflict abuse on pets. There, she sipped coffee with the "normal" people. She read books just like "normal" people and she placed her tips in the tip jar just like "normal" people. There were other attractive women married to rich men in this wealthy suburb. There, she was just another. In her heart she believed that her only true escape would be found in death. But in these acts of normalcy, she found courage to continue breathing each day. She had to be there, and it was inevitable that Chad would find her there.

"Hi," he said, as he sat down in the chair opposite Tiffany.

"Why are you doing this?" she whispered. "Chad, you're putting yourself in a bad spot. You don't know what you're doing, and you need to leave."

"You're not fooling me," answered Chad.

"You're a stupid fool!" Tiffany coldly stated.

"I never claimed to be an Einstein, but I'm keen enough to be able to read you like a book," replied Chad.

"Now, I know you are completely crazy," said Tiffany, still attempting to keep her voice down. "Do I need to call the manager and have you tossed out of here?"

"You aren't going to call anyone. You would never cause a stir or do anything to call attention to yourself here. You don't want to ruin this place for yourself. Things are bad at home, and this is a safe place. I saw your face in Larry's office. You're in real trouble. I want to help."

"You have no clue about anything, especially about me," she said. "It would be best for you to get as far away from me as you possibly can go. You can't help me, and I shouldn't have gone to see Larry. He can't help either. This is my life, and I have to live it. Look, you're a nice guy; but you don't have a clue about some things in the real world. You sit in your office and do marketing stuff – whatever that is. All I know is that you're some kind of pencil pusher who likes to give presentations to people about whatever. It doesn't matter. Your life is nothing like mine. You are just a naïve guy that sees a troubled woman and thinks he can come to her rescue. I've got news for you. I'm used to getting men to do things for me. The truth of the matter is that I use men, and you are a nice guy who doesn't need to be used by me. I'm trying to do you a favor, and you need to listen."

"I see something that most men don't see in you," replied Chad. "Most men can't see past your face or your body. To be honest, most men can't see past what's in their own pants."

"That's true," Tiffany said, with a chuckle.

"I'm usually not as talkative," Chad stated. "I watch and I listen, and I see things. You're a much better person than you let on."

"You don't really know me."

"I know that you went to prison for someone you cared

about," he stated. "You were willing to sacrifice yourself for someone else. That's rare."

"I was stupid, and I was a lousy judge of men," Tiffany said with a sigh.

"You're right about being a lousy judge of men, and apparently it also goes for this man," he replied. "However, there is nothing stupid about you. You said it yourself; you can get a lot of men to do just about whatever you want. You can out-think a number of people. In the case of you taking the rap and going to prison for that guy, you thought it out. You realized that the one you loved might be taken from you for a long time if he was convicted. The only way to shorten that time was for you to take the blame. That was the fastest way you could be with him again. You were willing to sacrifice yourself for someone else. Your problem was that he didn't deserve your sacrifice."

Her face hardened. She had learned to distance herself from those who reached deeply into that sacred place within her. This was a defensive mechanism, and it was almost automatic.

"You're just stupid," she replied. "You need to go. There's a chance you haven't been seen with me. My husband is the jealous type, and I never know when someone is watching. He has his people out and about, and they are often watching over me. My husband looks out for me, and anyone messing with me could be in big trouble."

"If your husband was looking out for you, you wouldn't have come to Larry scared out of your mind," answered Chad. "You're not going to play this act with me. You're in trouble, and your husband is the trouble. I want to help you, but you have to level with me."

"Go back to your safe office and your safe family," she said. "You can't help. You're only putting yourself and your family in danger."

It was apparent that she had seriously misjudged the man seated in front of her. She was conflicted, and her body began to tense. Chad was nothing like she had imagined. She suddenly saw something in him that she had loved in his father. He had the ability to peek into her soul. He was real. For the first time, Tiffany saw the real Chad.

"I don't have much in the line of a safe family," Chad said. "Both my parents are dead, and my only brother hasn't talked to me for more than ten years. I pretty much don't have a family. Larry has a family, and that's why Larry can't help. You know that. I am not just a marketing guy who has no clue about the real world. You knew my father. But you met him after he got it together, after he changed. You seem to forget that I was raised by an abusive alcoholic. Actually, you're the one who doesn't know what you are talking about. You didn't see me grow up. We are more alike than you think."

"We are nothing alike!" Tiffany blurted.

"You went to prison to help someone you loved," Chad said. "I got the dog crap beat out of me, while trying to help my father."

"You are a clean-cut pencil-pusher and I… I am… I'm a stupid whore," Tiffany whispered. "That's all. I'm a screwed-up whore, and you don't need to get involved. I've always been a crazy wild child. You are not at all like me."

"There's a part of me that nobody sees," he explained. "I can't afford to let that side of me show up, because it would screw up my career. I have to suppress some things. I learned early that it causes problems. Do you really think that someone who plays it safe would be sitting here with you?"

"Charlie would tell you to stay away from me," warned Tiffany.

"My father loved you, and he loved Brandy," Chad said. "He would not have told me to stay away."

"That's another reason you should stay away," whispered Tiffany. "People die when they become a part of my life. I wasn't even there to help my daughter when she needed my protection. I wasn't there for my little girl. Brandy didn't deserve that. She needed a good mother, and she needed a good father. She didn't deserve to die like that. I wasn't there for her. Why wasn't I killed in that car with him, instead of her? With both of her loser parents dead, she would have been free to be adopted and raised by good people. I wasn't there for her."

Tiffany was sobbing. She placed her hands over her eyes. Her small frame trembled. Chad reached for a stack of paper napkins, moved to her side of the table, and placed his arm around her.

"Get up and come with me," he whispered in her ear.

Obediently, she arose. He handed her the napkins and she immediately wiped her eyes. Chad quickly led her out the front door and escorted her to his parked car. Once seated, she looked down at the mascara-stained napkins.

"You should have stayed away," Tiffany said.

"Too late," Chad replied.

TWO WEEKS AFTER his meeting with Tiffany, Chad noticed a white van parked outside his apartment. It was the type used for commercial purposes. What puzzled him was the fact that it had no markings or lettering for commercial use. The only windows were those in the front for the driver and passenger. Within minutes of noticing the van he received a call on his cell phone from Larry.

"Chad, I tried to warn you to stay out the situation with Tiffany," he began. "You need to come to the mission tonight. There is someone that you need to meet."

"Did Tiffany tell you that we talked?" asked Chad.

"No. The situation has changed, and you need to be better informed. Just come to the center before 8:00 PM."

"I'll be there."

As soon as the call ended, Larry placed another call to Ryan.

"Chad will be here tonight to meet with the accountant."

"Chad?" Ryan questioned.

"He is determined to be involved with you know who, and now he has no choice," Larry explained. "In one sense, I hate the involvement of more people. There will be more people to keep track of; there is a greater chance that aspects of the plan could be leaked. This increases the chance that someone will screw up and blow the whole thing wide open. On the other hand, I think we have an answer to the handling of the funds."

"I'm glad you didn't ask me to handle the money," added Ryan. "I feel sick; I've come down with a case of chicken. I've recently broken out in a big yellow rash running the entire length of my back."

"Believe me, I understand," Larry replied. "I am so far in that the only way for me to escape is to keep moving forward. There isn't any backing out for me. I'm marked. My main concern has to do with my family."

"I'm sorry to be so distant," answered Ryan.

"Don't be so quick to apologize. We need to meet at the place this weekend to discuss the money. A certain accountant needs to meet with us there, and I think Chad will be brought along."

LARRY WAS FILLED with anxiety as he looked at his watch. He rose from his desk and began to nervously brush dust from books on a shelf.

"What's up?" Chad quizzed, as he stepped into Larry's office.

"Shut the door and take a seat," Larry quietly said. "We need to talk. You mentioned Tiffany in our earlier conversation, and that's what we need to talk about."

"Is she all right?"

"As far as I know. You've been spotted hanging around Tiffany by people working for her husband, and you're on his radar."

"From what Tiffany told me, the guy is a real jerk."

"He's worse than a jerk. That guy is a killer, and he sells weapons on the black market."

"Tiffany told me that he was bad, but she didn't go into details. How did you come by that information? Did Tiffany call you?"

"I haven't spoken to Tiffany recently. I need to explain to you that I've been working with the FBI regarding Mr. Molato. It wasn't really by choice. I'm being watched by both the FBI and Molato's men, and now you're being watched."

"Who cares if I'm watched by the FBI. I've done nothing wrong."

"I'm afraid the FBI has more in mind than just watching you," replied Larry. "Make sure that you are free this weekend. Someone will join us shortly, and he has plans for you."

Chad's eyes narrowed.

THE FOLLOWING WEEKEND, the cabin in Virginia offered an adult-only habitation. The children of the two couples were left with friends for the weekend. After supplies were put away for the weekend, Ryan, Layla, Larry, and Patsy seated themselves at the kitchen table for a game of cards. In one sense, it was like old times. There were no demands of children underfoot. The attention of parents was not tuned to the sounds of children at play. Though the setting afforded an opportunity for relaxation, none could be found. The safety of absent children nagged the minds of adults, and apprehension over an anticipated meeting left a cloud of dread hanging over each. Tension filled the air. The awkward telling of stupid jokes resulted in unwarranted bursts of laughter. Inwardly, each soul longed for simplicity once enjoyed.

As Larry finished telling the others of the visit by Russell Wells, they heard the sounds of an approaching car. Ryan opened the door to find Milton Holloway and Chad walking towards the cabin. The accountant for the FBI was unusually chipper.

"Did you bring enough food?" Holloway asked. "A rustic setting always gives me a huge appetite."

Ryan offered a nervous smile. It was apparent that the FBI agent briefed the plan to Chad while in route to the cabin. During the earlier meeting with Larry at the mission, Chad understood the real Milton Holloway for first time. Chad had paid little attention when the agent had been introduced to him as an accountant once before. In that second meeting, his eyes were fixed on the man as Holloway revealed to him the extent of the danger Tiffany faced. That night it became clear to Chad that his life was also very much at risk.

"This is a beautiful place," Holloway stated. "It's perfect. Chad and I have come up with a plan, and he has offered to play a large role. After sharing some of it with you, the two of us will need to leave – but not before we eat."

The men took seats around the plain wooden kitchen table, while Layla and Patsy brought out the ingredients for sandwiches and chips. They positioned the bread, meats, cheeses, paper plates, plastic cups, and condiments on the small counter near the sink. Soft drinks resided in an ice-filled cooler. Patsy set a large bowl of chips in the center of the table, and then took her place. After a quick, but sincere, prayer Patsy announced that it was time for each to prepare sandwiches for themselves. Nervous small talk filled the cabin until Holloway got down to business.

"Chad will set up a safe deposit box at a bank, and cash will be placed there," Milton began. "The FBI has paved the way for the IRS to ask no questions regarding the origin or handling of the money. A sting operation for Tony Molato and his associates has been set up, and Chad has offered complete cooperation. He will be heavily involved. Chad and Tiffany will be in very grave danger during a short window of time. Once Tiffany appears to be dead, Chad will withdraw the money and give cash to her. We aren't sure how long this stage of the plan will take, and multiple withdrawals of cash may have to be taken from the safe deposit box and given to Tiffany over an unspecified period of time. Very few people will know of her whereabouts. The FBI will handle complicated aspects of the plan, but there are no guarantees that everything will go as designed. Only after Molato and key associates have been taken down, will Tiffany enter a witness protection program. The FBI will then seize Molato's assets and use them to draw out other criminals. Tiffany will be given a new identity, and she will live under that name when she is relocated."

"What kind of danger?" asked Layla. "You said that both Tiffany and Chad will be in grave danger."

"I will only go into details with those who will be directly involved," explained Holloway. "The less other people know, the more likely we can keep what we are doing from Molato. The reason I am telling you this much is because I think you need to understand the risk that Chad will be taking. Tiffany is already in serious danger, and we have to be very careful not to place her in even worse peril. You have a right to know what I am telling you. If things go badly, I will contact you."

Studying the face of Chad, Larry had never seen him look so nervous. His face was tilted downward, but it was apparent there was nothing of interest on the table before him. His eyes darted around like a pair of squirrels doing synchronized dancing.

"Should we be in contact with Chad and Tiffany?" asked Larry.

"No," replied Holloway. "If they contact you, be extremely careful with your words. I think some of your calls may be monitored. Even after this is over, wait to be contacted. I'm sure you will want information, but you are not to try to contact Tiffany or Chad. Regardless of how this goes down, the FBI will have a story. Don't question it, and don't try to poke your noses where they don't belong. Don't be surprised by anything that happens. Once I tell you that it is over, leave it there. Hopefully you will have no future involvement in this – ever. That is best for you and your families. I want to assure you that if I think you are in greater danger, I will let you know. If you never hear from me again on the matter, know that you have nothing left to fear from Molato and his associates."

Each agreed to leave the matter alone unless contacted by Holloway. After the sandwiches were consumed, Chad was given the last of the charitable funds to place in the safe deposit box. He and Milton left. Those remaining in the cabin struggled to change the subject. Larry forced the conversation to recalling the events of charitable giving and what had been planned in that cabin over the years. They dealt out cards for another game, but the tension in the air was heavy.

"To be honest, I am relieved that the last of the money is gone," stated Larry.

"Agreed," answered Ryan.

The four talked for another hour, and plans of their own were put in place. Before leaving, the cabin was cleaned thoroughly by the four. Personal belongings were removed and placed in vehicles. Shared danger has a way of deepening bonds. It has a way of reminding people of matters of real importance. Sincere hugs were given, and each made promises to stay in touch on a more regular basis.

THE FOLLOWING SATURDAY afternoon, an elegant Lincoln entered the driveway of the home of Russell Wells. A man in a finely tailored gray suit exited the car and made his way to the front door of the house. In his left hand he carried a large envelope. It was exactly the same type of envelope which had been used by Ryan and Larry for all the cash donations made by them during their charitable efforts. Russell opened the heavy front door and stood behind the glass storm door.

""I am from the law firm of Whitten and Smith", the man said. Are you Russell Wells, the son of Sam Wells?"

"Yes," answered Russell.

"Let me see some identification," the man replied. "Do you have a driver's license?"

Still standing behind the glass door, Russell showed the license.

"What do you want?" Russell asked. "And what is this about?"

"I have been advised to present you with this envelope."

"Who advised you to give this to me?" asked Russell, as he opened the storm door and took the envelope.

"Just open the envelope," stated the man as he turned away.

Russell watched as the man returned to the car. Fear began to take hold of his mind as he watched the vehicle pull away from the home.

"*The last thing I need is to be sued or issued a subpoena*," he thought.

He locked the front door and nervously he retreated to the comfort of his home. Seated at the kitchen table, he closely examined the envelope. It had no markings, except for a label displaying his name and address. He tore open the envelope and emptied the contents on the table. There before him was a brief letter, the deed to the cabin and property in Virginia, and a set of keys. Both the deed and letter bore the seal of notary public. The letter bore the signatures of Larry and Ryan.

Mr. Russell Wells:

We realize that your father, Sam Wells, may not have been of sound mind during the days immediately preceding his death. Your father loved you and told us how proud he was of you. It is apparent that the cabin in Virginia afforded very special times for you and your father in years past. For this reason, we have placed this property in your name and all rights have been assigned to you. It now belongs to you.

Sincerely,

Larry Chatterson

Ryan Walker

Chapter 16

TWO MONTHS PASSED since Holloway shared the FBI's plan with Tiffany and Chad. In carrying it out they would be under intense physical and emotional duress, so he advised them both to seriously begin a regimen of exercise. Molato owned a private pool. Tiffany swam for hours each day after jogging. Chad began running like a maniac, and he pushed himself to relentlessly exercise in his apartment. During that two-month period, the stamina of each increased dramatically.

The plan carried serious risk to their lives. The slightest mistake could cause the situation to easily go very wrong. A larger slip-up would leave them completely under the power of a merciless killer. Chad found it difficult to concentrate on work. He had fallen behind in preparing a presentation for work to be given the following morning. Chad felt he had no choice but to work late into the evening. Just after 11:30 PM he finally felt comfortable about the content and style of the presentation. The next plan of action was to go home for a good night's sleep.

Chad's lone car was a welcoming sight when he walked out to the well-lit parking lot behind his place of work. As he reached to open the car door, two men in ski masks rushed out from behind his car and slammed him to the ground. Both of them used their combined weight to trap him against the asphalt. As one incredibly strong man fastened his hands behind his back, the other placed a knife against his neck.

"You will die right here if you struggle," the man with the knife warned.

Within seconds, a white van pulled alongside the three men. The man with the knife quickly rose and opened the side door of the vehicle and the stronger man forced Chad into the van. He was astonished at the speed and precision in which the abduction was carried out. Face down on the floor of the vehicle, he attempted to observe details of the van interior and the men who held him. His effort was short lived. Within seconds, Chad was blindfolded and shoved against the inner wall of the van. A rope was shoved between his tied hands, and he was fastened tightly to the wall of the vehicle. His arms ached. As he lay on his side, every bump in the road and every turn placed stress on his shoulder and wrists. Blindfolded, he could see nothing.

"It's obvious that I'm at your mercy," Chad said. "Please let me sit. My shoulder is really going to be sore."

"Shut up," grunted one of the men.

This voice was different from that of the man with the knife, so Chad ascertained that this must be the voice of the stronger of the two. The ride continued to punish the shoulder on which he lay.

Suddenly, the van came to a stop. He heard the front driver door open and close softly, and then he heard the slow opening of the side door. Chad listened to whispers of men, but he was able to pick out only a few words. Suddenly, the knife was against his throat again.

"I don't want to clean your blood from this van, but if you make a sound – you will die," the man whispered.

"*We're in agreement on that point*," thought Chad, as the van door quietly closed. "*I don't want you to have to clean my blood from this van either.*"

Within a couple of minutes, he heard the van door open again. Chad heard muffled moans of a female voice, and he guessed that the other victim was Tiffany. He listened to the sound of the van doors closing, and soon the vehicle was on its way into the blackness of the night. After a few minutes, the voice of the stronger man interrupted the sound of rolling tires meeting the pavement.

"I am going to readjust your bindings, and I advise against a struggle."

The man loosened the rope that held Chad to the van wall. Powerful hands lifted Chad into a sitting position. His strength spoke volumes to his victim. There was no use in struggle; there was no escape.

"Thank you," Chad said.

There was no answer.

"Tiffany?" Chad questioned.

He heard a slight muffled groan, and then the strong man gave a response.

"I was going to allow you to just be blindfolded, but you seem to want to have a conversation. I told you to shut up."

The man then placed duct tape across Chad's mouth. As he blindly and silently considered his situation, Chad struggled to encourage himself. He understood the fact that a fatalistic attitude during a crisis can seal one's doom. Chad attempted to calmly assess the situation.

"I am now sitting. If these people meant to hurt me, why would they have given any thought to my comfort? I just need to ride this out. I just wish I could talk with Tiffany."

It seemed to him that they traveled forever before turning off the highway and on to rougher surface. Chad imagined that they must be on rural county road. Within minutes the van pitched side to side and slowed.

"We've left the road and we must be traveling over bare ground or a poorly maintained dirt road," he thought.

The van stopped. Chad felt the hands of the strong man tug at the rope that tied him to the wall of the van. He heard some shuffling about, and then the side door opened. Chad heard more shuffling and then the muffled moan of a female voice.

"Your turn, lover boy," stated the strong man.

Chad couldn't help noticing the strength of the man escorting him from the van. He almost picked him up and carried him from the vehicle. The message was clearly communicated again – there would be no escape.

The side door of the van closed. Chad heard whispers. A host of chirping crickets made it impossible to understand the softly spoken words. Soon he heard the driver's door close, and the van lumbered slowly away. Only the retreating sound of the van traveling the rural road broke the continual chirp of crickets. As the sound of the van faded, the strong man tore the blindfold from Chad's face.

"You'll need to see where you are walking," he explained.

Standing directly in front of him was Tiffany. Her hands bound behind her, and her mouth silenced with duct tape, she seemed very small compared to her captor. Chad immediately forgot about his own aching bound wrists. His only concern was for Tiffany.

"Let's go" whispered Tiffany's escort.

Chad estimated that they walked about a hundred yards before reaching a small pier jutting slightly out into a remote lake. The men seated their captives on opposite sides in a pontoon boat, silently facing each other. The blindfolds were again placed on both. The engine started and the boat began moving.

SHORTLY AFTER TIFFANY and Chad went missing, Molato's warehouse was raided by the FBI and police.

Several of Molato's men were killed in a gun battle, but Tiffany's husband wasn't at the warehouse that evening. The police found him at his home and brought him in for questioning. The FBI and ATF immediately took total control of the investigation into the gun smuggling situation and the shootout. This was their turf. In an appearance to cooperate with the authorities, Molato suggested the possibility that the recent disappearance of his wife might be connected to the criminal activity found at the warehouse.

"Maybe she stumbled onto criminal activities of these employees, and they did something to her," said Molato.

With this statement suggesting a link between the two events, the FBI took over the investigation of missing persons. The CIA began investigating possible associations with foreign nationals. From this point on, the local police were given only filtered information regarding both cases. Most of the locals were surprised when the FBI set Molato free. The FBI believed that he would eventually lead them to more crime, but that didn't turn out to be the case. Molato died in a house fire a month later. An investigation ruled that it was a result of him smoking in bed.

Larry heard nothing from Holloway. This FBI agent had told him to ask no questions, that he would be contacted if his family was in any danger.

Larry's cell phone rang.

"I saw on the news that John Molato died in a house fire," Ryan said.

"I know as much as you do," replied Larry.

"Maybe no news is good news," Ryan nervously responded.

"That's what they say," stated Larry. "I've got a busy day; I'll call you back later."

Larry ended the call and leaned back into his chair. He found something comforting in the conversation. He convinced himself that this call was the beginning of the end of his fears. His mind rested in thoughts of his family being

safe.
"Maybe Tiffany and Chad are safe as well."

TWO BADLY DECOMPOSED bodies were pulled from High Rock Lake. Larry called Patsy and suggested that she watch the local news. The conversation was short and ended with both wishing to hear from Holloway.

Shortly after talking to Patsy, Larry's cell rang. He was relieved to hear the voice of Ryan.

"Larry, how are things at the mission?"

The mission is as unpredictable as ever," replied Larry.

Larry attempted to avoid conversation about the current situation reported on the news by injecting a light story.

"We never really know what to expect," Larry nervously continued. "Unpredictability is sometimes like a spreading virus."

"How so?"

"The pastor of the church that sponsors the mission dropped by yesterday to let me know that he's in the doghouse with his wife – and possibly with the denomination's regional superintendent."

"I met that old guy," replied Ryan. "He seems to be as solid as a rock. Are you telling me that he is in some kind of trouble?"

"He's mainly just embarrassed, but his wife is really ticked."

"Should you be telling me about something personally shared by the senior pastor?" asked Ryan.

"I'm not sharing something that is private; the entire church knows about it."

"Okay."

"This church is a regional flagship of the denomination, and you know how great it is. Last week, this church hosted a gathering of prominent pastors and denominational officials. There was a tour of the facility – they even came to the mission. There were lectures from a variety of people, raving about how this is a church that has gotten it right. I have to agree that Dr. Stevens is a great guy, and he has done something wonderful here."

"So, what is the big deal?" asked Ryan.

"Thursday evening, Mrs. Stevens had a select group of church officials at their home for dinner," Larry stated.

"I can't imagine that sweet old lady causing a problem."

"Dr. Steven's new dog caused the problem. They adopted this dog from the pound, and Dr. Stevens named him Moses. This Moses wouldn't be interested in parting any sea, but he was very interested in ramming his nose in the crotch of each church official seated with parted legs at the dinner table."

"Oh, no! I bet that made for a lively meal!"

"Once Dr. Stevens was notified of stealth attacks occurring under the table, Moses was promptly led outside to a fenced backyard. It didn't end there. The situation was complicated by a lack of proper timing. Mrs. Stevens was busy in the bathroom during the time when Moses was tossed out. She knew nothing of the fervent crotch sniffing, so she let the dog back inside. Within minutes the supper was again interrupted by a horrible odor that permeated the dining room. Dr. Stevens found Moses under the table again – this time chewing a fresh cat turd."

"Gross!" Ryan remarked. "That is just nasty! Where in the world did he find a fresh cat turd?"

"The turd belonged to Fluffy, Mrs. Steven's Persian cat. Moses had pillaged the litter box, snatched up the turd in his mouth, and brought it into the dining room. Sounds logical to me to consume a snack in the dining room, but those dining there didn't share that point of view. Moses was immediately banished to the backyard for the rest of the evening. Three of the guests lost their appetite and excused themselves before dessert was served – brownies, of course. Mrs. Stevens found the litter box turned upside down, with the contents dumped all over the floor. To make matters worse, Fluffy had recently peed in the spilt litter. She was busily kicking it around to cover up the deed."

"I sense an unhappy Mrs. Stevens?" quizzed Ryan.

"Indeed. Her evening had become as crappy as the mouth of a certain dog."

By this time, Ryan was laughing so hard he could hardly speak. "You're killing me!" Ryan blurted out.

"After the guests departed, Mrs. Stevens ordered Dr. Stevens to clean the litter mess while she cleaned the kitchen. He told me this morning that he is considering retirement. He asked me if I knew of a doggy rehab. It seems Moses is addicted to cat turds. I told Dr. Stevens that I didn't believe AAs had a program for that particular addiction."

"I can picture this dog Moses standing up at a meeting, raising his paw and stating, 'My name is Moses, and I am a turdoholic. It's been a week since I gobbled my last cat turd.'"

Laughter was heard on both ends of the call. Seconds later, it died away into an awkward silence.

"So, why did you call?" asked Larry.

"Patsy called Layla and asked for prayer. She told her that you have a lot on your mind – so what's going on?"

"Two bodies were pulled from High Rock Lake."

There was another moment of silence.

"I'm sure there are a lot of boaters on that lake," Ryan said, attempting to put a positive spin on the news. "Those could be bodies of anyone."

"I've never been to that lake, but you're probably right."

Talking with his friend usually calmed Larry, but not this time.

LARRY NERVOUSLY PACED his office at the mission. Patsy had just informed him that the bodies found in the lake were identified as Tiffany Molato and Chad Maddox. Passing by a window, he noticed dark clouds growing.

Larry didn't believe in omens, but the condition of the sky seemed fitting. Though the expanding thick vapors appeared to build slowly, he realized that those clouds were probably several miles above his head.

"They have to be growing at an enormous rate."

The ringing of his cell phone interrupted his fascination with the brewing storm.

"Holloway, here," announced the voice on the call.

"I've been thinking about you," replied Larry. "I understand that the bodies pulled from High Rock Lake were identified."

"I hear we are in for rough weather, but you shouldn't concern yourself," assured Holloway.

"Weather!" blurted Larry. "I'm not concerned about a stupid weather forecast!"

"Just consider what I am about to tell you," replied Holloway. "Pay careful attention to my words. You may want to write them down. Best observations today herald abundant local lightning and rain in great heaps tonight."

"What?"

"I said, best observations today herald abundant local lightning and rain in great heaps tonight," answered the caller.

With those words, Milton Holloway ended the phone call.

"That was about the weirdest phone call I have ever received," thought Larry. *"What in the world did he mean by that last statement. This isn't at all like Holloway. This man usually shoots as straight as an arrow. Holloway must have been weird on purpose. With so few words, and most of them weird, he must have chosen them carefully."*

Larry took a pen and pad and wrote out the odd phrase spoken by Holloway.

"Abundant local lightning and rain in great heaps tonight."

"Okay, a storm is coming on. So what? Is he trying to

warn me that storms in life are about to hit my family? No – he clearly stated that I had nothing to worry about. Why did he tell me to write down his words?"

He circled the first letter of each word, leaving out the conjunction "and". Immediately he recognized the phrase, "ALL RIGHT".

"Wow! You've got to be kidding me. He must be telling me that Tiffany and Chad are all right. This can't be a coincidence. This is just too weird."

He called Patsy immediately. "I just got the strangest call from Holloway. I think he was trying to tell me that Tiffany and Chad are alive and well. I believe it was some kind of word game. I'll show you when I come home tonight."

Before leaving for home, Larry called Ryan to explain the unusual message.

"What's up?" questioned Ryan.

"The FBI identified the two badly decomposed bodies found in High Rock Lake," answered Larry. "After several days of autopsy work, the FBI announced that they used dental x-rays to identify the bodies as those of Tiffany Molato and Chad Maddox. Both are being treated as homicides."

"I guess that's that," replied Ryan.

"Patsy and I hope that this is only an FBI plan to cover for Tiffany and Chad," Larry stated.

"Do you really think the FBI would go to such great lengths just for Tiffany and Chad?" Ryan asked. "Dental records are usually pretty good."

"Holloway called this afternoon with a really weird message," explained Larry. "I really think he was indicating that the two were all right. It's possible that I totally misunderstood him, but I don't think so. In either case, it is very doubtful that we will ever see them again. I just wanted to pass on the news."

"I guess it's easier to hope for the best," answered Ryan.

"We may never know what happened to them. I agree. In the remote chance that these bodies were incorrectly identified, I doubt we will ever see them again. At least we can take comfort that Molato is no longer around."

After the call, Ryan spent a few moments in prayer. He grieved for the two.

Chapter 17

CHAD AND TIFFANY were missed. However, they continued to live in the aging memories of those left behind. Whenever the Chattersons and Walkers gathered in Bandon Springs, private conversations among the four adults were ripe with speculation of what the missing pair could be doing if still alive. Time has a way of offering healing, but such mysteries offer little closure and are rarely forgotten.

"I can't believe it's been twenty years since Chad and Tiffany disappeared," said Layla.

"Maybe they are called in from time to time by the FBI to give information regarding mobsters," offered Ryan.

"If that was the case, the FBI would be interested in what only Tiffany could offer, leaving Chad to live a more normal life on his own somewhere," replied Larry.

"I hope both Chad and Tiffany are now experiencing enjoyable lives, but a part of me hopes Tiffany is as fat as a cow and has bags under those sexy blue eyes," chirped Patsy.

The other three burst into laughter at the thought of a fat Tiffany. Larry gave his wife a chastising look. Patsy puffed out her cheeks and pulled her bottom eyelids down in imitation of the woman she described. Layla let out a snort and cupped her hand over her mouth before stating, "That woman was knock-down gorgeous. It just wasn't fair to the rest of us."

"I'd take you over her any day of the week," Ryan stated.

"You'd better say that, and you had better mean it, if you know what's good for you!" Layla exclaimed, as she poked him in the ribs.

"She was a very troubled person," said Larry. "It's true that she caused trouble in the lives of others, but she experienced the horrible loss of her daughter. I think it sent her over the edge."

"That has to be the worst," replied Patsy. "I can't imagine the hell she went through at the hands of that dirt bag John Molato. I may joke around about Tiffany, but no one deserves to be abused like that. I'm glad she doesn't have to suffer under that evil jerk anymore."

"Let's eat lunch," suggested Larry. "I'm starved."

After lunch, Larry found his wife standing on the front porch looking out over the peaceful country setting. Walking up behind her, he wrapped his long arms around her and whispered in her left ear.

"Tiffany caused problems for a number of people, and I know that her actions toward me caused you tension."

"I should have done a better job of showing her God's love, but there were times that I wanted to choke the life out of her," answered Patsy. "She scared me."

"You never had anything to worry about. I've never loved anyone on earth like I love you. You know that don't you?"

Turning to face her husband, she kissed him and held him tightly. Hand in hand they walked back into the house. Stepping into the kitchen, they found Layla drying her hands from doing the dishes. Ryan had just finished sweeping the kitchen floor.

"I think it's time to do what we gathered here to do," announced Ryan.

Most of the conversations about Chad and Tiffany ended

whenever someone pointed out the obvious-- that the two were probably dead. Whether in celebration of new lives in the witness protection program, or as a memorial to the passing of the two, it was decided that two red maple trees should be planted in front of the old house in Brandon Springs. The families of Larry and Patsy, and of Ryan and Layla, met there for the occasion. Once the trees were planted, each offered a positive memory of the two. As Ryan watched the spring sun begin to set, the early buds on each tree caused him to consider the lives of the two.

"I feel like they have to be alive. Whether in this world or the next, I hope they've found peace."

THREE YEARS AFTER the planting of the trees, Ryan gave his old friend Larry a call.

"I've got an appointment with a doctor this Tuesday," said Ryan. "I've really been feeling run down lately. I stay tired all the time, and I have aches and pains."

"You and I are getting older!" blurted Larry. "Think about it. Speedy will soon graduate from college again."

"How is he doing?" asked Ryan.

"He is finishing his master's in business administration," explained Larry. "His undergraduate grades were excellent. He graduated with honors, but he still beats himself up for not being good enough to walk on with the college football team. I'm sure you remember that he was a star in high school, much like my dad, except for the fact that he has brains to go along with the athletics."

"That's a big-time college," replied Ryan. "If he had decided to attend a smaller college, I am sure that he would have played. Are his grades in graduate school still good?"

"His grades are great, and deep down he has enough sense to realize that the education will do more for him in the long run," Larry answered. "I'm really proud of him. He just hates to think of himself failing at anything. I keep reminding him that he might have suffered brain damage playing college football, but he doesn't seem to want to let it go. I'm not sure what we did wrong. He has an ego the size of an oil tanker. He grew up modestly with my work at the mission. Maybe he compared himself with the drunks at the center and got the big head. How are Kaylee and her husband Scott doing? Oh, and the kids?"

"They're all doing great," said Ryan. "After Kaylee and Scott lost the first child to SIDS, I was really worried about how they would handle it. When Kaylee became pregnant again, Scott asked if it would be alright to build a sand box beside one of the maple trees at the place in Brandon Springs. I think it was his way of showing faith that the pregnancy would go well."

"I'm glad things turned out all right," Larry said.

"I talked with them this year about replacing the sand box with a swing set," said Ryan. "I put a picnic table near the other maple. Kaylee loves to come out to the place and cook big meals with her mother. She has turned out to be a real princess. Kaylee has grown up to be such a good mother, and a strong person of faith."

"About your appointment, make sure you let me know what the doctor says," replied Larry. "I need to go."

RYAN CALLED LARRY the following week.

"I've decided to retire this year," began Ryan, speaking quietly into the phone. "Layla and I plan to sell the house in Charlotte and move to Brandon Springs."

"We've all enjoyed times at that place over the past thirty years, but you told me last year that you planned to work at least seven more years," said Larry.

"The tests were positive," explained Ryan.

The recipient of the call remained silent for a few seconds before Larry asked, "How bad is it?"

"Stage four means pretty bad," replied Ryan. "There's

not much use in beginning a regimen, as it would possibly only add about a month. I would be miserable during the time I have left. They give me maybe four months."

"What are your plans?" asked Larry.

"Layla and I plan to visit a few folks while I'm still able. We plan to sell the house in town and move to the farmhouse in Brandon Springs. The kids are grown and gone, so there is no use in having a large house in the city. Everyone loves the old place in the country. Layla still has a few relatives in the area."

"When can Patsy and I come to visit?"

"Anytime. We plan to move to Brandon Springs this month. We'll leave our current home in the hands of realtors."

AS LARRY STOPPED the car in the gravel drive, Layla came out onto the porch of the old home in Brandon Springs. Wiping her hands on a dish towel, she tried to present a welcoming smile.

"She really looks tired," Larry whispered to his wife.

Exiting the car, the fresh familiar rural air reminded him of better times shared there with Ryan. Memories flooded his mind. Despite the unfortunate situation, he felt at home there.

"The place looks great!" commented Larry as he pulled a suitcase from the trunk.

Layla held open the screen door to allow him to carry the suitcase more easily into the house.

"You know where the spare bedroom is, so just make yourself at home," Layla said as he entered.

Patsy stopped and held her old friend in a genuine embrace.

"How are you holding up?" Patsy asked.

"I'm fine," replied Layla through quivering lips.

Patsy responded with another warm embrace and the

two entered the home together arm in arm.

Obediently, Larry placed the suitcase in the spare bedroom and then stepped back into the main room. There, slowly rising from a chair, was his old friend Ryan. Thin and pale, he appeared to be half the man he once was.

"Larry, it's so good to see you," greeted Ryan.

Larry gave his friend a gentle hug, mindful of the pain that racked Ryan's body. A similar hug was given by Patsy.

"Patsy, I need a little help in the kitchen," Layla stated as she made her way past the three.

Patsy gave her husband a wink as she left the room. Larry watched in sadness as Ryan slowly settled himself onto the couch.

"Out of all the people in this world, why you?" questioned Larry. "Why couldn't it be one of the many sleazy dirt bags that we've run across?"

"Maybe God is giving them more time to turn things around," Ryan responded. "God knows, and that is good enough for me."

"I'm just saying….," Larry stopped in mid-sentence.

"Just saying what?" asked Ryan. "Either God knows what He is doing, or He doesn't. I've found that He has a lot more sense than I do."

"You know the saying about the good dying young," Larry said.

"Yeah, I've heard something to that effect."

"Well, it stinks – if you ask me, it stinks."

"I've been reading the book of Job in the Bible," stated Ryan.

"I guess that's fitting," replied Larry. "There's an example of a good guy catching a really hard time."

"It's more than that," said Ryan, picking up his Bible from the end table. "I think we all should read chapters 38 and 39 a little more often. It really puts things into perspective. Who are we to question God? Here, let me read Job 40: 1-14."

Moreover the Lord answered Job, and said,
Shall he that contendeth with the Almighty instruct
him? he that reproveth God, let him answer it.
Then Job answered the Lord, and said,
Behold, I am vile; what shall I answer thee? I will lay
mine hand upon my mouth.
Once have I spoken; but I will not answer: yea, twice;
but I will proceed no further.
Then answered the Lord unto Job out of the whirlwind,
and said, Gird up thy loins now like a man: I will demand
of thee, and declare thou unto me.
Wilt thou also disannul my judgment? wilt thou
condemn me, that thou mayest be righteous?
Hast thou an arm like God? or canst thou thunder with
a voice like him?
Deck thyself now with majesty and excellency; and
array thyself with glory and beauty.
Cast abroad the rage of thy wrath: and behold every
one that is proud, and abase him.
Look on every one that is proud, and bring him low;
and tread down the wicked in their place.
Hide them in the dust together; and bind their faces in
secret.
Then will I also confess unto thee that thine own right
hand can save thee.

"Job was a good man, but it wasn't until that point in his life that he got the message," Ryan explained.

"What message?" Larry asked. "I'm supposed to be the preacher here, but I have always avoided that book in the Bible. To be honest, I don't really like it. I never have. It sort of scares me. I know that Job passed the test, but who wants a test like that?"

"Job finally understood God, and that is no small

thing," Ryan said. "He finally understood that God is always right. No matter the situation, He is always right. In our heads, most Christians will say that God is righteous. However, we want to make Him right on our terms. We decide what is right, we decide what is fair, we decide what love means – then we try to fit God into our definitions. We humans tend to establish criteria in which we believe that a righteous God should meet, and then we are sometimes disturbed when we find that He doesn't measure up to what we have in mind. That is totally backwards. Deep down, we know this – but we don't like it. It scares us to not be in control of the terms of life. In a sense, we tend to define God in our own image. But that is backwards. We are created in His image. Who are we to pass judgment on our Creator, the Creator of the universe? Who do we think we are?"

"You're absolutely right in what you're saying," confessed Larry. "I know this in my mind, but in my heart, I still don't feel that a lot of things that God allows to happen to good people are right."

"A lot of things in this world are wrong," said Ryan. "People do wrong things. The subject is God, and He is never wrong… never. We struggle with the existence of bad things in this life because we feel that God shouldn't let those things happen. However, we would be mad at God if He didn't give us choices. Either way, we want God to fit in our concept of right and wrong. That is backwards thinking. The fact is, God is right – and Job finally got it. He got this truth deep down in his soul… not just in his head."

"I guess I figure that you're the type of person that grandkids need for a grandfather," Larry said. "I just wish God would take some of the trash out of this world and leave the good stuff around."

"We're God's creation, living on a large ball, flying through space, circling a star, one of 100 billion stars that make up the Milky Way galaxy, one of the billions of galaxies that make up the known universe. I want to stress the term *known universe*. This is just what we know of the universe. Who are we to question the Creator? Who are we to set criteria by which to judge God? Half of us can't even muster enough good judgment to pick a marriage partner who will stay with us for life. What the heck do we know? Daily, we make mistakes in judgment. Yet in our arrogance, we think we can judge God. In our ridiculous ignorance, we think we can be smarter than God regarding certain things. In our self-centered mentality, we think that we can be more just than God. Look at the mess we make of God's creation. How small-minded can we be, and how arrogant?"

"I have to admit that I don't understand all that God does," stated Larry.

"In the Bible, Paul said that in this life we see things as if we were looking through stained glass," replied Ryan. "We can only see a shadow image of what is on the other side of the glass. God sees everything with crystal clarity. Over time, some of us learn a few things. God is eternal. He isn't bound by time. He created time. He created the three dimensions of height, width, and depth that we live in. He created the fourth dimension, time, in which those three dimensions reside. He's not bound to live in the realm where He has placed us. He can see my entire life in one glance. In fact, He doesn't even have to glance. He just knows. We get upset and shake our puny little fists at God. We judge Him with our tiny understanding. Still, He loves us. His mercies are incredible, and the Bible says they are new every morning."

"I like mornings," said Larry. "Mornings can be pretty busy. We meant to leave out earlier this morning, but I got a call from the center."

"I thought you were through with the mission work," stated Ryan.

"I still get a call from time to time for advice, but I rarely go there," answered Larry. "Are you feeling all right? You seem to be a little short of breath."

"Larry, I'm a little tired. I run out of energy so quickly. Please read something for me. Read Lamentations 3:17-26."

Looking into the eyes of his old friend, Larry began to realize something. Outwardly, Ryan was a shell of the man he once was. He had grown weak and frail. Yet, he sensed a strength of soul that beamed through his broken exterior like light emitting through the cracks of a broken lamp shade. There was something brilliant and pure that was waiting to get out. It was in this moment of physical weakness that Larry felt he was clearly witnessing the soul of his dear ailing friend.

"Sure, just let me turn to it," replied Larry. He began to read.

And thou hast removed my soul far off from peace: I forgot prosperity.

And I said, My strength and my hope is perished from the Lord:

Remembering mine affliction and my misery, the wormwood and the gall.

My soul hath them still in remembrance, and is humbled in me.

This I recall to my mind, therefore have I hope.

It is of the Lord's mercies that we are not consumed, because his compassions fail not.

They are new every morning: great is thy faithfulness.

The Lord is my portion, saith my soul; therefore will I hope in him.

The Lord is good unto them that wait for him, to the soul that seeketh him.

It is good that a man should both hope and quietly wait for the salvation of the Lord.

"Thanks," Ryan said. "I've had a lot of time on my hands lately, and I've been reading the Bible a lot. Maybe it's a little like reading a road map before taking a trip," he said with a grin.

"Like you said, God's mercies are new every morning," Larry replied. "I feel like I've just been to church."

"I hate to be a party pooper, but would you mind if I took a quick nap?" asked Ryan.

"No, not at all," replied Larry. "Do whatever is best for you. Can I do something? Is there something that you need help with while I'm here?"

"Nope. I've gotten to the point where I can drop off just about wherever I am. Nothing bothers me when I am asleep. I just didn't want to conk out on you during our conversation. Part of it is the medication, I think. I won't sleep long."

Leaving his friend to rest, Larry made his way to the kitchen. He found the two women seated at the small rustic kitchen table.

"I thought you two were fixing a meal," he said while offering a slight smile.

"Everything but the rolls are either baking in the oven or cooking on the top," answered Patsy. "We're keeping an eye on things."

Realizing that the women had been in serious conversation before the interruption, he excused himself.

"I'm going out on the front porch while Ryan takes a nap."

"He stays pretty tired," said Layla. "He takes several short naps during the day, and I'm guessing he will wake up about the time the food is ready. One of us will let you know when it's time to eat."

As Larry walked quietly past his sleeping friend, he stopped momentarily to study the gaunt features now marking this familiar still face.

"He is so frail. I guess time catches up on all of us. I can't believe how fast life has passed, and the fact that Ryan is now sixty. When I was washing dishes in Boston, I never thought I would live to be fifty-eight."

Closing the screen door behind him, he took a seat in a chair on the porch. He reflected on how easy life had become for him and Pasty, and how difficult it was becoming for Ryan and Layla. Larry had done well with speaking engagements and publishing two books, one on missions for the homeless and one on investment strategies for Christian families. Since going into the ministry, Larry and Patsy tithed 10% of their income to God and invested 10% of his income into retirement funds. Eventually, he and Pasty had made adjustments of personal frugality that allowed them to place another 10% of his income for their children's education. All those years, he and Patsy lived a simple life in the small home in Charlotte. Since retiring from full-time ministry at age fifty-four, he and Patsy moved into a nicer home in a better part of town. He now ran the mission only as Chairman of the Board, leaving the handling of the daily duties and operations to younger ministers.

Larry breathed in the country air and remembered shared times with Ryan, Layla, and Patsy. Nowhere in the world did he feel more at peace than this small house in Brandon Springs. The house and land belonged to Ryan, yet Larry felt as if they were his. He thought about the repairs he and Ryan had made on the place, the hikes to the top of the mountain, and of the many charitable acts planned there by all four over the years.

His thoughts were interrupted by Layla.

"The meal is on the table and Ryan is awake," she instructed.

The hours passed as though they were minutes, as they ate and played cards afterwards. It was like old times, except for the fact that one of them showed heavy signs of weariness. However, no one wanted the fellowship to end. It was evident to all that there was a strong possibility that this might be the last gathering of the four.

"I think we've done some good," stated Larry. "We invested most of our adult lives in making this place a better world for some people."

"No book was written about anything that we've done," stated Ryan. "No record of any of this is being passed down. But we know, and God knows. That's all we need. It doesn't matter what other people know or don't know."

"I've been recognized for some of my mission work, but nothing compares to the fun of being able to secretly give away thousands upon thousands of dollars to worthy people in need," Larry added. "This was the best. I was having a blast."

"I never dreamed of where God would take us," replied Ryan. "Think about the adventures God may have in mind for our children."

"I want to thank you for being my best friend," Larry said to Ryan.

"I want to thank you for all those stock tips," Ryan said with a chuckle. "Layla is in great shape financially, and our kids have lived very comfortably."

"My life changed because of you." Larry stated.

"Think of all the lives changed because of your work at the mission, and there are still people blessed by that work," Ryan said. "There must be thousands. Think of the millions who have been helped by your books."

"None of it would have happened if I had not met you," Larry reminded his friend.

"I would have been a much different person if it hadn't been for my Aunt Sally," explained Ryan. "In a way, that small woman changed the lives of a lot of people-- either directly, or indirectly. She was someone special."

"I wish I could have met her," said Larry.

"Without her, I wouldn't have this place in Brandon

Springs," stated Ryan. "Brandon Springs is a good place to rest, and I'm feeling pretty tired."

"It's time that Patsy and I let you go to bed," said Larry. "I think this visit has worn you out."

"It is so good to see you," Ryan answered.

"I'll see you in the morning," replied Larry. "We plan to return to Charlotte right after lunch tomorrow."

AS RYAN SAT ON the front porch of the house in Brandon Springs, he reflected on Larry's visit the previous month. The colors of the red maples seemed unusually majestic in the setting fall sun. He was enraptured by the reds, oranges, and yellows as they created an explosion of color. His enjoyment was interrupted by a tap on his left shoulder. A familiar face looked down on him.

"Sorry, I haven't been well lately," stated Ryan. "I didn't even see you walk up. What can I do for you?"

"I've come here to do something for you," said the visitor.

"You must be good medicine, because I am feeling a lot better than I did this morning," said Ryan. "You look familiar. Do I know you?"

"My name is Jerry, and we've crossed paths on more than one occasion."

At that moment, Ryan remembered the accident when his Aunt Sally was fatally injured.

"I do remember you," said Ryan. "You were there when my Aunt Sally was killed in the accident. It makes sense. I wouldn't have suspected you to be what an angel looks like, but you make a pretty good one."

Beyond the maple trees, he saw a bright glowing light, but Ryan knew the warmth he felt wasn't from the rays of the sun. An unusual sense of peace spread throughout him.

"Is it time to go?" Ryan asked.

Jerry nodded and reached out to take Ryan by the arm. As Ryan rose from the chair, all the cancerous pain slipped from his body.

ROB WILLIAMS

Chapter 18

THE LITTLE VILLAGE OF Brandon Springs
had never witnessed such attention. Ryan Walker had made
it clear in his will that he was to be buried in the same church
cemetery where his Aunt Sally had been laid to rest. The
press swooped down upon the town like vultures on a fresh
carcass. Most of them had little interest in Ryan or his
family. They were interested in an event. The event was a
famous minister conducting the eulogy of a little-known
person at a tiny church located in a small remote
Appalachian community. The event was Larry Chatterson.

A young minister stepped to the pulpit and nervously
addressed members of the press. "As a show of reverence
during the service, please refrain from taking pictures in the
sanctuary. I'm going to ask you to leave cameras outside."

Ryan's parents were no longer living, and he was an only
child. He had no living blood relatives except for his
children. However, Ryan's parents and other deceased
relatives were all from this tiny hamlet. That being the case,
he was accepted as one of their own. He had never lived in
the area until he inherited his late Aunt Sally's property
there, but her love for him made him welcome. Some of
them had come to know him since the inheritance, and most
of those gained an appreciation for Ryan.

Only a select few members of press were approved to stand in the back of the small sanctuary. The front pews of the sanctuary were reserved for family and were populated by friends and people waiting to see and hear Larry. Most attempted to sit as close to the front as allowed. Some felt genuine concern for the grieving members of the family, but Larry was the draw for many. On occasions visiting the area with Ryan, some of the locals had the opportunity to meet him. It didn't take long for the sanctuary to fill. The church building was completely out of character with the worship of such a celebrity. There was warmth in that small wooden church that spoke of simplicity and honesty. There were no elaborate furnishings or ornately stained-glass windows. This plain and simple building offered a place of worship to those desiring it, and spiritual refreshment for those in need of it. No one came to this building to be in awe of the architecture or grandeur.

Within minutes after Ryan's family was seated, the initial silence and reverence of the setting gave way to the hum of voices. The church quieted again as Larry and Patsy Chatterson entered the sanctuary and moved slowly up the aisle toward the area reserved for them. Larry and his wife made their way to Layla and Ryan's children. Upon seeing him, Layla rose to her feet and gave Larry a deep long hug. Passing him off to her children, she approached Patsy. Larry's wife experienced difficulties walking, as osteoarthritis and disk problems in her back now impacted her once capable body. Years of lifting heavy patients and constant standing in her nursing career had taken a toll. She was scheduled for back fusion, but that surgery would only address part of her intense pain. Damaged cartilage in joints caused a degree of pain with each step. Her face was worn, but her smile echoed the goodness of her soul. She reminded Layla of an ancient and weather battered lighthouse which still emitted a radiant beam of comfort to those sailing near a coast. She was a signal to all who approached her that the robust soul of those suffering physically can still shine brightly. Layla's hug with Patsy was more ginger, but it was just as deep and heartfelt as the one she had given to Larry. Patsy and Larry took their reserved seats, and the organist began to play. Larry caught the eye of the young minister who was seated alone on the platform. He easily read the relief on the young man's face and clearly understood the situation. Fresh out of school, this young minister had recently begun to exercise his first pastoral duty in this small rural church. The presence of the press caused him to be exceptionally on edge, and he had been nervous about Larry's slightly late arrival. In addition, he really didn't know Ryan very well. Prior to this, he had never officiated at a funeral and he had absolutely no desire to assume the duty of giving the eulogy in Larry's absence. The nervous smile spoke volumes to the older minister seated with the family.

Larry was a gifted individual, but singing was not one of his talents. He couldn't hold a pitch to save his life and he knew it. He usually quietly mouthed the words so silently that only his wife could tell that he was making an attempt to sing. She had grown accustomed to it. In fact, it became one of his endearing qualities – or better stated as a lack of quality. Often, he would only read the words of a hymn as he followed the singing of those around him. This was not his practice this day. This was the funeral of his best friend, and Larry expressed each word of the hymns sung.

Those in attendance sang "Blessed Assurance," "Leaning on the Everlasting Arms," and "Amazing Grace". However, Larry experienced a warm sensation deep within him as they began singing "The Unclouded Day."

> *1. Oh, they tell me of a home far beyond the skies,*
> *Oh, they tell me of a home far away;*
> *Oh, they tell me of a home where no storm clouds*

rise,
Oh, they tell me of an unclouded day.
     o   *Refrain:*
     Oh, the land of cloudless day,
     Oh, the land of an unclouded sky,
     Oh, they tell me of a home where no storm
     clouds rise,
     Oh, they tell me of an unclouded day.
  2. *Oh, they tell me of a home where my friends*
have gone,
Oh, they tell me of that land far away,
Where the tree of life in eternal bloom
Sheds its fragrance through the unclouded day.
     o   *Refrain:*
     Oh, the land of cloudless day,
     Oh, the land of an unclouded sky,
     Oh, they tell me of a home where no storm
     clouds rise,
     Oh, they tell me of an unclouded day.
  3. *Oh, they tell me of a King in His beauty*
there,
And they tell me that mine eyes shall behold
Where He sits on the throne that is whiter than
snow,
In the city that is made of gold.
     o   *Refrain:*
     Oh, the land of cloudless day,
     Oh, the land of an unclouded sky,
     Oh, they tell me of a home where no storm
     clouds rise,
     Oh, they tell me of an unclouded day.
  4. *Oh, they tell me that He smiles on His*
children there,
And His smile drives their sorrows all away;
And they tell me that no tears ever come again
In that lovely land of unclouded day.

o   *Refrain:*
Oh, the land of cloudless day,
Oh, the land of an unclouded sky,
Oh, they tell me of a home where no storm
clouds rise,
Oh, they tell me of an unclouded day.

Larry thought of a rural home in Heaven, much like the farmhouse in Brandon Springs. He remembered standing on top of the mountain that rose behind the place, beneath a clear blue sky containing a single small puffy cloud. In his imagination, Larry breathed in the bittersweet smell of large hardwoods, and he imagined wild dogwoods in bloom. He dreamed of breezes blowing across the mountaintop and imagined how it might feel to sense the radiance of the Creator of the universe.

It became very real to him that his friend was now residing in that Holy Presence, and tears began to spill from Larry's eyes. Without saying a word, he threw both hands straight up in the air. His expression was the same as when an athlete crosses the goal line for the winning touchdown. His friend Ryan had run the race of life and had crossed the finish line.

At the conclusion of this fourth hymn, the young minister approached the pulpit to introduce the man who would be giving the eulogy. Glancing at the older minister, he found encouragement. Approving eyes assured him of shared comradery. Larry rose and made his way to the pulpit. Though he was beginning to show the signs of age, he was still an imposing figure. Every face was turned toward his.

"We sometimes compare our lives to others, and question God," Larry began. "Please listen to the words of the Bible in John 21:18-23."

Truly, truly, I say to you, when you were young, you used to dress yourself and walk wherever you wanted, but when you are old, you will stretch out your hands, and another will dress you and carry you where you do not want to go.

(This he said to show by what kind of death he was to glorify God.) And after saying this he said to him, 'Follow me.'

Peter turned and saw the disciple whom Jesus loved following them, the one who also had leaned back against him during the supper and had said, Lord, who is it that is going to betray you?' When Peter saw him, he said to Jesus, 'Lord, what about this man?

Jesus said to him, If it is my will that he remain until I come, what is that to you? You follow me!

So the saying spread abroad among the brothers that this disciple was not to die; yet Jesus did not say to him that he was not to die, but, If it is my will that he remain until I come, what is that to you?

"Jesus told Simon Peter what his death would be like. Peter's immediate reaction was to point to the disciple John and to ask Jesus 'what about this man?' Jesus replied by asking Peter, 'What if I decide to allow him to live until I return?' Jesus basically told Peter that what God does in the lives of others was none of his business.

God deals with each of us on an individual basis. When we, as people, look out onto the sea of humanity we are a bit overwhelmed. We can't cope with dealing with everyone on earth on an individual basis, so we basically take the ethical position that everyone should be treated the same. God doesn't have our limitations. He can deal with each of us individually. The scripture says that He knows the number of hairs on each of our heads. God has a personal relationship with each of us. This isn't a cliché, it's absolutely the truth. He knows our personal strengths and weaknesses because He is our Creator. God knows us intimately. He knows us better than we know ourselves. As beings with a relatively short lifetime, we are very limited in our understanding. God is eternal, and His understanding is all knowing. We understand things based on personal experiences we have in this realm of space and time. God's perspective is not limited by space and time. He created both. His view is all inclusive. He sees the big picture of our lives, the true picture.

We see things happen differently in the life of one person than for another, and we tend to judge God and think that He is not being fair. Yet, if God treated us all the same, we would still tend to say that God is unfair for not allowing people to be unique. It wouldn't matter what God did, we would find something to complain about.

Should God expect an extremely poor person in a third world country to be able to provide the care for his brother that God requires of a rich man in the United States? We would say that God should consider each person's situation in life and allow us all personal freedom to choose. Other times we might state that God should place us all in the same situations, thus limiting our choices. Which is it? If we think about it, it's obvious that we are the ones who are confused. We really don't know what the heck we are doing or what God should be doing. Out of that confusion and frustration we lash out at God. In truth, we are not very qualified to judge the fairness of God.

When God deals with us in a particular way (perhaps in a way that we don't like), we should not compare our lives with what He is doing in another person's life. We should not be asking the question, 'what about this man?' We should be thankful that God deals with each of us on a very personal basis. Wise parents understand that each child is different, and what works with one child doesn't necessarily work with another child. We are God's children, and He is wise enough to understand how to work with us on an individual basis. Again, we are not very qualified to judge the fairness of God.

To take this a step further, because of our sins we deserve judgment. Unlike us, Jesus never sinned. God gave

His sinless Son over to be punished in our place, and at His crucifixion God placed all the sins of humanity on Him. In doing so, when Jesus died on that cross, our sins died with Him. Though we may be thankful for God providing this amazing Grace toward us, did Jesus deserve the punishment meant for us? Judging by our criteria for fairness, was this fair? Was it fair to Jesus to have our sins and punishment placed on Him? He had done nothing wrong. Yet, this was God's plan from the foundation of the world. We are not very qualified to judge the fairness of God.

When Jesus rose from the dead, and before He ascended into Heaven, He told His followers that after He was gone, they would do the work He had done. From the beginning of Jesus' ministry here on earth, signified at His baptism by John the Baptist, the Spirit of God rested on Jesus. Jesus told His followers that after His ascension to Heaven this same Holy Spirit would be sent to fill them. After His departure, these followers of Christ would become His body (vessel for the Spirit of God), and they would be empowered by the Holy Spirit to do great things. The physical body of Jesus is gone, and we now make up a sort of replacement body in Christ's stead. When the Bible explains the fact that we Christians are now the body of Christ, it states that we are not all hands or feet. In other words, we are not all the same. God has different plans for each of us, and we have different functions in making up this replacement body for the Spirit of God to operate through. We each make up a different part of the body of Christ, and each part is needed. We are all different, and God deals with us differently. A shoe belongs on a foot, not a face. A hat belongs on a head, not a foot. Each part of the body of Christ is treated a bit differently. When we see God deal with someone differently than how He deals with us, we should not think of God as being unfair. We should celebrate the fact that God cares so much about us that He deals with us on an individual basis. He loves us individually."

Larry stopped briefly and allowed this message to settle in the minds of those attending. In the still silence, only the faint song of a distant bird could be heard. When Larry continued, the message became more personal.

"As a minister, I've been a more visible part of the body of Christ than Ryan Walker. It certainly doesn't mean that I am more important in God's plan for humanity, and that Ryan's life had a lesser role. I came to know Christ because of Ryan. So, who is more important in the scheme of things? I truthfully tell you that I have never known a greater man of God than Ryan Walker.

Each life impacts the lives of others, and those lives impact generations to come. I've experienced a lot of recognition through the ministry in Charlotte. I want you to know that there are many great people whose contributions to the lives of others are known but to very few and to God. Ryan Walker was one of those men. My life would never have had a positive influence on other people if it had not been for him. He befriended me when I was a dishwasher in Boston. He was an educated professional, and I was an uneducated person who was lost. My first marriage had failed, and my hopes for the future were almost nonexistent. I came from a dysfunctional family in south Alabama, and I had tried to run away from the situation. You can't run away from your problems because a person is usually part of the problem. You carry your problems with you wherever you go.

Ryan introduced me to the woman who became my wife, the mother of my children. Without this man's influence, I never would have been inspired to obtain a degree in finance and later become a minister after completing theological studies. I was inspired by a continual stream of encouragement flowing from Ryan Walker. In ministry, he and my wife Patsy were my confidants. These were the two people I leaned on when I found it difficult to continue to lean on God. I can't begin to tell you how much I miss him.

I am so thankful to still have my wife, Patsy. Ryan and Layla were our best friends for life, and Layla knows that she will always be like family to us.

I would have never been a positive influence on anyone's life without Ryan's influence on mine. I might not have reconnected with my brother and my mother. God's hand reached through Ryan to redirect my life. I hope he understood how grateful I will always be. I hope his wife Layla understands how indebted I am to him. She knows that we were like brothers, but I don't know that she fully understands what Ryan meant to me. He was my hero. He wasn't a world class athlete, or a famous inventor, or a military hero, or a statesman in politics. He was consistently my friend and a faithful follower of Christ. He wasn't the type of person to be in anyone's face about his faith; he just lived it, and he was a man of great internal strength.

This is a small out-of-the-way town. Ryan wasn't from here; he didn't grow up here. His parents and their families were from this area. In time, he began to understand that Brandon Springs is a very special place. It is special because of the beautiful mountains and the countryside. However, he found it special because of the special people here. Many of those who live here have come to understand that this is the place Ryan called home, even during times when he lived away. His grave will be here in Brandon Springs, near that of his Aunt Sally. I've heard many stories about that woman, and I wish I had been able to meet her. We are about to bury the body of a great man. His greatness may not be realized by many outside of his family and close friends. But he is known by God, the Creator of us all. He was my friend, and I will forever be grateful."

As Larry asked those in attendance to bow for prayer, his eyes met those of an old friend seated at the rear of the church.

Chapter 19

AT THE CONCLUSION of the service, the younger minister announced that a private graveside gathering would be held momentarily for only the immediate family and a few friends. A small crowd consoled Layla and the children, but a larger one formed around Larry. He briefly entertained the group before excusing himself to attend to his ailing wife and a grieving friend. As he spoke with Layla, his eyes periodically drifted to someone still seated on the last pew. Turning to assist his ailing wife down the aisle, he motioned for Layla to follow him.

"Take a glance at the rear pew," he whispered to his wife as he gently took her arm.

As her eyes made contact with the man, the fellow gave her a slight acknowledging wave with his right hand. A very attractive aging woman sat just to the right of him. As her eyes met Patsy's, a broad smile spread across the familiar face.

"Tiffany," Patsy whispered to Larry.

Patsy had no trouble recognizing her, but that face showed more change than just age. Her eyes reflected an inner peace. When Larry told Holloway of Ryan's passing, the retired FBI accountant confessed to Larry that the two were alive and had entered a witness protection program.

247

Larry and Patsy hadn't seen or spoken to them for more than two decades. Patsy was stopped by a visitor momentarily and motioned for Larry to continue to escort his wife to greet the old friends.

"It's so good to see you," Larry said as he embraced them both in his long arms.

"In case you've forgotten our names, let me introduce the two of us," offered Chad. "My name is Charlie Wilson, and this is my wife, Becky."

Patsy gave Tiffany a long hug. As Layla approached, Larry turned to introduce the couple.

"Let me introduce you to Charlie and Becky Wilson," he said.

"Do you have somewhere we can go to have a private conversation?' asked Chad.

"Absolutely," answered Layla, with a wink. "I have a farmhouse just outside town."

"Perfect," replied Tiffany. Reaching out to embrace her old friend, she whispered, "I am so sorry about Ryan."

"Me too," answered Layla. "I miss him so much already."

Patsy demonstrated a great deal of patience attending to questions from the visitor. Seeing that she was beginning to tire, Tiffany immediately took her hand and suggested that she take a seat on the back pew. The friends waited several minutes until those in attendance had finished consoling Ryan's widow. By now it was apparent that Layla's grandchildren were becoming restless with the situation. The younger minister approached and asked if they were ready for the graveside moment. Layla agreed. As they were about to start toward the door of the church, she gave her children a hug and explained that she wished to spend time later at the house visiting with friends.

"I have some catching up to do with this couple, and I'm sure you and my grandchildren could use a break," Layla began. "After the graveside, why don't you take the grandkids out for lunch and maybe treat them to a movie. They've been cooped up far too long in a depressing environment."

Since arriving in Brandon Springs her children had not left her side. They were now somewhat relieved for her to spend a little time in the company of friends. Her children agreed to take the grandchildren out to eat and check out the only local movie theater. Once the brief private graveside service concluded, the old friends made their way to the farmhouse just outside Brandon Springs.

"Help yourselves to the food in the kitchen, while I change clothes," offered Layla. "I can't believe all the food brought by people."

The other four sat down at the rustic wooden kitchen table. Immediately, Tiffany opened her wallet to show pictures of two children and a grandchild. Patsy smiled as she glanced over them. "I am so happy for you both."

Layla entered the room wearing jeans and one of Ryan's old flannel shirts. "Does it seem cold to anyone else but me?" she asked.

"I feel fine," answered Patsy. "Come look at these pictures. Chad and Tiffany…. I meant to say, Charlie and Becky have two children."

Layla's eyes, tired and puffy from days of weeping, danced as she studied the pictures. "I can see a little of both of you in each of them," she said. "They're very attractive. I bet they were cute kids."

"They are back in Iowa," Tiffany explained. "We drove here without them. They have busy lives of their own now."

"Iowa?" questioned Layla. "Thank you so much for coming. I bet you're tired."

"Actually, we arrived yesterday, and we stayed in a hotel here last night," said Chad.

"What in the world have you been doing for the last twenty-four years?" asked Patsy.

"All right, you've got to fill us in," added Layla.

"I'm sure Holloway told you about us both being in the witness security program, so I won't start with that," offered Chad.

"No, I think that would be the perfect place to start!" exclaimed Larry. "Holloway has been pretty secretive. He's been fairly silent about you both until I called to inform him about Ryan. I wasn't sure you were still alive until that conversation. After the bodies were found in that lake, he inferred that I had nothing to worry about. But he never gave me any solid confirmation until that call."

"He does his job well, and that's probably why we're still alive," stated Chad. "I guess he never told you what happened the night we went into the program."

"I know nothing about that," stated Patsy. "I've got to hear what happened."

"It may be weird to you, but it's important that we use our new names in conversation," explained Tiffany. "We can't afford to revert back to original names, even with you."

"I understand," said Larry. "Charlie and Becky, it is. I once knew a man named Charlie, and he was a good man."

"The first thing that the FBI had me do was to place a bug in John's car," Becky said. "This enabled them to track where he drove. They keyed off cell towers when he used his cell phone while in transit. They recorded many of his cell phone conversations. It all kicked into high gear when John gave the big guy the order to kill Charlie and me. He told him when and where to do it, so the FBI was aware of all but the method. John told the guy that I had not learned my lesson from the earlier warning given to me, and that it was now too late. The big guy must have been afraid that John thought he had been too easy with me, with the earlier warning. That goon told John he would use the same method as he had used in the past for killing two women who were family members of a rival gun-running group. He bragged to him about horrible things he did to them before killing them. My husband must have had some feelings for me, because he instructed the man not to do that to me. I was to be simply disposed of in a manner that wouldn't be painful. He didn't care how Charlie was to be murdered. In his view, my conversations with Charlie could not be tolerated. He was concerned that I might talk about his illegal activities, especially if my loyalty went to another man. This conversation between John and the guy was picked up by the FBI and recorded. Holloway told me that John viewed this as strictly about business."

"That's pretty weird business," said Layla. "You must have been absolutely scared to death when you heard about this."

"I was terrified," said Becky. "On the other hand, I desperately wanted out of the situation, and this was my opportunity. I was hopeful that the FBI could protect me. They couldn't use the recordings in court against John, but they used the tape of the conversation to bring an inside man into their plans. Milton Holloway is an amazing judge of people. He has sort of a gift for it. They initially wouldn't tell me who the person on the inside was, but I later found out that they used the tape against the big man. Who would have guessed that huge cold-blooded killer would be concerned about what his mother and sister thought of him? The FBI threatened to let family members of that big goon hear him bragging about doing horrible things to those two women. It worked, and the man turned."

"Things were precisely planned in detail, and Holloway coached us on what was to go down," explained Charlie. "However, we had no assurance that the plan would work out. I didn't even know exactly when it would go into effect. As I came out to my car one evening, after a long day at work, two guys jumped me. One of them threatened to cut my throat if I made a sound. My hands were bound behind my back with plastic cable ties. Those guys were really fast. Before I knew it, I was placed in the back of a van and blindfolded. I couldn't see a thing, but I could hear much of what was going on around me. There were three of them in all. Someone drove as the other two stayed in the back of the van with me. As we drove off, one of them put a rope around the cable ties on my wrists and fastened me to the inside panel of the van. Generally, I knew what was supposed to happen. But it still scared the crap out of me."

Becky placed her hand on Charlie's forearm and gave him a gentle kiss on the cheek. Turning to the others, she continued the story.

"I woke up in bed one night with a huge guy on top of me," explained Becky. "There were two of them in the room. I recognized the big guy, because he was the same man John had used to teach me a lesson on another occasion. I wasn't sure if the plan was being put in motion, or if I was being taught another lesson. If it was to be the lesson, I would have been in serious trouble. I would not have lived, for sure. I would have been sexually abused and roughed up until I was dead. I had been warned. I was scared to death. My hands were bound behind my back, my mouth was taped, and I was taken to a van wearing only panties under a small night gown. Once there, I heard Charlie's voice. I then knew that the plan was underway. They immediately taped his mouth, but he had communicated the message that I needed to hear."

"A while after they abducted me, the van stopped," said Charlie. "I could hear the three of them whispering to each other. One of them started whispering threats in my ear. He told me that I would die if I made a sound. After a few minutes I heard the van side door open and close, and I heard the muffled moan of a woman. I knew it was Becky. With the blindfold on, I couldn't tell what shape she was in. I couldn't tell if they were doing something really bad to her or not. I called her name out, and they taped up my mouth. I had to let her know that I was there, and that things were in motion. We drove for a long time. I recognized it when we left the city and traveled a highway. The shoulder I was laying on was becoming pretty sore as well. We exited onto a small road for a while, and then another. The last road was in bad shape. With all the bumps in the road, the ropes and ties were killing my wrists. The vehicle finally stopped and two of them manhandled us out of the van. The third guy drove off. They removed our blindfolds, escorted us across a grassy area, and put us in a boat. This was very close to what Holloway had told us would happen. After the boat pulled away from the small pier things got crazy. The blindfolds were put back on our heads. They fastened us by the wrist to something, and I could hear one of them talk about what he planned to do to Becky. This guy was sick, really sick. I heard the large guy tell him to stop what he was doing, but I could see nothing.

The boat stopped. I felt them tie a rope around my waist, and a rope around each ankle. My wrists were unfastened from the boat. I had a very bad feeling about what was about to happen. I guess they were doing the same to Becky. The sick guy kept asking if he could do nasty things to her. It was obvious that the big guy was in charge, and he told him that they had been given orders to do certain things and nothing more."

"What Charlie couldn't see was that the nasty jerk was feeling me up and down as he talked," interrupted Becky. "I had been dragged out of bed, and I was wearing that small night gown. That jerk had ripped my panties off just after the boat started in motion. He did more than just talk. If it hadn't been for the big guy calling him down, there is no telling what he would have done. Actually, I was surprised he stopped the man. As I said, I had come across that huge man before. On that other occasion, as a warning not to talk about his business activities, John gave him orders to rape me. That was one of the worst days of my life. My life began to be a living hell after that day."

Charlie reached over and took his wife's hand. "Those

days are long gone now," he reminded her.

She took the back of his hand to her lips and kissed it. "I am so grateful for you," she said.

"They stood us up and again removed the blindfolds," Charlie explained. "That is when I realized that the riskiest aspects of the plan were about to happen. Those ropes on us were tied to three concrete blocks, which were positioned on the sides of the pontoon boat. The three blocks for her were placed on the port side, and my three were placed on the starboard side. She and I were facing each other, and I felt relieved that she seemed physically unharmed. However, it still didn't mean we would make it out alive. A number of things could have gone wrong. The huge guy was the man in charge of handling us. Like she said, this was the same big jerk who had earlier raped her and warned her about being disloyal to Molato. He reminded her that John Molato gave him orders to do worse for continued disloyalty, and he said that was exactly what he was about to carry out. Turning to me, he told me that he was about to share a story that his mother had told him when he was fourteen. It went like this:

'There was dog that loved to sleep next to railroad tracks. On one occasion, the dog's tail wagged over one of the rails while he was having a happy dream. Just as that happened, a train came down the tracks and cut the dog's tail off. As a reaction, the dog whipped his head around to see what had happened. This resulted in the dog's head being cut off by the moving train. The moral of the story is, don't lose your head over a piece of tail.'

I think the big guy enjoyed this. He told me that this was my problem, and now it was time for me to pay up."

"I can't argue with the premise of the story, but I can't see this guy as being a suitable judge in matters of sexual purity," said Larry.

"My thoughts exactly," replied Charlie. "This fellow was not someone who should give a lecture on morality.

With our wrists still bound behind our backs, facing each other, with our mouths still covered with duct tape, the huge guy asked us if we had any last words. Both of them burst out laughing, and then simultaneously shoved us overboard. The concrete blocks followed, dragging us both to the bottom. We trained for two months for this. She spent four hours each day swimming in Molato's pool. I ran miles every day, building endurance in my lungs."

"I even practiced dropping to the bottom of the deep end and holding my breath for long periods of time," explained Becky. "The real thing was much different, and it was really hard not to panic."

"We had gone over the plan several times with FBI personnel, and I practiced holding my breath while at work," stated Charlie. "Even though I was somewhat prepared for this, there is no way I can describe having your hands tied behind your back while sinking deeper and deeper into cold darkness."

"Good Lord!" cried Layla. "Oh, dear God! How are you still alive?"

"The FBI had prepared air for us down below the boat," replied Charlie. "I didn't know whether I would be able to hold my breath long enough to make it to the air. I can't begin to describe how it feels to be weighed down in dark waters, trying to anticipate when you might come to a stop. I had been told about the plan, but I had to fight being overwhelmed by horror the entire way down. If I panicked, it would have been over for me. I wasn't even sure that we had been dumped overboard in the right place. I just concentrated on holding my breath for as long as I could. The water became colder the deeper I went. When I reached the bottom, I tried to think of something else to keep the fear away. I began to try to figure out which of the two men in the boat was the inside man. Holloway told us that he had inside help, but at the time I wasn't sure which one. My gut feeling was that it was the big guy, because he drove the boat. It turned out that I was right."

"Never mind the inside man, how did you reach the air?" asked Patsy.

"The inside man was important," said Charlie. "The FBI had given him the exact position of where this was to occur on High Rock Lake. I had never been to that lake before, so it was totally unfamiliar to me. The pontoon boat was equipped with a GPS and a fish finder. That is how the driver of the boat positioned it in the correct place. Below the boat were two FBI agents wearing re-breathing devices, as not to show bubbles on the surface. The boat was also over an old, junked car, resting about 20 feet below the surface. However, at the time, I had no clue as to how deep the water was. Earlier the FBI had prepared the vehicle for us. They forced open the doors and lined the inside of the car with a type of plastic tarp. It was secured to the car and had been filled with about eighteen inches of air. Holloway had coached us well. He told us not to panic, but to just hold our breath as long as possible. The divers found us quickly, cut the ropes attached to the blocks, and shoved us into the car and under the plastic tarp. They immediately pulled the tape from our mouths and made sure we could breathe well. It was unbelievably dark, until one of them presented a small glow stick. I have never been so glad to see light."

"If the car held air, what kept it from floating up to the surface?" questioned Larry.

"That car sunk into the mud years ago, and eighteen inches of air was not enough to pull a heavy old car out of the mud," Charlie explained. "I'm sure it was a real effort preparing the vehicle for us. They had to pry open a door and position the tarp so that it held air and remained stable. The seats were removed to make more room for us."

"One diver stayed with us, removing the ties from our wrists," said Becky. "He helped us stay calm and catch our breath. He kept telling us that it was all over. I couldn't help it. I started bawling my eyes out and I was shaking almost uncontrollably. The other diver kept a look out to make sure the boat was gone."

"It seemed like forever to Becky," Charlie added, as he nodded in the direction of his wife. "For some weird reason, I felt secure inside that junked car. In fact, I was a little afraid to leave it. I really didn't know how deep we were, and I was afraid those guys in the boat might come back after we surfaced."

"Sure enough, the pontoon boat was gone when we surfaced," explained Becky. "In its place was another boat, a cabin cruiser with no lights turned on. This was a nice boat. Dry clothes were provided for us, and we placed our wet ones in bags. As I climbed on board, all I could think about was the fact that I had no panties. Just before they shoved us overboard, the big guy tied my ripped panties to the rope tied around my waist. He said something about getting rid of evidence. I hated that man, but I guess he saved my life that night. I still feel sick when I think about him. It's hard to shake something like that."

"Holloway told us that those guys met up with the driver of the van at a boat dock," said Charlie. "The FBI had people in the woods around the lake watching everything. They watched those guys clean up the boat. They later watched them cap off the night with a cooler of beer back at the motel where they were staying. These guys were cold-blooded."

"A couple of days later, John reported me as missing," added Becky. "Two months later, the FBI raided the warehouse used for storing black market weapons. All but the big guy were either killed or arrested. They caught them while in the process of loading a huge stash of weapons for a delivery. The big guy had conveniently gone for a pack of smokes when the raid occurred. Instead, he was actually giving the FBI the signal that it was time for the raid. Afterwards the big man left town. Since it was Molato's warehouse, they took my ex-husband in for questioning. The FBI let John go, and then sent a copy of the tape of what the big guy had done to those women to the rival gun-running group. Those women had been connected to that group. John was left without the protection of his men, and I understand the rival group took care of him. A few days later, it was reported that John Molato died in a house fire."

"I read about that in the papers," said Larry. "The article said it was a result of smoking in bed."

"John had given up smoking," stated Becky. "I should know. He was taken out. That rival group made it look like an accidental death. Holloway told us that the big guy was found dead a year later. It looked like a suicide, but I wouldn't be surprised if that group tracked him down. He had bragged about brutally murdering those two women, and I am pretty sure family members of guys in that group were looking for him. John was taken out and so was the big guy. It was a sure bet that rival group would be looking to settle up with anyone in John's family. That's another reason I had to remain in the witness security program. For a few years, Holloway contacted me from time to time to ask questions about John's contacts and about things I knew about the rival group. I had to appear to be dead."

"Holloway said that you attended our funerals," said Charlie. "How were they?"

"No open casket for you," replied Larry. "You were cremated."

"Holloway told me that the FBI collected a John Doe and a Jane Doe and put them in a freezer until time for them to be used," explained Charlie. "In North Carolina, some unidentified bodies are used as cadaver bodies in medical schools. In this case, a couple of unidentified bodies were frozen by the FBI and used to mask our disappearance. The bodies were dressed in the clothes we wore that night, and divers tied the bodies to those concrete blocks in the bottom of the lake. After a period of underwater decomposition, a part washed up on the bank. The police put the information out. Since our disappearance had been handled by the FBI, the FBI swooped in and took it from there. The lake was dragged, and the bodies were found. I would guess those bodies would be pretty unrecognizable after being under water for so long. They pretended dental X-rays of ours matched those taken from the bodies. We were officially declared dead, the bodies were cremated, and funerals held."

"Looks like you two probably owe a couple of dead homeless people that were used to cover your disappearances," observed Larry.

"You know, I never thought of that," replied Charlie. "You're probably right. That's pretty ironic don't you think."

"Ironic?" questioned Larry.

"My father was a homeless guy for years," answered Charlie. "If it weren't for him, and the mess he got me into, I might have never gotten to know you. I doubt I would have met my wife. I hope those two souls are in heaven now. I hope they found peace."

"Maybe so," stated Layla. "It is ironic, and this entire story is fascinating." She had been mostly quiet while listening to the explanation offered by Charlie and Becky. She welcomed the good news of their survival. It seemed to lessen her own personal grief.

"Chad became Charlie Wilson, and I became Becky Millwood," explained Tiffany. "We moved to Denver under new paperwork and things began to settle down a bit. Charlie Wilson went to work as an accountant for the FBI office there."

That brought out a laugh from everyone in the room. Milton Holloway had presented himself as an accountant for the FBI, but they had found him to be much more than an accountant.

"No, I really became an accountant," added Charlie. "The FBI doesn't really need someone in marketing, so they retrained me to be an accountant. It wasn't all that difficult, as I had taken a few accounting classes in college. Becky had a job as a waitress in a café and I pretended to meet her there. We hit it off and got married. After a few years of calm in this new life we decided to start a family. The FBI later let me leave and take an accounting job with a firm in Davenport, Iowa. We have a house just outside of town. It's a good place to raise kids. Holloway was in contact with us even more than before. In fact, he became a friend of the family. We told the kids that he and I became friends while working in the Denver FBI office. The kids see him as sort of an uncle, since they have no other family."

"Sounds like you've both enjoyed a great life since those days in Charlotte," said Patsy.

"I was a much different person back then," answered Becky. "I caused problems for so many people, including you. I hope you can forgive me for my behavior."

"I'll have to admit there were times when I was tempted to grab you by your hair and shake the daylights out of you," replied Patsy. "Larry was quick to put things into perspective for me. You had undergone the loss of your daughter and your life was horrible. I can't imagine what I would have done under your circumstances."

"We all have things that require forgiveness," said Larry. "I killed a man. You didn't do that."

"You saved your brother's life at the time!" exclaimed Patsy.

"I was protecting my brother, but I totally lost control," answered Larry. "I completely lost it. I was like a crazed animal. When I came to myself, a man was dying. I was scared to death."

"I didn't kill a guy, but I can relate," said Charlie. "When I was young, I had an extremely violent temper. I know what it is like to be afraid of yourself, afraid of what you might be capable of doing. I think I understand."

Reaching into his coat, Larry pulled out a pocket New Testament of the Bible. He opened it to a familiar passage.

"John 8:1-11," he announced.

1 Jesus went unto the mount of Olives.

2 And early in the morning he came again into the temple, and all the people came unto him; and he sat down, and taught them.

3 And the scribes and Pharisees brought unto him a woman taken in adultery; and when they had set her in the midst,

4 They say unto him, Master, this woman was taken in adultery, in the very act.

5 Now Moses in the law commanded us, that such should be stoned: but what sayest thou?

6 This they said, tempting him, that they might have to accuse him. But Jesus stooped down, and with his finger wrote on the ground, as though he heard them not.

7 So when they continued asking him, he lifted up himself, and said unto them, He that is without sin among you, let him first cast a stone at her.

8 And again he stooped down, and wrote on the ground.

9 And they which heard it, being convicted by their own conscience, went out one by one, beginning at the eldest, even unto the last: and Jesus was left alone, and the woman standing in the midst.

10 When Jesus had lifted up himself, and saw none but the woman, he said unto her, Woman, where are those thine accusers? hath no man condemned thee?

11 She said, No man, Lord. And Jesus said unto her, Neither do I condemn thee: go, and sin no more.

"What came to mind when you heard these verses?" Larry asked.

"We shouldn't be so quick to judge someone else," offered Layla.

"Jesus was really wise," stated Charlie.

"Each of her accusers realized they were sinners as well," said Patsy.

"Jesus forgave her," answered Becky.

"You all are right," said Larry. "What strikes me is that

there was one person present who was without sin. Jesus. Jesus was qualified to pick up a stone and begin stoning her to death, because He never sinned. However, He chose not to. He was telling her that God was in the process of granting Grace to mankind. God was still just as displeased with sin as He was in the Old Testament, but He was in the process of granting forgiveness to sinners – to people – to everyone. God has forgiven us, and we should forgive each other. What is sometimes most difficult is to forgive ourselves. It took years before I was able to be at peace with myself."

"I forgave you a long time ago," said Patsy, looking squarely into the eyes of Becky. "I hope you're at peace with yourself."

Becky stood and moved quickly to Patsy's side of the table. She wrapped her arms around Patsy's neck. "Thank you, so much."

Changing the conversation to a lighter subject, Larry said, "Layla, I see a loaf of banana bread on the counter, along with piles of other goodies. I thought you said something about chowing down on of some of the food brought by people in the community."

"I'm on it," said Layla, as she rose from her chair. "I'll put on some coffee to go with it."

"Perfect!" stated Larry.

"Larry, we have a favor to ask of you," said Becky.

"What can I do?" asked Larry.

"It's been tough not telling our kids the truth," explained Becky. "We told them that we never talk about our childhood because it is too painful. They were told that our difficult childhoods were something that seemed to bring us together. We told our children that their grandparents are dead, which is true. It's not fair to our kids not to have a family history. At least, they should know about Charlie's father and Brandy. We have a safe deposit box at a bank, containing old pictures of us and others from our past. We want them to have access to that safe deposit box after we die. They need to know at least part of the truth one day, and it will be in that bank box. Milton Holloway gave us permission to do this. Would you mind writing about the old man Charlie, Chad's dad? Would you help tell them what kind of man he became?"

"That's really an interesting request," began Larry. "I've prayed about whether to write my autobiography, and maybe this is an answer. Maybe I should do it. Charlie played a big role in my life. Patsy and I thought it would be a good idea to leave that legacy for our kids. I would be honored to do that. I could write my autobiography in series of three novels. We might want to check with Holloway regarding the use of real names. I wouldn't have to tell everything, and I could change the names of some of the people. I can give you two copies of the unpublished work for your kids, and I could explain things to them in a letter left with the books. I could leave instructions for the letter to be destroyed. If an attorney handles the reading of your will, the letter could be destroyed immediately after being read. No one outside of our families would need to know about the connection of you two and the characters in the novel. Others would not only know about Charlie and Brandy, but your children would know about their mom and dad. It's not all wonderful stuff, but it's the truth."

"Thank you so much," said Charlie.

"That's a good idea," stated Patsy.

"Then it's settled," said Larry.

"What would you call the three novels?" asked Layla.

"I have always loved this property in Brandon Springs," said Larry. "This was Ryan's favorite place, and he was my best friend. We had great times here. Maybe I will call the novels the *Brandon Springs* series."

JUST BEFORE EVENING, Larry, Patsy, and Layla returned to the church cemetery and viewed the ground where Ryan's body had been laid to rest. The setting sun cast a warm glow across headstones. As Larry's eyes shifted to the small grave marker of Ryan's Aunt Sally, he thought about her influence on Ryan's life. He gave God thanks for sending Ryan his way in Boston and for his friendship. He considered the thousands of souls God had touched through his own life. Larry realized how each life impacts others, and he attempted to envision how all those he had encountered might touch lives of others in a series of chain reactions.

Sally's influence on her nephew Ryan Walker profoundly and positively changed him for the remainder of his life. The three days he spent with her in Brandon Springs resulted in a tremendous awakening of his soul. Through Ryan, the lives of Larry, Patsy, Layla, Kaylee and others were enriched. Without the life of Sally, Ryan and Larry would not have carried on the charitable works begun by the older men. None of those people receiving monetary packages would have been financially blessed in times of need. Larry's mind filled with thoughts of how each would inevitably leave this world and pass on to the next.

Because of Ryan, the change in my life exploded into the lives of my brother Ronnie and my mother. Because of Ryan, I was able to minister to Charlie, Tiffany, Brandy, and Dr. David Clarkston. As a result, God used David to bless the lives of his family and his congregation, including Chad. The gifts of such a talented man might have been buried in failure. None of the thousands of lives passing through the mission would have been ministered to without this chain reaction begun by a relatively unknown woman, Sally. Countless lives on earth and souls in heaven were rocked in a positive way by the remarkable life of Ryan's Aunt Sally, whose small body resides in such an unremarkable grave.

Studying the small tombstone of the woman who had been an inspiration for Ryan, he contemplated the fact that she was the original catalyst for change in so many lives.

This woman, buried in a simple grave, behind a small church, in a rural community, was royalty in spirit. Only a handful of individuals realized her contribution to so many. However, Larry understood that God knew. *In her life, Sally had experienced poverty, heartache, and grief. Yet, she didn't allow it to cripple her soul. Sally didn't attempt to console her own crushed heart through self-absorbed bitterness. She openly reached out to others in God's love. Sally allowed God's Spirit to bathe her wounded soul. God's presence filled her, spilling over into the lives of those around her. She carried greatness around in a broken vessel, not thinking of herself. Her inner peace and strength had been passed down from Sally to possibly thousands.*

Larry Chatterson stared at his open hands - hands which had brutally taken the life of another individual. The grief and fear that troubled him in earlier years had long melted away, replaced by a deep inner peace. He understood the Grace of God. Larry had witnessed this Grace within his friend, as Ryan's body was being eaten away by cancer. He understood what Ryan had learned from his Aunt Sally. Without Sally, none of what he and his friend experienced would have come to pass. He imagined Ryan and Sally joined in Heaven, rejoicing and free from the cares of this world. So many lives touched. He knew that Ryan had lived to fully understand his aunt's secret.

Both souls deserve great reward in heaven. Only God knows how much I'm going to miss Ryan, but it is fitting that his soul, released from his expended and broken body, takes rest in Brandon Springs.

ROB WILLIAMS

About the Author:

Rob Williams, currently residing in Nacogdoches Texas, has served in multiple roles supporting the Christian community. Included in this long list of mentorships was his service as youth director of an inner-city church in Atlanta and working with children in some of the toughest housing projects in that city. Rob worked at a rehabilitation center for five years, where he became acquainted with the homeless. The center helped those on work release from jail and those who were physically and mentally handicapped. He has taught adult Sunday school classes for more than thirty years and led youth in Boy Scouts and Cub Scouts for twenty years. Retired from the high-tech industry in Huntsville Alabama, he writes Christian fiction and science fiction in his free time. Rob is a husband, a father of four, and a grandfather. He is the author of the three novel *Brandon Springs* Christian fiction series, the dystopian science fiction novel *Sins of Variance*, the Christian crime novel *Gathering of Six*, and Christian mystery *Cabin by the Stream*.

ROB WILLIAMS